The Book of

Illumination

The Book of
Illumination

A Novel from the Ghost Files

Mary Ann Winkowski
Maureen Foley

THREE RIVERS PRESS
NEW YORK

All rights reserved. Published in the United States by
Three Rivers Press, an imprint of the Crown Publishing Group,
a division of Random House, Inc., New York.
www.crownpublishing.com

Three Rivers Press and the Tugboat design are
registered trademarks of Random House, Inc.

Library of Congress Cataloging-in-Publication Data is available upon request.

ISBN 978-0-307-45244-3

Printed in the United States of America

Design by Jo Anne Metsch

10 9 8 7 6 5 4 3 2 1

First Edition

To my husband, Ted,
and our daughters, Amber and Tara.
I love you.

—MAW

For Rob, Grace, and Charlie

—MF

The Book of
Illumination

Chapter One

I SHOULD NOT have answered the phone.

But that's one more thing they fail to mention in those books you buy to try to prepare for parenthood. What the books should say is this: unless your child is in sight or within shouting distance, you will never again be comfortable letting a phone ring.

My five-year-old, Henry, was spending the weekend with his father, Declan; his stepmother, Kelly; and his two half sisters, Delia and Nell. Kelly's brother has a cottage on Lake Sunapee, and since it was Columbus Day weekend, which happened to fall very early this year, they'd all set off on Friday for three days of boating and campfires.

"Anza? It's Nat."

"Oh, hi!"

My friend Natalie was everything I wasn't: cool, willowy, able to get through life with a few faultlessly chosen pieces of clothing— one cashmere sweater, one black pencil skirt, one perfect pair of jeans. The jewelry she made was just like her wardrobe, spare and tasteful. She was also a secret smoker with somewhat unfortunate taste in men.

"What are you doing?" she asked.

"Nothing." I had just settled down with a glass of Sancerre and a DVD.

"Nothing?"

"Well, I was just about to fire up the third season of *24*."

"Oh!" She sounded a little too enthusiastic. With anyone else, I'd wonder if they were angling for an invitation. But Nat didn't need one, any more than I needed to call before showing up at her place or her grandmother's. Pasquina, Nat's grandmother, had grown up with my nona in Palermo. I'd appeased Nona's early fears about my living alone in Boston by spending every Sunday with her childhood friend and the dozens of relatives and hangers-on who floated in and out of three family apartments in the same building in Boston's Italian North End.

I could hear many of these relatives in the background right now. Maybe Nat needed out.

"You want to come over?"

"No, no, I can't, but . . . listen. You remember Sylvia Cremaldi?"

At the mention of the name, I recalled Sylvia's pale and worried face, the face of someone who grew up hearing nothing but "No!"

"I think so."

"She was ahead of us."

We'd attended the North Bennet Street School, where Nat got her training in jewelry making and I learned the deeply rewarding yet highly impractical and not very lucrative trade of bookbinding. Well, I had to do something. Books seemed . . . logical. I'd just spent four years as an English major, and reading was what I did. Reading is what I would still be doing, if I could pay my rent by lying on the couch with a good novel.

"She did that folio of Danish woodcuts," Nat went on.

"Yeah, I remember."

She paused, possibly distracted by what sounded like a platter hitting the floor, followed by lots of yelling.

"She got a job at the Athenaeum."

The Boston Athenaeum was one of the oldest private lending libraries in America. It was located in a jewel of a building on Beacon Hill.

What I said was, "Really? That's fantastic."

What I thought was, *I'd kill to get a job there! How come she got it?*

To which I answered myself, *She stopped waiting for the people conducting the door-to-door search for bookbinders specializing in bookcalf and marbled boards. She went looking for a job, and when she found that one, she applied.*

"Well," Nat said, "they seem to be having a little problem."

"What kind of problem?"

"Your kind."

I knew it. Nat had dropped her voice to a whisper, maintaining the illusion that this was just between us—that is, if you didn't count all the relatives who were probably standing around the phone: Pasquina and Nat's aunt, Marcella, and of course Camille, and probably Nat's brother, Franco.

"Would you just . . . talk to her? She's kind of freaked out."

I let out a beleaguered sigh. I really didn't want to get involved in this. I took a sip of my wine and stared at the paused image on my TV screen: a fuzzy Jack Bauer with a cell phone pressed to his ear.

"Are you there?" Nat asked.

"I'm here." Here, and feeling guilty. According to Nona, who may not have read the Bible but who sure had listened to her share of Sunday sermons, the problem-solving ability Nat was hoping to enlist fell into the category of talents one was not supposed to bury, and lights one was not supposed to "hide under a barrel."

This parable had baffled me as a child. Not that I didn't understand the message, but hearing the story always brought to mind the image of a circle of Old Testament guys in robes and beards placing a wooden basket—the kind we used for apples and garden clippings—over a lighted candle, which even a kid knows is a bad idea.

I sighed again.

"Okay," said Nat. "I get it." And she did, which was one reason why I loved her. But I'd moved halfway across the country to get away from all this: from the police and the FBI and strangers calling me up in the middle of the night to drag me into messes I had no part in creating and would just as soon not even have known about, thank you very much.

I didn't have a choice when I was a kid. But I wasn't a kid anymore.

And Nat wasn't a stranger. She was the closest thing I had to a sister.

"Okaaaaay."

"You don't have to. Really."

"I know. You think she can keep quiet?"

"She's desperate. She'll do anything you ask."

Nat paused, and when I didn't respond, went on. "The Athenaeum is closed tomorrow, but she has a key. She said she could meet you anytime."

"Tell her I'll come by around eleven."

"Thanks. And just so you know, this wasn't my idea."

"Pasquina?"

"Marcella. Sylvia's mom was in her wedding."

Given the way Nat's family had folded me in when I first moved to Boston, this practically made Marcella *my* aunt.

We chatted for a few more minutes before hanging up. I don't remember finishing my wine, but I must have. I thought about pouring another glass but decided against it. I was always kind of lonesome on Sunday afternoons, especially as darkness started to fall, especially in the autumn, especially if I let myself start thinking about Nona and Dad back in Cleveland, and how they were probably missing me, too, and wondering why Henry and I had to live so far away.

What was Daddy doing right now? Was he down at his workbench in the basement, putting a coat of varnish on something he would give to one of us? Sitting at the kitchen table as the afternoon light faded, wearing a flannel shirt and his old reading glasses, the radio on low, leafing through *Yankee* magazine or the ads in the Sunday paper?

What do you do, when you're seventy-one and the kids you struggled so hard to raise are grown and gone? Do you think about the drunk driver who picked off your bride in the middle of a May afternoon while she was walking to collect your boys at her mother's with your only daughter in a stroller? Do you go back to Ireland and attempt to resume a life you left off four decades ago, when there was not a lick of work to be had, for carpenters or anyone else? Do you throw in your lot with snowbirds like the Costellos and Colm and Ann McInerny, flying south for a condo on a golf course?

I have no idea what you do if you're Owen James O'Malley. I only know what you don't do. Complain.

So, about that other . . . uh, aspect of things. It's kind of hard to explain, but here goes.

I am not musical. Even though I love to listen to jazz and old time and anything Joni Mitchell ever sang, I myself couldn't hum a recognizable "Jingle Bells," much less write it.

But I once saw a musical prodigy being interviewed on *60 Minutes*. He couldn't have been more than ten or eleven, and all his life, people had been comparing him to Mozart, who was entertaining kings and princes by the time he was six and writing symphonies soon after that.

Morley Safer or Dan Rather, or whoever it was, asked him if he could describe what went on for him as he wrote music. And this little boy said that it didn't really feel as if he were *composing* it; he was just copying it down. He didn't sit there trying to come up with a melody. He just listened for it in the air, and there it was. It was the same with harmonies and all the different parts. He just listened for the moments when the instruments floated in and out, all the time writing as fast as he possibly could.

It's kind of like that for me, too.

Whereas most people hear everyday sounds in the air—a siren in the distance, a power drill a few yards over, birds, cars—he hears music. A quartet. A symphony.

And where he hears music, I hear, and see, and can speak with . . .

Ghosts.

Chapter Two

I TOOK THE train to Park Street. The sky was a deep, fall blue
and the Charles River glittered brightly as the train surfaced after
Kendall. Sailboats dipped and bobbed in the basin, toylike and
cheery.

For a holiday, the train had been crowded, and when I climbed
the stairs to Boston Common, I realized why: the Tufts 10K, held
every year on the second Monday in October, Columbus Day.
Tents of every shape and size lined the sidewalks, and loud plastic
banners heralded competing brands of yogurt, power bars, energy
drinks, and cell phones.

Behind me, four aerobics instructors wearing headsets were
leading an entire field of women in a prerace warm-up, to the
boom and thrust of "It's Raining Men." A boy about Henry's
age was groovin' on the sidelines, and I couldn't help thinking, *Too
much MTV*.

As I paused at the top of the hill, though, and looked back
down at the swirl of humanity in shades of khaki and Day-
Glo—the sleep-deprived dads clutching their Starbucks ventis
and manning the strollers, the toddlers careening wildly toward

meltdown, the little clumps of hopeful, average women, about to subject themselves to 6.2 miles of asphalt and concrete—I remembered an Updike story I'd read in college.

In it, a man had gotten sick on a trip and had found himself completely at the mercy of strangers. As his homebound plane cleared the clouds, the sparkling lights of his city came into view: lining the streets and lighting the hospitals and the pools, the ball fields and bridges. Seeing them, he was overcome by tenderness at all the things people come together to do with, and for, one another.

The Athenaeum was only a few blocks away and I was early, so I took my time walking up Park Street. As usual, a van from one of the local TV affiliates was parked within sight of the golden dome, and a reporter I recognized was interviewing a cluster of protesters on the State House steps. It was a scruffy bunch and none too well organized, judging from the size and illegibility of their signs. I hazarded a guess: the legalize pot lobby.

Sylvia must have been watching for me, because the front door of the Athenaeum opened before I even had a chance to scan the granite for a doorbell.

"Thanks for coming, Anza," said Sylvia quietly.

"That's okay."

I stepped inside and she locked the door behind us, then proceeded to an alarm panel in the adjoining coatroom and punched in a code. Six years' time and gainful employment had done little to dispel her timid and furtive air. She was dressed in fawn wool slacks, a pale pink turtleneck, and a beige cardigan. I couldn't be sure, but I would have bet she had a couple of crumpled Kleenexes tucked up her sleeve.

We stood awkwardly for a moment before she said, as though asking my permission, "We could go to my office?"

"Sure."

She attempted a smile, then led me through a succession of rooms right out of *Masterpiece Theatre*, rooms lined with marble statues and gilded portraits, leather wing chairs and highly buffed mahogany tables.

"Have you been here before?" she asked.

I shook my head.

"I could give you a tour," she offered. Anything to delay the conversation we were about to have.

"Maybe later," I said.

"It's beautiful." Her tiny office was painted a pearly sage, and two tall windows offered a view of the old Granary Burying Ground and King's Chapel.

"Thanks. This whole floor was a painting studio, lit by sky-lights. They added on the fourth and fifth floors in the 1900s."

I walked to the windows and gazed out, feeling centuries away from the cheerful throngs on the common.

"How long have you worked here?" I asked. I crossed the room and sat down in a wooden armchair by her desk.

"A few months. It's not permanent; at least not yet."

My ears pricked up. I could *really* see myself in this office. "What do you mean?"

Sylvia didn't sit at her desk, choosing instead one of two up-holstered chairs that formed what decorators call a "conversation area." I wasn't sure if I should move, but she patted the seat be-side her, in a curiously personal gesture that made me feel like a cat or a two-year-old. I hopped up obediently and toddled over.

"I was working for John Winslow," she said.

"Winslow, as in Winslow Paper?"

"And the Winslow Building at Mass. General, the Winslow gym at Harvard . . ."

"The Winslow Room at the MFA?" I asked.

She nodded. "He died in January. His collection came here and I came with it. I was restoring about forty volumes, and he left a fund in place for me to finish the job. Once his kids donated the books, it just made sense for me to work out of the bindery here."

"What's in the collection?" I asked.

Her smile became conspiratorial. "Daniell's *Oriental Scenery*, for starters."

"No!"

She smiled, with a hint of satisfaction in her eyes. "Gabriel Lory's *Swiss Illustrations*, Gould and Elliot plates."

I caught my breath. "Plants or birds?"

"Both!" A little color had come to her cheeks. For book geeks like Sylvia and me, these were emeralds and rubies. She paused, savoring the moment. She pulled her chair a little closer and leaned in.

"And something else," she whispered, her gaze meeting mine full-on for the first time, as though she was trying to decide whether she could really trust me with what she was about to reveal.

I waited for her to go on, but instead, she sat back. "You'll think I'm crazy."

"No, I won't."

She didn't seem convinced. "Look," I said, "*I'm* the one who talks to ghosts!"

She laughed and I saw her relax a little. There was another long pause before she spoke.

"Finny bought it in the sixties. In Switzerland."

"Who's Finny?" I asked.

"Oh, sorry—Mr. Winslow. His middle name was Phineas; he went by Finny."

I nodded.

"An illuminated manuscript," she continued.

This got my attention. These manuscripts dated from the Middle Ages and had been calligraphed and painted by monks in scriptoriums on the skin of calves, sheep, or goats. Most were religious, many were painted with real gold, and all were priceless.

"We think it might be the Book of Kildare," she whispered.

I stared at her. She *was* crazy. She had to be. The Book of Kildare, said to be the most splendid illustration of the Gospels ever produced, was created in the twelfth century by monks at Kildare Abbey, founded by Saint Brigid in County Kildare, Ireland. Reputed to be even more magnificent than the legendary Book of Kells, it disappeared during the Reformation and was never seen again.

"What makes you think . . . ?"

"A few things," she answered. "We were in touch with some art historians at Yale and The Cloisters. They led us to the writings of a medieval ecclesiastic called Gerald of Wales. He saw the manuscript before it disappeared and wrote about it in detail. He described some pretty unusual images."

"Such as?"

"A snake devouring a lion cub. An eagle wearing a bloody crown. Pages that look like oriental carpets, with intricate coils and knots."

"How many of the things he described are in your book?"

"All of them."

"Wow," I whispered.

She nodded, scanning my face. "We were so close to proving it. We only had to verify a few more details. Hardly anyone knew about it, because if word got out too early, before we'd really built an airtight case, well, you know how it goes with the art establishment."

She was giving me way too much credit. I had no idea how it went with the art establishment.

"You read about that Caravaggio," she prompted, apparently assuming that I just needed to be reminded of how much I actually knew. "The one in that monastery?"

I dimly recalled an article in *The New Yorker,* years ago.

"The *experts* don't like *amateurs* claiming to have discovered long-lost treasures," she explained.

"Why not?"

"They spend their lives hoping to make those headlines. And God help you if you poke your nose in before you've got absolute proof. They'll pick you apart. Besides, if the manuscript really is what we—"

She broke off. There was no more "we."

"What it appears to be, Finny wanted the right thing done with it."

"What would that be?"

"I'm not sure."

I nodded. We sat quietly for a few moments.

"Does anyone else know about it?" I finally asked.

"Only Sam, Sam Blake. He ran the bindery here for forty years. He retired in August."

"You felt you could trust him?"

"Oh, completely." She smiled. "Sam's life is books. I was nervous about the manuscript being here in the bindery, so he kept it at his place with his own collection, in this little room he's outfitted for climate and humidity control. He made me take it back here when he retired, though."

"Where is it now?" I whispered.

"Downstairs."

"On the *shelves?*" I dearly hoped not.

She shook her head. "I've hidden it. In the bindery."

"Didn't they inventory the collection when they took possession?"

"I made a false cover." Her eyes were shining brightly. "For all intents and purposes, there *is* no illuminated manuscript. There's just a newly rebound second edition of Hoeffler's *Mysterium Musicum*."

Well, well. Furtive, yes. Timid, no.

"But why?"

"Because I promised Finny I'd see it through. Tad would probably have sold it to the highest bidder, and that's not what Finny wanted."

"I take it Tad's his son."

"Son, and executor. Finny also had two daughters, Josie and Esther. Josie's all right. As long as she can go to Kripalu and Aspen, she doesn't really care what Tad does. But she would never stand up to her brother. Esther I like. She's much younger than the other two. She's a sculptor in the Berkshires."

"Is Finny's wife still alive?"

"She died a long time ago."

Neither of us spoke for a few moments. The sun had shifted, and it suddenly felt much later in the day.

"This may be a stupid question," I finally said. "But why didn't Finny just leave the book to you?"

She appeared surprised, then smiled sadly and shook her head. "Oh, no, he wouldn't have done that. He didn't feel that anyone should own it—not me, not his kids, not even him. He felt it belonged to the world. Besides, he died very suddenly. He'd been sick for a while, but in the end, he went in two days."

No doubt this was all true, but I had a nagging sense that if Finny had felt for Sylvia what she so obviously felt for him, he might have entrusted her with the disposition of the book. Time might tell if my hunch was correct.

"So," I said, changing the subject. "You heard about me through Marcella."

She nodded.

"What did she tell you?"

She shifted nervously and couldn't seem to meet my gaze.

"That I can see ghosts? And talk to them?"

She looked up sharply. "Is it true?"

"It is."

"How did you . . . When did you . . . ?" She faltered helplessly.

Oh, good. She wasn't going to put me through the usual tests. Though that sometimes comes later.

"My grandmother basically raised me. My mom died when I was a baby and my dad had all he could do to keep track of my two brothers. So I spent a lot of time with Nona. One day, when I was four, she overheard me talking to someone in the next room. She came in to see who it was, but there was nobody there. Just me. She asked me who I'd been talking to, and I told her he said his name was Vinny and his dog's name was Lola and he came from Italy.

"She sat down and started to cry. She knew who it was, or rather whose *spirit* it was—that of Vinny Sottosanto, a boy she'd been in love with but wasn't allowed to marry. Her cousin called her an hour later, but Nona already knew—Vinny had died of a stroke. What broke her heart was, he could have come to her, talked to her."

"Your grandmother can . . . do this, too?"

I nodded. "She was so upset. She knew he had seen her as an old woman, but he hadn't wanted her to see him as an old man. He broke her heart all over again."

"So he just . . . flew over the ocean?" Sylvia asked softly. She wasn't being snarky, just struggling to understand.

"Spirits can do that after they die."

She stood up. She crossed the room to the window and struggled to open it. She flipped on a table lamp, then turned and sat down on the windowsill, searching my face.

"I know it's a lot to take in," I said.

"No, no."

I proceeded gently. Some people find this to be terrifying, and I can understand why. But for me, it's normal. Ghosts are just another category of people, with the same quirks and qualities they possessed in life.

"Some people aren't quite ready to leave. When they die."

"Like who?" she asked.

"Oh, parents of small children. Victims of crime, especially murder victims. They want their murderers caught. People get really attached—to places, to objects, to other people—and they just can't give them up. But if they hang around too long, then they *can't* leave. It's like they're *stuck*. Sometimes I can help them."

"Leave?" She was pale.

"Deal with what's keeping them from leaving."

"Where do they go? When they 'leave'?"

"That I couldn't tell you."

Chapter Three

I COULD FEEL the force of their fury before I even caught a glimpse of them. And a glimpse it was, for we had no sooner passed through the first floor in the creaky old cage of an elevator than the lights began to flicker and then went out, plunging us into darkness as we hit the basement floor.

"My God," said Sylvia, fumbling for the door handle. I was afraid we might be trapped, if the electricity was truly out, but at least we weren't dangling between floors. They were monks, no doubt about that, and from the thickness and color of their worn linen robes, I guessed they were seven or eight centuries past their use-by date. The younger one had a blank, impassive gaze, but the sight of the older monk raised the hair on the back of my neck. It wasn't danger I felt—he was dead; he couldn't hurt us—but a shock of surprise at being on the receiving end of his blazing contempt. I felt like saying, "Hey, what did *I* do?"

The lights flickered and came back on, so Sylvia was able to open the door.

"Does that happen often?" I asked.

"Yes. It's one of the things that made me think we might have . . .

a ghost." She let out a bright, nervous giggle, as though she was a little embarrassed to be saying this out loud. She closed the elevator door with precise care, and I remembered from childhood that if the accordion door wasn't fully closed, completing the electrical connection, the elevator couldn't be called to another floor.

"You do," I said.

"We *do*?"

I nodded.

"How do you know?"

I shrugged. Wasn't it obvious? "I saw them."

"Where?" She glanced around quickly. "Here?"

"Just now. That's why the power went out. It's one of the few things earthbound spirits can actually do: disrupt the flow of energy."

We started down the hall to the bindery, where she was going to show me the manuscript. Though it didn't have the elegance of the upper floors, the basement was well maintained: the floors glazed and buffed, the walls painted the pale and reputedly "calming" green of grammar school classrooms and 1940s kitchens.

"What do they look like?" she asked softly.

"Ghosts in general? Or these in particular?"

She was struggling to appear calm, but I could tell she was rattled, so I chatted on in a tone intended to convey nonchalance.

"They look just like they did when they were alive, just not . . . solid."

She paused and turned.

"These two," I said, my glance indicating the floor above us, "were monks."

"Oh my God." The color had drained from her face and she suddenly had the dazed and chalky look of someone about to pass out. I steered her toward a nearby chair and had her hang her head over her knees and take a few deep breaths.

"Don't worry," I said, rubbing her back the way I rub Henry's when he's not feeling well. "They can't hurt you. They're just trying to get your attention."

She took a few more breaths and then sat up. "But why?"

"That's what we have to find out."

She nodded trustingly. I sat down on the floor beside her chair.

"What else happened? To make you . . . look for help?"

She let out a sigh. I suspected she was now sorry she had crossed the line separating the abstract possibility of ghosts from my confirming that they were, in fact, absolutely *here*. But it was too late now.

"Well, I'd come into the bindery, and it would look like a tornado had touched down. My things would be thrown all over the place. Not the books themselves, but all my tools and supplies. And where Chandler, the other bookbinder, works, not a pin would be out of place."

"That's pretty standard," I said.

"And another thing—this ring." She held out her hand. "I always leave it in my top drawer upstairs. Opals are really porous, and some of the substances I work with—"

"I know."

"Oh, right. Sorry! I keep it in a little alabaster box, but sometimes, when I go to put it on at the end of the day, the box is empty. It's happened a number of times, so I know it's not just my memory. I always find it eventually—in the middle of the floor or right on my bookshelf—always in plain sight. Just not where I left it."

"And nothing else is missing?"

"No. The door's locked. Could a ghost do something like that?"

"Move something light, like a ring? Yeah, sure. They're pure energy. The things you're talking about, whipping up a little wind, moving light objects, messing with electronics and electricity—that's the usual bag of tricks."

She nodded. I sensed she was trying to absorb all of this.

"I can see the book some other time," I said, though I was desperate for a glimpse.

"No, I'm fine." She stood up, testing whether she really was fine, then started down the hall. I got to my feet and followed.

"That's funny," she said, when we were just a few paces from the bindery door. "The lights in the bindery are on."

"Don't worry," I said. "It wouldn't be ghosts. They don't need light."

I saw her hand hesitate on the doorknob, then she took a deep breath, turned it, and flung the door open with such force that it slammed back against the interior wall.

"Chandler!"

"Jesus, Sylvia!"

"Sorry!"

"You scared the shit out of me!"

Which didn't look as though it would take too much. Granted, we were in a basement, and the reflection from the green walls could have made just about anyone look sickly, but the man had a sallow and sour quality, as though he rarely breathed fresh air.

So much for seeing the manuscript.

"This is . . . my friend, Anza," Sylvia sputtered. "She's a bookbinder, too."

Chandler looked peeved at being disturbed. He had twelve or fourteen architectural plates laid out on a table and was cutting layers of tissue.

"She wanted to see where we work," Sylvia managed, nodding overenthusiastically.

"Well, here it is," Chandler said grouchily.

"What are you working on?" I stupidly asked, the result being that fifteen minutes later, we were still listening to a discourse on lesser-known details of Palladian influence in the buildings of nineteenth-century Philadelphia. He had really warmed up—to the sound of his own voice.

"Well," Sylvia broke in, "we should probably let you get back to work. Anza has . . ."

I could see her searching helplessly for something I had . . . to do? To get to? To treat with an immediate dose of . . . something?

". . . a friend running the Tufts 10K!" I offered brilliantly. I beamed at Sylvia.

"How unpleasant," he mumbled. A horrifying image of Chandler in spandex, and too little of it, sprang unbidden to mind.

I had to agree.

———※———

Sylvia unlocked her office door, switched on the light, and stepped inside. A strangled cry escaped her lips, and as my gaze swept the room, my stomach did a little flip. Desk drawers were pulled out and their contents spilled across the carpet, and several beautiful shells I had noticed, pearly varieties in various shapes, had been shattered.

Man, these guys were mad!

Then I saw him again, the older monk. He had apparently just finished his rampage, because he was red and breathless.

"What's *this* all about?" I demanded, fixing him with a direct stare. "You should be ashamed of yourself! This is no way for a man of God to behave! Trashing people's offices!"

I have to admit, I always enjoy the look of shock on their faces. Ghosts don't know I can see them. Until I speak to them directly or wave or something, they assume I'm like every other clueless human being.

They were thinking in a language that was unfamiliar to me, a language I had never heard spoken. But words are not, and never have been, barriers for me. I have no idea how or why, but I understand what is being thought. That's how it's always been.

"Oh my God," Sylvia said. Miraculously, she was still on her feet.

"Thou shalt not take the name of the Lord, thy God, in vain!" the older monk bellowed.

"Knock off the swearing," I said to Sylvia. "You're pissing him off."

"I didn't swear," she said.

" 'God' is a swear," I explained, "when you say it like that."

"I'm sorry! I didn't know!" I noticed that her hands were shaking.

"What do you want?" I asked him.

"I demand to speak with the cardinal!"

He was quavering with fury, and I tried to keep from smiling by biting the inside of my cheek. He was giving my son some real competition in the tantrum department.

"I don't think that's possible, Brother. As you probably know."

He didn't answer, but I had his attention.

"I'm sure you've tried. And he couldn't see you, could he?"

He seemed to deflate before my eyes. Behind him, the younger monk shook his head silently.

"I'll be glad to help if I can."

"You?" The sneer had returned to his expression.

I speculated on which part of me he would find most objectionable, and the list was long: I was a lapsed Catholic, an unwed mother, a female wearing jeans and a torn T-shirt that might be a tad too tight, a female wearing red(dish) lipstick, a female who didn't feel she had to genuflect before him and ask for his blessing. In short, a female who wasn't a nun.

"Suit yourself," I said. "You probably have people showing up here all the time who can see you and talk to you."

He glared at me, but I could see that this had hit home. "I must speak with the cardinal!"

"Not going to happen, Brother. I'd do it if I could but I seriously doubt that someone like me could get Cardinal O'Shea here to do the bidding of someone like you."

"And by that you mean . . . ?"

"A ghost. With all due respect. You should know that better than anyone: the Church doesn't believe in ghosts."

Officially, that is. Unofficially, I have friendly working relationships with a number of men of the cloth, some of whom wear black, and some of whom wear scarlet. Cardinal O'Shea might not take my call if I phoned up his office and asked to speak with him, but I had people I could get to call him.

I glanced over at Sylvia. She had found her way to a chair and sat down. As though to compensate for her profane lapse, her posture was perfect and her ankles were primly crossed.

The older monk began to pace as his younger companion watched nervously. I could tell that the younger ghost wanted to speak but didn't dare. From their relationship, I inferred that the older monk was his abbot.

"So it's really up to you," I ventured. "If you want my help, you have to tell me what's going on."

The older monk paused, then turned toward me slowly.

I'll tell you . . . *nothing,* he thought coldly.

"Not even what language you're speaking?"

He could not prevent me from hearing what he was thinking, so as first he, then the younger monk vanished into air, I heard my answer as that young musical prodigy might hear a snatch of melody in the wind:

Irish.

Clouds had gathered during the course of the day, and the few sailboats left on the river looked lonesome and vulnerable, like toys in danger of being picked up and tossed by an irritable child. I had stayed longer at the Athenaeum than I'd planned and was anxious to get home; Declan and Henry would be back anytime now, and I wanted to have a meal ready. I glanced at my watch and relaxed a little: it was only a quarter to four.

It had taken Sylvia and me half an hour to put her office back together. We'd replaced the items in her desk drawer, straightened the books on her shelves, and swept the opalescent shards of shell into her wastebasket. Her delicate pearly nautilus had been shattered, and a shell with a chestnut zebra pattern had taken a pretty hard hit, but a couple of the smaller, harder shells had survived with only chips.

"Why would they do this?" she asked, positioning the surviving shells so that the chips would be hidden.

"I don't know. The younger one seems nicer, but I don't think we'll get anything out of him unless he comes to see you alone. Which poses a problem."

Sylvia was straightening the items on her desk. She looked up. "You're the only one they can communicate with."

"Yeah."

I sat down. All of a sudden I felt very tired, and then I remembered that I had forgotten to pick up the blueberry muffin I'd intended to buy with my Starbucks on my way in this morning. I was fading. Maybe they'd be giving out leftover Luna bars on the common. I liked those Chocolate Pecan Pie ones.

Sylvia wiped off the top of her desk—aha! She did tuck Kleenex up her sleeve! She came over and sat down beside me.

"Are you . . . crazy busy right now?" she asked.

"My son's getting home in a little while. I really have to—"

"No," she interrupted, "I mean, are you working full-time?"

"I wish." She had no idea how I wished. We were getting by, but just barely.

She nodded and smiled. "Could we meet for coffee tomorrow?"

"I have a meeting at two in Carlisle, but I'm free in the morning."

"There's a café on the corner of Mass. Ave. and Commonwealth. Would eight thirty be too early?"

"Not at all," I said.

Chapter Four

THE CANNELLONI WERE warming up when I heard Declan's truck pull into the driveway. I glanced out the window, but the doors didn't open right away. Transitions were hard. As much as Henry might want to see me, he hated saying good-bye to his dad. On Fridays, it went the other way.

Declan and his wife, Kelly, had been separated for eight months when he and I met one night at a bar in the North End. I wish I could blame the luscious and vaguely tawdry turn the evening took (backseat of a car parked up by the ocean in Swampscott) on something like euphoria over Italy's winning the World Cup or the Patriots' winning the Super Bowl, but I can't. It was the fatal . . . No, fatal is not a word I could ever use in a sentence that leads directly to Henry. Nothing ended that night. In fact, just the opposite.

It was the . . . *irresistible* combination of eyes the blue of faded jeans, a spring sea breeze wafting sweetly up Hanover Street, and, well, let's just say *more than two* whiskey sours, a throwback of a cocktail choice I later had reason to regret. Briefly.

A violin maker from North Bennet had introduced us. He knew Declan from a soccer league.

"How are you?" Declan had asked, with his soft Galway lilt.

"Can't complain." Or wouldn't dream of it, when standing in front of a dead ringer for Gabriel Byrne.

"Sure you can." He had smiled.

"Who would listen?"

"I would."

That's all it took. That and the crooked little smile I now see on Henry every so often, when he's pretty sure I'll appreciate the humor in a sticky situation, or at least forgive him without a lot of drama.

When the Wild Cherry nail polish, for example, that he was secretly using to paint in the heart on a card he was making for me accidentally tipped over onto my expensive, handmade Italian paper, paper that took weeks to arrive.

Well, he *was* making me a card.

I took a sip of my wine. Declan had opened his door, and rather than exiting through the door on the passenger side, Henry was sliding across the seat. He liked to hang out in the driver's seat for a minute or two, hands on the wheel, just getting the feel of things. I knocked on the window, but they didn't hear me.

Declan had been truthful that first night. He and Kelly were separated, they'd been unhappy, they were trying to work things out. They didn't have Delia and Nell at the time, or I like to think I would have exercised a little more restraint.

What can I say?

I was weak.

"Hi, sweetie!" I called down as they clomped up the stairs to our second floor apartment. "How *was* it?"

His face told me a lot: that it had been great, but he wasn't great right now because it was over. He appeared to need what I knew he would want the least: a hot bath, an early bedtime, Mommy love. The cannelloni might revive him for a while, but it wasn't going to be an easy night.

In the past few months, ever since starting kindergarten at St. Enda's, he'd become acutely conscious that he lived with—a girl. And Delia and Nell were girls. So was Kelly. The only two guys in the whole sorry picture were him and his dad. This had made the weekly return to Mom-land all the more difficult.

I wasn't sure where this was coming from. He'd had very little awareness of boys and girls—or rather, boys versus girls—at the touchy-feely preschool he'd attended for two years. In fact, he'd been shocked to learn that his best friend, Carey, who'd had the cubby next to his for two years and whose Lego-building skills were universally admired, *was* a girl.

It didn't come from Declan, either; I was pretty sure of that. Though he *is* a police officer, which might lead you to draw certain conclusions, he had only one brother in a house full of girls. He got it. His sisters had made very sure of that.

"You must be starving!" I said as Declan swung Henry's backpack onto the kitchen table.

"We had McDonald's," Henry said.

"At one o'clock!" Declan added, seeing the look on my face.

I really wanted to kiss him (Henry, that is) but I could tell this would not be a good idea. I ruffled his hair a bit, and he pulled away.

"Go dump your stuff and wash up," I said. And then, in an attempt to cheer him up, I added, "I have a surprise for you after supper." I didn't, but I'd think of something.

"What?" he demanded.

"Never mind," I said.

"Come on!" he wheedled.

"After supper," I said in a singsong voice. He made a face but headed off toward the bathroom. I heard the water blasting out at full force.

"How was it?" I asked Declan.

"Oh, grand, yeah."

"How are the girls?"

"Right as rain; everybody's good."

He'd seen some sun and wind in the past few days, and my stomach did a little swoop.

"You want a beer? Glass of wine?" I wished I felt the way most divorced women feel when the dads make the return drop: relieved to see the back of him. But then, you can't be divorced if you were never married.

"No, thanks." He smiled. "I should probably—" He glanced in the direction of the driveway.

"Sure," I said. "No problem."

I knew he would have stayed for a while if I invoked Henry, the difficulty of the transition, all of that, but that would be cheating. This whole weird arrangement of ours worked because nobody played games, and I wasn't about to start.

Kelly and I had a couple of rough patches in the first year or two, but things have gradually worked out. I like her, and I think she likes me; well enough, anyway. She treats Henry like a son, not a stepson, and I will never be able to repay her for that. They're sending the girls to St. Enda's—Delia will start in the fall and Nell the year after—in part so the kids can be in school together. And Dec never misses a T-ball game or a parents' night. Kelly wouldn't let him. Given that I had an affair with her husband while they were still technically married, adding one more obstacle to their process of reconciliation, she's been a regular Mother Teresa. The least I can do is act like a grown-up and not confuse—or represent—a need or desire of my own as Henry's.

"The canoe tipped over!" Henry announced excitedly, bouncing over to the table, where the pan of cannelloni sat cooling.

"Good thing you had your life jacket on!" I said.

The glance I shot Declan said, *He did have his life jacket on, didn't he?*

The glance he shot back said, *Of course he had his life jacket on! What kind of idiot do you think I am?*

"I hate life jackets," Henry announced. "I know how to swim."

He peeled off some of the cheese topping and popped it into his mouth before I could stop him. I'd recently pointed out that this was kind of like cheating, because everybody knows that the cheese topping is the best part and everybody wants their own. To which he responded by pointing out that since I always let him have my cheese anyway, and it's just the two of us here, what was the problem? I had a glimpse of what he might be like as a teenager.

"And there was a *ghost!*" he said.

I snapped to. I have always feared (a lot) and hoped (a tiny bit) that Henry might have inherited my ability, as I inherited Nona's, but so far, no sign in sight.

"There was the *story* of a ghost," Declan clarified, shooting me a significant glance.

Declan knows about me. Depending on how you look at it, either he has helped me out a number of times or I have helped him. He might well have made detective without my "anonymous tips" (that's what we decided to call them), pieces of information I picked up from the earthbound spirits of crime victims. He might have cracked those very cold cases on his own. But we shall never know.

"She fell in the lake and died!" Henry said, his mouth full of cheese.

"Don't talk with your mouth full," I said. "Who?"

He tried to answer without opening his mouth very much. "The little girl. In the olden days."

"I thought you didn't believe in ghosts," I said, scooping some cannelloni onto a plate and setting it on the table. Henry grabbed a fork from the drawer, sat down, and tucked in. He appeared to be ravenous.

He looked up at Declan. "Do you think there's ghosts, Daddy?" I sensed that this might break along gender lines.

"Oh, I'm keeping an open mind," Declan said.

What he had said to me, when we had *the conversation*, was, "Well, there's more than one meaning to the word, true." I think he has his doubts, to be honest, but he grew up on his granny's fireside tales from the west of Ireland, so he's pretty used to talk of faeries and changelings and great, gray horses striding through the surf and carrying off wives and children.

"You can hear her crying," Henry said. "At night sometimes."

"Did *you* hear her?" I asked.

He nodded earnestly, eyes wide. "I think I did." He paused. "I *might* have."

Declan's wry grin said, *No way.*

"What's my surprise?" Henry asked. He had just gotten out of the tub and into his pj's, and he had that clean baby-hair smell that I found hard to resist.

"Nat's taking you to the movies!" She wasn't, but she would. She owed me.

"Oh," he said, sounding a little disappointed.

"I thought you were dying to see . . ." The name of the movie momentarily escaped me, but not the image of an army of insects preparing to do battle with a muskrat, a ferret, and a mole. "That ant one," I finished lamely.

"I thought maybe we were getting cable," he said sadly. Much to his continuing disappointment, I drew the line at cable and microwaves. I didn't want us eating Hot Pockets, and I didn't want to be called "Dude."

I smiled. "Sorry."

"When?" he asked.

"When what?" I had forgotten I was in the middle of a lie.

"When's Nat taking me?"

"Oh! Soon! This week!" I hoped.

"Okay," he said sweetly, and I immediately hated myself. He was so trusting. Not that I didn't plan to make good on this fake promise of mine—I did; I would—but still, it was a small betrayal.

Like telling him he could turn the traffic light green if he blew hard enough. Like the father in a story I'd read one time burning the grilled cheeses and serving them to his kids anyway, black side down.

Oh, well.

"I'll read you two chapters tonight!" I said. We were making our way through *Redwall,* one chapter a night, and two would be a treat.

"But I was gone *three* nights," he reasoned.

I did a swift, silent calculation—three chapters would take us an hour. But if I read quietly and had him all tucked in, warm and cozy, he'd probably last about twenty minutes.

"All right," I said, as though he had won a huge victory.

Momentarily forgetting that I was a girl, he gave me a hard hug, then pulled back, looked me straight in the eyes, and gave me a kiss.

Chapter Five

A HEAVY OVERNIGHT rainstorm had washed the streets and the sidewalks and stripped the trees of leaves that might otherwise have hung on for a few more days. The low clouds were breaking up as I ordered my coffee and settled in at a table by the window. A police car roared by. A beautiful fat woman, who must have lived or worked in the building just in from the corner, was using a lime green power hose to wash the slippery fallen leaves into the street.

Inside the Café Rouge, a stack of cornstalks paid incongruous homage to the season, tucked in as they were among the stylish French posters and alabaster lamps. It was my second time in the place, and the guy who poured my coffee was so nice, and so cute, that I folded a dollar into the tip cup.

I was hoping that this meeting wouldn't take too long. I had a two o'clock appointment in Carlisle with a demanding client and I needed to have my ducks in a row. It was the kind of job that fed the bank account but not the spirit. A wealthy developer in the western exurbs had hired me to create thirteen identical coffee-table books celebrating his completion of a dozen virtually identical trophy houses on the former site of a hundred-year-old orchard.

He'd hired an architectural photographer to document the destruction of the orchard and all the phases of construction. Now that the houses had all been sold, presumably to people who hadn't caught up with the news that two-story "great rooms" were hard to furnish and had a tendency to make one feel small and unsettled, he'd hired me to make the actual books. They were to be bound in leather and embossed in gilt. He would present them to the buyers at the closings. Of course, he also wanted a copy of the book for himself.

I caught sight of Sylvia across the way. It was cruel to notice, but she already had the air of an old-lady-in-the-making, waiting patiently for the light to change with her umbrella and rain boots and bags. I stopped myself. This was mean. Still, I couldn't help wondering if she had one of those clear, fold-up rain hats, the kind in the little vinyl sleeve, tucked into a compartment in her purse.

"Coffee?" I asked as she caught sight of me and approached the table.

"Tea, please. With lemon."

"I've been thinking," she said moments later, stirring honey into the steamy liquid in front of her, "that maybe I could hire you."

I took a deep breath. While I have gotten paid (sometimes extravagantly) for my work with earthbound spirits, I had already decided that I was not going to take any money from Sylvia. This—uh, consultation—was a deposit in the checkbook of my soul.

"No, I really . . . I couldn't."

"But I thought you weren't working full-time."

"I'm not."

She gave me a puzzled look, then shook her head. "I meant, hire you to bind some books."

Oh.

"I've got some discretionary funds." She smiled slyly.

I saw the logic immediately: I would have access to the monks and the monks would have access to me.

"I'd love to," I said. "But is there enough work?"

"Oh, yeah. Dozens of books on British history, memoirs of the Great Indian Uprising, Kashmiri travelogues. Finny's father-in-law was a diplomat in Hyderabad. I could probably keep you busy for a couple of months."

"That'd be great."

"You could start anytime. In fact, you could even come in with me now. I could show you around."

"Sure." I didn't have to leave for Carlisle until one.

Sylvia looked a little relieved. "We just have to stop by Finny's house on the way," she said. "Tad's cleaning it out to put it on the market. He asked me to look at a couple of books that have turned up."

We chatted, finishing our drinks slowly, then took our time walking down Commonwealth Avenue. The "house" was, well, frankly, a mansion in the middle of the block between Clarendon and Dartmouth streets. It was flanked by two other buildings that looked recently restored, and though its tiny front garden had been allowed to go to seed, the place had the worn and comfortable air of money. Old money. Sylvia rang the bell. The remaining leaves on the magnolia tree beside us glowed brightly in a shaft of sunlight.

I had learned to recognize some of the signs of vast, inherited wealth shortly after I moved to Boston. I was walking around this very neighborhood, looking for a studio or a one-bedroom to rent. It was the first of September and many of the apartments were turning over—students were leaving town and others were arriving, and U-Hauls were everywhere you looked. I happened upon an elegant matron having a conversation with someone I took to be a neighborhood "character," if not actually a homeless person, resting on the building's granite stoop.

I asked if by chance they (meaning the well-fed matron, of course) knew of any small apartments becoming available, and the vagrant offered to take me inside. To my surprise, she owned the building. And three or four others in Back Bay. She had a studio apartment for rent.

I moved in a week later, and over the next two years, I learned a lot about old money, Boston style. That the people who had it didn't tend to put in "cook's kitchens" with polished-granite countertops and Sub-Zero freezers and didn't tend to worry too much about the sofas sagging and the walls cracking and the oriental rugs wearing thin. They rode old three-speed bikes and wore sweaters with holes in the elbows, and their summer places were less like the McMansions ruining Nantucket than like the cabins at Girl Scout camp.

A housekeeper, whom Sylvia introduced to me as Mrs. Martin, answered the door swiftly, greeted Sylvia warmly, and offered us banana bread, the nostalgic waft of which nearly brought tears to my eyes. Sylvia declined for us both (*Speak for yourself!* I felt like saying), so Mrs. Martin led us right up a formal staircase to Mr. Winslow's second-floor study, where we were supposed to wait for Tad, who was on the phone. I longed for more than a glimpse of the first-floor rooms, being categorically in love with all things forlorn—falling-down houses, homely little kids in eyeglasses—but all I had time to notice were sheets covering the furniture, floors in need of refinishing, and large, dark rectangles on the faded wallpaper where paintings had formerly hung.

The study was partially disassembled, and Sylvia sank down on a hassock as soon as Mrs. Martin closed the door. It *was* sad, and I didn't even know him. Half of the books were gone from the shelves, and the drawers of the tables waiting to be taken to Skinner, where they were going to be auctioned off with the rest of the furniture the heirs didn't want, had all been emptied out. Cardboard boxes under the windows were filled with papers, notebooks, and small, old volumes, and an open shoe box (Brooks Brothers) on top of Mr. Winslow's desk held what I took to be the intimate contents of his top desk drawer: coins, old pens, a key chain, some faded Polaroids curling at the edges.

I thought of my mother and father in one such photo, sitting in the sand at a beach on Lake Erie. It was taken before they were married, when I imagine that the word *husband* on my mother's tongue still had the tang of a rare, exotic fruit. I can easily recall the image, the way she's leaning in under my father's arm, her head tilted slightly in the softening light, caught in the middle of a word she is speaking to whomever clicked the shutter. Ten years later, she was dead.

We heard brisk, confident footsteps in the hall and Tad opened the door. He was probably in his late thirties, was uncommonly tall—six four or five—and had the healthy, even glow of a person who eats perfectly at all times, engages in regular, vigorous exercise (atop a polo pony? a windsurfing board? skis?), and drinks sparingly of very fine wine. As opposed to me, who gets her ass to the pool maybe three times a month, eats too little, followed by too much, and drinks whatever's on sale in the two-for-ten-dollars bin. That Sancerre was a gift.

Sylvia stood up and introduced us, identifying me as a bookbinder she had hired to help complete "the Winslow Collection." The phrase brought a flicker of a smile to Tad's lips.

"That's an unusual name," he said to me.

"It's short for Speranza."

"Ah."

"Which means *hope*," I blundered on. "In Italian." I smiled weakly.

He nodded vaguely. I could tell he wasn't the least bit interested in either my name or me. He had a stack of books in his arms, and Sylvia hurried to clear off space on a nearby table.

"Thank you for coming," he said, laying the volumes down one by one. "These were in the boxes from Father's office. I doubt they're valuable, but I thought I'd have you look at them."

"Sure." Sylvia picked up the first book and opened it to the flyleaf. I could see the faded, bubbly swirl of the marbled paper, which, from the looks of it, was probably French, probably mid–eighteenth century. I knew she wouldn't be able to give Tad any definitive answers without examining the books closely and doing some research, so we'd probably be taking them all back to the Athenaeum with us. If I wanted to have a sneak peek at any more of the house, I had to act quickly.

"Excuse me," I said, "but would you mind if I used the ladies' room?"

Ladies' room. How ridiculous a term was that? It was silly to be embarrassed about asking to use the bathroom—I had potty-trained Henry with the help of a book called *Everyone Poops*—but I still felt a little sheepish drawing attention to bodily functions, especially because I had no intention of using a bathroom. I just wanted to snoop.

Tad looked up distractedly. "Down the hall, then take a left. It'll be on your right."

"Thanks." I made a quick escape and closed the door quietly behind me. The hall stretched all the way to the rear of the building, and I walked back slowly, peeping into one gloomy room after another. You forget that the only windows in these buildings are the grand ones in the front and the considerably less grand ones overlooking the alleys in the back.

I turned the corner and there he was, the ghost of a butler. He was dressed in a formal uniform: dark gray tails over a pale gray vest. Though he didn't wear gloves, there were links in his cuffs, and his feathery white hair appeared to have resisted a recent effort to smooth it into place.

"Hello," I said. Though he was clearly stunned that I could see him, he bowed politely. His sweet, faded gallantry just about broke my heart.

"Who are you?" I asked gently.

"John Grady," he answered. "Ma'am." He pronounced it "Mum."

"Did you . . . work here?" I asked. I often meet the ghosts of lonely old men who had lived for their jobs—ushers and waiters and doormen who had eaten most of their meals at lunch counters and spent most of their nights in boardinghouse rooms, counting the hours until they could return to life at work.

"Yes, ma'am."

"For the Winslows?"

"For Miss Edlyn's family, ma'am, the Shand-Thompsons. In London, and in Brighton in the summer. My Mairead, God rest her soul, she was Miss Edlyn's—Mrs. Winslow's—nurse."

"After she got sick?" I was guessing.

"No, ma'am—when she was born. And every day of her life until—"

He broke off. I nodded.

"You came here with her? From England?"

Now he smiled. "We did, indeed. The missus and I, we like to say we were His Lordship's wedding gift. So Miss Edlyn wouldn't be alone in America. We loved her like our own."

Suddenly, I heard voices; Tad or Sylvia had opened the study door. I hated to interrupt John Grady's sweet reminiscences, but I had to.

"We don't have much time. Could I ask you . . . ?"

He nodded.

"Why are you here?"

"The deed, to the house in Swansea. I kept it in Gwennie's rhyme book—*The Butterfly's Ball.*"

I heard footsteps approaching and recognized just whose they were.

"Gwennie?" I whispered.

"Our daughter. She and Miss Edlyn were like—"

The footsteps were nearly upon us.

"I'll come back," I whispered.

"Don't go!" he moaned, loudly enough that Tad would have heard him, if Tad could hear the voices of ghosts. I wheeled around sharply, nearly colliding with all six and a half feet of the family executor as he rounded the corner. Which would have put me nose to chest, given my height of five six.

"Oh, sorry!" I said.

Tad nodded distractedly. "I'll be back in a minute," he responded, hurrying off down the hall, right through the spot where the butler's ghost had hovered, before he had faded into the air. I thought that if I waited around for a moment or two, Mr. Grady might reappear. So I did. But he didn't. Leaving me with the problem of how I was going to get back into this house, so that I could help him.

Help him do what? I haven't explained that part, have I?

Earthbound spirits are just the ghosts of people who get stuck between this world and whatever comes next, assuming there *is* a next, which I firmly believe there is. But I can't see into it. I don't know any more about it than any other living person. What I *can* see is almost like a doorway of light, and when ghosts are finally at peace, they walk right through the light into . . . who knows? Whatever's on the other side.

The doorway appears when a person is dying. When a spirit leaves its body after the last breath of life has been taken, many don't go through the doorway right away. First off, there's a lot of really fascinating action unfolding on the ground. Doctors and nurses performing useless medical heroics, loved ones wailing and weeping, high drama bursting out left and right. It's like the season finale of *ER*, or the climax of an Italian opera.

Second, every ghost wants to go to their own funeral. And they always go. Always. After all, who *wouldn't* be curious to see who shows up, who sends flowers, who fakes their way through crocodile tears, and who is truly hobbled by honest-to-goodness grief? What a show! Even for an audience of one.

The problem is, the doorway of light doesn't burn brightly forever, and when the light goes out, the spirit is marooned in the in-between. Ghosts of people who still have an earthly agenda—something important they've left unfinished, one final task they feel they simply have to do—hardly ever notice that the light is fading, and if they do, they don't care. But once the light goes out for them, it's out. They're stranded.

I can help them in two ways. First, I can find out what it is that's keeping them here, in the land of the living. I try to resolve that earthly problem so the spirit can feel free to move on. I don't yet know why the monks have been hanging around for eight or nine hundred years, but it sounds as though Mr. Grady just needs to locate the deed to a house. That's the kind of problem I like. Simple. Straightforward. Except for gaining access to the house, of course, and then actually finding the piece of paper.

Once the real-life problem has been resolved, I can do one more thing to help a waylaid spirit move on. I can create a doorway of white light for them or lead them to a place, like a hospital or a funeral home, where the light is glowing for someone else, another person who has recently died. This white light illuminates the passageway to the next world.

It took me a while to learn how to create the light. When I was seven or eight, I realized that there was a difference between the spirits of people who had just died and the spirits of people who had been dead for three or four days. The doorway of white light glowed brightly for the very recently dead, but not for the others. For them, the light had gone out.

Nona taught me how to open up that passageway for a spirit who has waited too long to cross over. It was summertime. We had just finished supper, hot dogs and corn on the cob, and she took me out into the backyard to look at the sunset. She told me to concentrate on the light of the fading sun, really to think about it and observe it, and then to try to visualize that very same light on the side of the barn.

I tried hard. Nothing. There was no light at all when I opened my eyes. I tried again and again, and on my fourth or fifth attempt, I was able to create a tiny pinpoint of light. I practiced for weeks and weeks before I was able to make the passageway big enough and bright enough for an adult spirit to fit through and to keep it open long enough so that the spirit actually had time to enter it and cross over. But once I learned how to do it, the gift never left me. I only have to envision the white light and a spirit can walk through it as easily as I was now reentering Mr. Winslow's study.

Sylvia was perched stiffly on the edge of her chair. She looked pale. "There are a couple of letters. Tad's gone to get them."

"From who? Whom?"

"James Wescott at the British Library and Paola Moretti at The Cloisters. We wrote to them just before Finny died. I drafted the letters myself."

"Who are they?"

"Two of the most respected authorities on illuminated manuscripts. Tad wasn't sure what 'book' they were referring to; he just explained that the whole collection had been donated to the Athenaeum. He put them in touch with Amanda."

I must have looked puzzled, because she added, "Amanda Perkins—my boss."

"When was this?"

"Sometime in June. The letters had been addressed to Finny, so it took a while before they were forwarded to Tad. He was in France for the summer."

She gave me a look, but I wasn't sure what it meant.

"You'd think he would have picked up the phone."

I nodded. "What did they say?"

Sylvia stood up and brushed dust from the books off her skirt. "We shall see," she said.

The British Library
96 Euston Road
London NW1 2DB
ENGLAND

Dear Mr. Winslow and Ms. Cremaldi:

Thank you for your interest in the British Library and for your intriguing letter regarding the illuminated manuscript in your possession. It is, no doubt, a precious treasure, and I should have been overjoyed to be able to validate your suspicion that it might be the legendary lost manuscript of Kildare.

Sadly, however, I cannot, for I am among those not persuaded that the so-called Book of Kildare ever actually existed. I took the liberty of sharing your letter (in confidence, of course) with two trusted colleagues, Professor Julian Rowan at the Royal Foundation for Illuminated Manuscripts and Dr. Susan McCasson at the Windsor Institute of Art. They share my opinion on the mystery of the manuscript and know of no recent findings in our field that might call our shared conclusions into question.

It is, of course, well documented that Giraldus Cabrenses (Gerald of Wales) paid a twelfth-century visit to St. Brigid's Abbey in Cill-Dara. Many historians believe, and Professor

Rowan, Dr. McCasson, and I are among them, that the book he examined there, the book he described as being so exquisite that it had to be "the work of an angel, and not of a man" was none other than the well-known Book of Kells.

Undoubtedly you are aware that the Book of Kells has been safely in the possession of Trinity College, Dublin, since 1661. Though I would love to be proven wrong, our research has yet to yield any persuasive evidence that a second manuscript of this magnificent caliber emerged from the scriptorium at "the Church of the Oak." Would that it were so!

I do believe that I may be able to help you, though, and I would be happy to do so. We have in our possession, thanks to the generosity of the bibliophile and collector Charles Burney, an illuminated manuscript that has come to be known as the "Glossed Gospel of Luke." This manuscript is believed to have been produced in the west country of England sometime between 1150 and 1180.

From your description, I am of the opinion that the book you have in your possession may be English in origin and may date from roughly the same period as the volume we possess. There is even a slim chance that it may have emerged from the selfsame scriptorium.

I shall be coming to Boston in early October. Lady Annabel Barnes, a dear friend and patron of the British Library, is donating her collection of theatrical and literary papers to the Houghton Library at Harvard, and the university has planned a weekend symposium to celebrate her bequest.

My visit is scheduled for October 10–11, after which I plan to spend time with friends in Vermont, returning to London on November 2. I should be happy to meet with you to examine the manuscript and advise you if I can.

Please be in touch with my office before September 21 if

you would like to meet. I shall be traveling on business for the two weeks prior to my departure for Boston.

My best wishes to you both.

Sincerely yours,
James Wescott, Curator
Manuscript Department
The British Library

———————

We were sitting on a bench on the Commonwealth Mall, a luxuriant pedestrian boulevard running between eight tasteful blocks of ersatz French brownstones. It was turning out to be a beautiful day, air and sky alike having been washed clean by the overnight storm. The late-morning sun was bright and crisp, the nearly cloudless sky a deep blue, the bark on the linden and sweetgum trees dampened to shades of deep silver and slate.

"Why on earth didn't Tad get in touch with me?" Sylvia asked. Then she went on to answer her own question.

"Because vacations are *very* important, when you work as hard as Tad does."

"What does he do?" I asked.

She gave me a sly smile. "I was kidding."

Ooh, I was starting to like her.

"If it's not about scuba diving off islands no one's heard of, trekking in the Himalayas, or hanging out with hipster filmmakers who lose money for him, it's not on Tad's radar screen."

"Might be just as well," I suggested.

She turned to me, suddenly earnest. "You're right!"

"You could call Wescott's office," I suggested. "They must know how to reach him. It's only—what is it?—the thirteenth. He might still be in town."

"I think I'll show these to Sam," she said. "He'll know what to do."

We certainly didn't. In the letter we'd read right before West-cott's, Paola Moretti from The Cloisters, the branch of the Metropolitan Museum devoted to medieval art, had sounded thrilled and breathless. She urged Sylvia and Finny to call Professor Rory Concannon at Harvard and asked for a phone number at which Finny could be reached.

So much for consensus among "the experts."

Sylvia tucked the letters into her briefcase and we set off toward Arlington Street. The Public Garden was alive with activity. Toddlers from a nearby preschool, each attired for quick location in a tangerine T-shirt and clutching the rung of a rope ladder, inched along communally like a huge, orange caterpillar. A beaming Japanese couple posed for photographs on the bridge over the pond. They were wearing suits. The woman held a small nosegay. It took me a moment to realize that they must just have been married.

The line for the Swan Boats snaked halfway up the hill, and I remembered the time I took Henry here to be paddled around for fifteen minutes in the white swan catamaran. In his excitement, he grabbed my sunglasses right off my face and promptly dropped them into the pond. I watched them sink into the murk. They were probably still down there.

Our plan, hatched as we headed up Beacon Street, was first to fetch the manuscript from the bindery and bring it up to Sylvia's office so I could see it, and then to set the wheels of my employment into motion. Strictly speaking, my hiring didn't have to be approved by the institutional powers-that-be, since Sylvia controlled the restoration fund, but she wanted to introduce me to a couple of people before I suddenly showed up for work.

I never got to see the book.

Chapter Six

Since the former orchard, known to the locals for decades as Brookside Farm, had been renamed Sherwood Glen, my client, Trip Hollister, thought the commemorative books should have a medieval flair. He liked those stripey tents they erected at jousting matches, with the little triangular flags at the pinnacle, and he liked magenta, cobalt blue, and anything with a sleek, metallic sheen.

He had rejected my suggestion of a dark green suede cover and pages made of a gorgeous handmade paper from France: thick, bumpy sheaves in a deep shade of chocolate. It looked like tree bark, which is probably why I loved it and he didn't: he didn't want to be reminded of what he had razed and uprooted.

My cheeks were hurting when I got back into my car, likely from grinding my teeth while pretending to smile for close to two hours. I had an hour and a half before it would be time to pick up Henry, so I drove home via Wilson Farms in Lexington, filling the backseat of my car with macoun apples and parsnips and fresh spinach. I have to be careful at Wilson Farms. Everything looks and smells so good, everything *is* so good, that you can easily end up buying way more food than it's possible for two people to eat.

But that's okay. Ellie and Max Meisel, who own the two-family house where we live, are always happy for a little care package, and God knows they help me out with Henry often enough. It works out well for everyone. Their son and his family live in San Francisco, and their daughter and her husband and kids are in Chicago, so Ellie's always delighted to have a messy little guy like mine drinking her root beer floats and bringing her wilting bouquets of dandelions. Max is teaching him chess. Once Henry's asleep, I can even go out at night; all I have to do is let them know and leave open the second-floor door that separates our apartments. Henry never wakes up once he gets to sleep, though I think they wish he would, so they could rush to the rescue with drinks of water and cuddle him on their couch in a blanket.

I took the back road over Belmont Hill and down Concord Avenue. There was so little traffic that I decided to go home before picking up Henry at after-school. I could dump the groceries, throw in a load of laundry, and still get to the school in plenty of time.

Sorting laundry, I thought back to the turn things had taken when we opened the bindery door. Amanda Perkins, Sylvia's boss, was leading some very well dressed individuals—trustees? potential benefactors?—on what I presumed to be a private backstage tour.

Chandler, flushed and damp, was holding forth with animation (and a slight British accent that he seemed to have acquired overnight) about a book on British and Irish ferns that had been donated to the library by the architect John Sturgis. He wore weird German glasses, the kind they made fun of on *Saturday Night Live*. These apparently represented a random stab at sartorial edginess, as he was otherwise attired in faded Dockers, a blue oxford shirt that appeared to be no-iron, and sneakers that definitely hailed from the "Comfort Shoe" aisle of the New Balance factory outlet. I know, because I checked it out when I took Henry there for soccer cleats. Not being opposed to comfort, I even tried some on, and they sure did feel great. But I just couldn't. The day may come, but I'm not there yet.

Amanda, a slight, trim blonde in a sleek navy suit, eyed me over horn-rimmed half glasses. Her hair, expertly frosted, was cut short in the manner of a chic Parisian. I could tell she wasn't thrilled by the interruption. I suspected she was buttering up these CEOs for donations.

I was starting to get a little worried about time, so as soon as I could politely pull Sylvia away from the group, I did. It was obvious that we wouldn't have the opportunity to sneak the manuscript out of there anytime soon, and Amanda, whom Sylvia had particularly wanted me to meet, was clearly engaged for the time being.

"I'll talk to her this afternoon," she whispered. "I'm sure she won't have a problem with me bringing you on."

"All right," I said. I was walking kind of slowly, half-hoping that the monks would deign to appear to us as Sylvia escorted me to the elevator. They didn't.

"Could I maybe start on Monday? I've got some loose ends to tie up, and I have to chaperone my son's field trip on Friday."

She smiled. "Sure. Where are you going?"

"Apple picking."

"Sounds like fun."

I nodded. To be honest, I don't much look forward to these things. I'd put in so much time "parent helping" at Henry's nursery school—scrubbing toilets, washing out the dozens of yogurt tubs used for painting projects, freezing my tail off on the weekends before Christmas, serving my obligatory shifts at the annual tree sale—that I hoped never again to be asked to sign up for anything. But so many of the parents have "real" jobs, sometimes two, that the teachers tend to rely on people like me, who apparently don't have to be anywhere at any special time. And the trips are always nicer than I think they'll be. There's often a moment when I unexpectedly find myself on the verge of tears, thinking of Henry going off to college.

"What time should I come in?" I asked.

"Ten all right?"

The rain woke me up in the wee hours of Friday morning and my first thought was, *Oh no!* Followed instantly by, *Oh, yeah! Maybe they'll cancel the field trip and reschedule it for next week, when I won't be able to chaperone because* I have a job.

I particularly looked forward to making this fact known, somehow, to my nemesis, Julia Swensen, who had absolutely no idea how largely she figured in my imagination. We rarely spoke more than a couple of words, as she was as unaware of me as I was aware of her.

I'd stopped introducing myself to her after the third or fourth time, when it became abundantly clear that she had filed my name, and me, in the folder marked "No Reason to Remember." Julia was always perfectly turned out, with great shoes that I coveted, waiting to usher little Neela inside the minute the school doors opened at seven thirty. School doesn't start until eight; I have only been there earlier than that a couple of times, and never by choice.

Julia's cell phone would already be ringing, and you could practically smell how important it made her feel to have people absolutely desperate to reach her at seven twenty-five in the morning. She would roll her eyes at the rest of us, huddled in a dazed little group, clutching our travel mugs. Her look said, *Can't I please be left in peace to drop my only child at school? Am I that indispensable?*

Julia didn't chaperone. Ever. She didn't have time. She was very,

very busy, terribly busy, crushingly busy. According to my friend Lianne, who volunteered part-time in the school's newly established development office, she gave the school money, instead.

Lying in bed listening to the rain on the eaves, I imagined the interaction unfolding like this.

I would show up at seven thirty some morning in my one nice suit (if it still fit—I hadn't had it on since before Henry was born). Julia would practically do a double take and say:

"It's—Anne, isn't it?"

Wrong, sister, but we'll let it pass.

"Uh, Anza, actually."

Julia would secretly be congratulating herself for dredging something fairly close to my name up from the depths of her memory. She'd smile wearily. "Early meeting?"

I'd sigh and nod but offer no details, making her work for the information she wanted.

"Where do you work?" she would finally ask, curious to place me somewhere on the grid.

"Oh, at the Boston Athenaeum," I'd coolly respond, in a tone of voice that conveyed my surprise at the fact that she didn't already know this. My suit would send the signal: *And not sweeping floors, baby.*

"Really? I had no idea," she would no doubt go on, relegating to her thoughts the second half of the sentence, *Because you always struck me as such a schlump.*

"I'm restoring a collection of rare books," I could now say, casually. Topping *that* with, "and consulting on the provenance of a priceless medieval manuscript."

Julia would then respond with, "Wow!" Or something like that. Which is all I really wanted. That one moment in which she instantly understood how profoundly she had underestimated me.

I didn't like Julia at all. I didn't want to be friends with her. I didn't want to meet her husband or be invited to dinner or asked to a party to which I would have nothing fun to wear. I just didn't want her to look at me first thing in the morning through her chic, tasteful glasses and think, *Loser.*

Henry was up in a tree. I wasn't sure that the owners of the orchard would be crazy about this, the health of their branches being closely tied to the wealth in their coffers, but the low-hanging limbs were proving irresistible, not only to Henry, but also to several other kids.

"Henry," I called.

He ignored me.

"Henry!" He looked down.

"Come on down. It's not good for the branches."

"I'm not hurting them!"

I gave him a look, the kind that meant, *Did you hear what I just said?*

"I'm not," he insisted. Then I heard, much more quietly, "You're not in charge."

He glanced at me guiltily. He knew I had heard him. I took a deep breath, recalling this phenomenon from my days of parent helping. You show up. Your kid seems overjoyed to have you there, and for five minutes, you cannot peel him off your leg. Then, for the rest of the day, he acts like a monster.

"Henry!" I heard his teacher, Miss O'Hara, say sharply. "Hannah! Miles! Get down this minute and come over here!" They scrambled down the trees so quickly they hardly could have fallen faster.

I was a little in awe of Miss O'Hara, whom the kids called Miss O. Where did they get these teachers? These attractive, smart, organized young women, and a couple of men, who are so woefully underpaid that they have to support their teaching habit with second jobs?

The children squirmed and threw glances at one another. Miss O. stood for a few moments without speaking. Then she said quietly, "Did the three of you sign a contract this morning?"

They nodded.

"Henry?"

"Yes."

"Yes, what?"

"Yes, Miss O."

"And what is a contract, Hannah?"

"A pwomith," Hannah lisped. She was missing all four of her front teeth.

"Louder, please." Her tone was even and kind.

"A pwomith."

"A promise, what?"

"A pwomith, Mith O."

Miss O'Hara nodded. "Miles, did the contract say anything about trees?"

"It said I will not climb on trees. Miss O."

The teacher nodded.

"All right. Since I'm sure you have all learned from your mistake, I'm going to give you *one—more—chance*. One."

She sounded like me when I say, "I am going to count to three." You hope the tone of voice does the trick, because you haven't got a clue what you'll do if the standoff continues past three. But Miss O. probably knows. She is definitely a person with a plan.

The phone in the kitchen was ringing as Henry and I climbed the stairs, but the call went to the machine before I could get the door open. I figured it was just Hollywood Express, calling to let me know that the 24 DVD was overdue.

It was nearly seven o'clock. Sunshine, fresh air, and the excitement of the day had worn the kids out, but I was still surprised when Henry followed me to a seat on the bus and slid in beside me. He was asleep before we hit Route 2 and slept all the way back to Cambridge, waking only when the bus pulled into the schoolyard. He sat up sharply, damp from the heat of the sun through the window, momentarily disoriented. Then he smiled, sighed, and slumped back down.

I'd forgotten to pick up coffee at Wilson Farms, so we'd driven to Whole Foods before heading home. I had steeled myself to resist the rows of delectable out-of-season fruit shipped halfway around the globe, but the scent of the ever-expanding take-out section captured us the minute we walked in the door. Sure, I had a fridge full of fresh produce and a chicken just waiting to be roasted, but that would take a while. We were both starving, and I wasn't up for the effort it would take to hold Henry off until I could get a proper meal on the table. Besides, the time would come when I would no longer be able to delight my son simply by springing for a six-inch pizza. Me, I went for chowder and corn bread. We ate at a table by the windows.

I checked for a phone message, but it was too soon. Normally I'd be steering Henry toward the tub at this point, but his hour-long nap had revived him, so I decided to let him play while I cleaned up the kitchen. Junk mail had been piling up, offers from credit card companies and hopeful postcards from local Realtors, who had obviously bought the wrong mailing list. The phone rang again. I picked it up.

"Anza!" someone said, but I couldn't tell who. There was a little series of sobs, and then a whisper so low I could hardly hear. "The book," I heard her say. I recognized the voice: it was Sylvia's.

"The manuscript! It's gone."

Chapter Seven

MAX AND ELLIE had just finished supper when I knocked on their door. Ellie was about to leave, already late for a class she was taking, something to do with home organization and freeing your spirit by getting rid of clutter. I hoped she didn't get rid of too much; I loved her eccentric arrangements of shells and stones, the tables strewn with old magazines and dishes of hard candy, postcards and photos propped against the books on the bookshelves, and her kitchen, which seemed not to have two matching anything, each plate and cup apparently a lone survivor of a set an aunt or a friend had formerly owned.

Max was more than happy to have company, so I hustled Henry into the tub, extracting from him a promise that he would go to bed without any drama if nine o'clock came and I still wasn't home.

Max was setting up the chessboard when we arrived. Henry pulled over his favorite chair, piling it up with the pillows he needed to be able to see the board. A package of Oreos, two glasses, and a quart of milk were on the table. I bit my tongue, thanked Max again, and promised to be back as quickly as I could.

"Don't hurry," Max said.

"Yeah," Henry chimed in.

It took me half an hour to get to Sylvia's. I'd been stunned to hear that the manuscript had disappeared from her apartment, not the bindery, but that was all I knew so far. I had convinced her not to touch anything or to call anyone—not the police, not the Athenaeum, nobody—until I got there. Having a detective in the family, at least *sort of* in the family, can be handy. My plan was to get in touch with Declan as soon as I got the lay of the land.

Sylvia lives in a well-kept brick building near Cleveland Circle in Brookline, on a street lined with elegant postwar apartment buildings. In the downstairs lobby, unlocked from the street, were eight brass doorbells and mailboxes. Anyone could walk right in and follow a resident into the inner stairwell, or even be buzzed inside by a careless resident of one of the other apartments. I pressed her button, waiting on the polished-granite landing until I heard her buzz me in. I paused inside to see if the inner door closed all the way on its own. It did.

I climbed to the fourth floor, where Sylvia stood in her doorway. She launched right in as she led me into her living room, a floral, feminine nest that looked out onto the treetops.

"My door was locked, like nothing was wrong," she began. "I must have been home for half an hour before I realized something had happened. I can't believe it. I feel sick."

She sat down on the sofa, looking pasty and distraught.

"It's okay," I said. "My . . . son's dad is a Boston cop, a detective."

"Really?"

I nodded. "I'll call him in a minute. Just tell me what happened."

I sat down beside her. She closed her eyes, as though trying to collect her thoughts.

"I don't know where to start," she finally admitted. "I'm just—"

"I thought the book was at the Athenaeum," I interrupted.

"Okay," she said, taking a deep breath. "After you left on Tuesday, I went back to talk to Amanda. Let her know you were going to be starting."

"Who were those people she was showing around?"

"Two guys from Oxford and a rare books dealer from Sussex. And a *viscount*. Lord Brisley or Risley or something." Sylvia shrugged. "They're in town for a conference at Harvard."

"The same one?"

She gave me a puzzled look.

"The same what?"

"The symposium at Harvard? The reason James Wescott said he was coming over."

Her expression went blank and she let out a deep sigh. "Oh my God. I never put it together. Maybe that's where Sam's been."

"You're losing me. Back up."

"Sorry." She took another breath and started over. "I worked in the bindery until about five thirty. Chandler was there all afternoon, so I couldn't get the manuscript out of the back room. He's so nosy; he would have been all over me. I had to wait until he left, which he did, at about six o'clock. I figured he was gone for the night, but I took the book up to my office, just to be safe. That thing Paola Moretti said about the knot pattern in the borders? I wanted to see if I could find it."

I nodded. In the letter Tad had given Sylvia, Paola Moretti had described a variation on the classic Celtic knot: a rare symmetrical pattern in which the four knots forming the painted symbol point toward the center of the illustration. The presence of this variation in Sylvia's manuscript could help to establish the time and place of its creation.

"I found them. In seven or eight places. They were *so* beautiful. Anyway, about an hour later, I took the book back downstairs, but when I got off the elevator, I saw Chandler unlocking the bindery door. He had a Starbucks and a shopping bag from DeLuca's—"

"So he was settling in for the night," I concluded.

"Lately, he's there when I get to work in the morning and he's there when I leave. Sometimes I wonder if he even goes home. I don't know what's going on in his personal life—"

"Not much, apparently," I commented.

"Right, which is why I decided to bring the book home with me and take it over to Sam's. Who knows what Chandler does when he gets bored? I could easily see him poking around late at night and finding it."

"Couldn't you have left it in your office?"

"The cleaners come in every night, plus the temperature's always up and down. I knew Sam would be really excited about the letter, and I knew I could talk him into keeping the book for me. But I couldn't get in touch with him. I called the house four or five times. I even drove down there."

"Doesn't he have a cell phone?" I asked.

"He doesn't even have an answering machine," she said.

She paused, leaned forward, and straightened some magazines that were already straight. She didn't say anything for a minute or two. Finally she looked over.

"Could the ghosts have taken it? The monks?" she asked.

I shook my head.

"Are you sure?"

"They probably didn't even know it was here. Ghosts are like people that way: they only know about what they've actually seen and heard."

Sylvia looked completely baffled.

"They're not omniscient. They don't see and know everything that happens in the world just because they're—in the air. If they didn't actually *see* you take the book out of the bindery, carry it to your office, and then bring it here, they wouldn't have any idea where it went. We'll probably hear from them on Monday, when they suddenly notice it's missing."

"Thank God you're going to be there."

"Yeah, lucky me." I smiled and glanced around the room. My apartment had been broken into once when I lived on Commonwealth Avenue. It had been easy for the thief, or thieves; the building's outer doors didn't lock properly, and the lock to my apartment was loose and old. They just popped the bolt with a screwdriver, scooped up a bag of my stuff, and were out the door in a couple of minutes. The only thing that shattered me was losing my mother's engagement ring.

"What else did they take?" I asked Sylvia gently, remembering the sorrowful task of making a list for the police, who acted as though the break-in was my own fault, for being so lax about the locks.

"That's the thing," she said urgently. "Nothing."

"Nothing? Only the book?"

Sylvia buried her face in her hands and let out a little moan.

———

Declan was there within the hour. I try to keep my mind on business when he's in detective mode, but it's hard. He just smells so . . . he seems so . . . Okay, I am *not* going down that road.

The book had been taken from Sylvia's bedroom. On Tuesday, the same day she and I read the letters from James Wescott and Paola Moretti, she'd taken the book home and placed it on a shelf in her closet. Arriving home from work today, she'd gone into the kitchen, where everything seemed fine. She poured herself a glass of wine and went into the living room to read the *Globe*. After ten or fifteen minutes, she was cold, so she went into the bedroom to get a sweater.

Her closet door was open, and her bedroom had been messed up, but pretty halfheartedly, when you looked at things closely. A couple of drawers had been pulled out and their contents casually tossed, and a jewelry box was tipped over on the bureau, spilling pins and necklaces onto the floor. But it was the sight of a gold bracelet and a pair of expensive emerald earrings, worn to a family dinner over the weekend and lying in plain sight on a bedside table, that sent Sylvia flying to the closet.

That, she told me, was when she first suspected that the thief or thieves weren't after jewelry or money. In the panicked moments after realizing the manuscript was gone, she said, she'd wandered through the apartment in a state of shock. They hadn't touched the PowerBook on her desk. The rose-gold flute on her music stand was just where she had left it. Whoever broke in had been after one thing, and only one thing. And they had gotten it.

I'd related these details to Declan over the phone, and now he was making a thorough inspection of Sylvia's doors and windows. The door to her back hallway had been locked, and was still locked, from the inside. So was the window opening onto her fire escape, the only one accessible from the street. That left only her front door, made of solid oak, which locked by itself when you closed it. There was a second deadbolt, which Sylvia admitted to being casual about locking, as the main lock seemed so secure, but she was absolutely sure she had locked it every morning since Wednesday of this week, being mindful that she was leaving the book inside.

"Who has keys to the place?" Declan asked, examining the area around the doorknob. The finish was undamaged; it seemed pretty unlikely that access had been gained by crowbar or screwdriver.

"My parents," Sylvia said. "They live in Providence. And my brother in Medford. And a friend of mine from San Francisco.

She stayed with me last summer and took them home with her by mistake."

Declan glanced at me, then back at Sylvia. "Any . . . other visitors?"

"You mean men?"

"Not necessarily," Declan said, open-mindedly.

She shook her head. He nodded and wrote something on his notepad.

"Have you had any work done in here lately?" he went on. "Painting or carpentry? Anyone in to fix anything?"

Sylvia shook her head and let out a little sigh.

"Window washers?"

She glanced at me. I suspected she was getting impatient. We all knew this wasn't a crime of opportunity. There were plenty of valuable items in sight, objects easily tucked into a pocket or a backpack and sold for quick cash.

Declan must have read her mind. He stopped short of asking her if she'd noticed suspicious cars idling in the street or spooky strangers hanging around in the halls. He put down his notepad.

"I'd say he picked the lock. Cheeky bastard." Dec shook his head and gave Sylvia his lopsided grin, which, together with his tone and inflection, had the effect of entirely transforming the atmosphere in the room. Suddenly we weren't dealing with a frightening villain, someone potentially capable of murder or rape. We were dealing with . . . a burglar! The cheeky kind. The brilliant and ingenious kind. The kind who wore a funny black half mask and quiet slipper shoes and who swung from a rope, scaling the wall like a cat. It might not be true, but we sure felt better.

Sylvia let out a surprised little laugh. Her gaze went from Declan, to me, then back to him. A flush of color rose to her cheeks.

Get in line, I thought.

According to Sylvia, the building was managed by a realty corporation and did not have a live-in superintendent. This made our task a little simpler: we didn't have to deal with a suspicious old curmudgeon who had keys to every apartment, a nose for intrigue, and an inclination to place a matter like breaking and entering hastily and irrevocably into the hands of the Boston Police Department.

We had our own detective, thank you very much, and several good reasons for keeping this quiet for now. First of all, on paper at least, the book didn't actually exist. Sylvia didn't own it. Nor did the Athenaeum—it was not on any of the lists compiled and cross-checked when the museum took possession of Finny Winslow's collection. Of course, there *was* a newly rebound second edition of Hoeffler's *Mysterium Musicum* that was going to be a little hard to locate at the moment, should anyone care to look. But since Sylvia had been responsible for entering (or in this case, not entering) Finny's books into the library's database, no one was going to be looking.

Tad didn't own the manuscript, either, though the letters from Moretti and Wescott had certainly piqued his curiosity. What *was* this rare and ancient volume? he'd asked us before handing over the letters. Why hadn't he ever seen it or heard about it? When had his father acquired it, and where? Sylvia sidestepped Tad's thrusts and parries with commendable dexterity, finally reassuring him that the book was safe and sound at the Athenaeum and was clearly *not* what they had once dared to hope it was. Still, he should come down and see it. It was really something. She'd be delighted to show it to him.

"It'll never happen," she'd whispered to me as we'd left the mansion on Commonwealth Avenue. "He just smells money."

If we reported the theft, it would come out that Sylvia had been bending the rules a little, to put it mildly. Or, to put it not so mildly, she had deliberately defrauded both the Athenaeum and the Winslow heirs, and acted in a manner that would certainly cost her her job and likely her professional reputation. She might even go to jail.

Declan has no problem with jail, or with any kind of punishment that people have rightfully earned. But he does have a soft spot for Kildare, a county in which one of his favorite uncles still lives. Maybe he was intrigued by the idea of helping out old Saint Brigid, icon of the homeland. Imagine delivering into her hands, at least symbolically, the priceless treasure. Pull off a coup of that magnitude for a saint like Brigid, and, come time for the Big Tally in the Sky, he might even find his slate wiped clean of . . . me.

I doubt Declan really thinks that way. It was probably just my own guilty conscience spinning webs. All he said was, "Let's give this a day or two before we let it out of the bag."

He knew, because we'd explained it all, that if the manuscript really was the Book of Kildare, and it was located and authenticated, everybody and their brother would get involved in a fierce public battle for ownership and disposition rights. There would go the one and only chance we ever might have to do the right thing with it, whatever that might be. Although Declan plays by the rules, he does appreciate the occasional distinction between what's legal and what's right. Up to a point. The point was Monday morning. If he, or we, hadn't made any progress in tracking down the book by then, he was going to insist that we bring in the bigger guns.

He told us he would start with a couple of guys who "worked art." They'd been full-time on the Gardner Museum case for a couple of years and knew most of the art-world lowlifes on the eastern seaboard. I had hoped that Dec and I would have a few minutes alone together, if only while walking out to our respective vehicles, but it was not to be. He was now in detective mode. He left, and left to us the job of canvassing the residents in the building, just in case anyone had buzzed in an unfamiliar repairman or noticed someone tiptoeing around wearing a little black mask.

We decided to tell Sylvia's neighbors a partial truth: that there had been a robbery. But we'd leave out the fact that Sylvia's lock had been picked; there was no sense alarming everyone in the building, when the thief was so obviously disinterested in the baubles and doodads of the average Brookline pad.

"My bike was stolen," Sylvia lied to the first person who opened a door, a gloomy-looking man in his sixties. The cooking aroma of an unfamiliar meat—something gray, I intuited, and not normally consumed in the continental United States—drifted into the hall. It was carried on strains of what sounded like Tchaikovsky or Rachmaninoff.

"Oh, no!" he said. Was he looking slightly more cheerful? No, he couldn't be.

"It's my own fault—it wasn't locked," Sylvia went on. "I thought it would be safe on the landing. I was just wondering if you might have seen anyone. If anyone asked to be buzzed in, or—"

No, no, he hadn't seen anyone. He'd been at Symphony Hall all day (turned out he was a cellist) and had only been home for an hour.

The woman who lived below him had spent most of the day in the bathroom, she overshared enthusiastically, because she was having a colonoscopy in the morning. So no, she hadn't been outside of her apartment or heard anything unusual. We wished her luck with her procedure and headed down to the first floor.

Sylvia knew the two guys who lived on the right, married gay men who owned a housewares shop called Chez Nous in the South End. She had been to a couple of their Academy Awards parties, once winning a bottle of Perrier-Jouet for being the only person to predict that Adrien Brody would take home an Oscar for *The Pianist*. I thought they would be fun to meet. They weren't home.

Nor was the couple across the hall, a lawyer and her graduate student/high school baseball coach husband, who had just moved in within the past six months. Nor were the occupants of 2A or 3A. Well, we reminded ourselves, it *was* Friday night.

We hit pay dirt, though, with the woman who lived across the hall from Sylvia. She was a statuesque faux blonde named Carlotta McKay, employed, I later learned, as a writer of technical manuals four days a week. On Fridays, she worked from home, on a screenplay she was writing with her boyfriend, who lived in LA and was trying to break into the film business. If they could sell the screenplay, she was planning to move there.

Carlotta didn't know anything about the bike—she had never even noticed it in the hallway—but she had met Sylvia's new *friend*.

"Oh!" Sylvia said, a smile frozen on her face. She glanced at me.

They had run into each other in the hall. Carlotta had hit a wall with her writing, at about two thirty, and she'd decided to walk down to Trader Joe's to pick up a few things and get some fresh air. As she was locking her own door—

"What's his name?" she asked us.

I jumped in with "John." Dull, but serviceable.

"He was just coming out of your place. You guys must have had a late night!"

"Kind of," Sylvia said, unconvincingly.

Carlotta liked older guys, too, she volunteered. In fact, Craig, that was her boyfriend, he was going to be forty-three in April, but she was sworn to secrecy on that, because if it got out, it might work against him when he went up for the younger parts. Which was really unfair, because he really did not look his age at all, on account of all the yoga and internal cleansing.

"You didn't tell me he was *older*," I said teasingly to Sylvia, then turned to Carlotta. "How old would you say he is?"

Carlotta looked questioningly at Sylvia.

"Guess!" Sylvia had the presence of mind to respond.

"Forty-five? Forty-six?"

Sylvia nodded. "Pretty close."

"She's hardly told me anything," I confided, girlfriendlike, to the woman I had met thirty seconds ago. "She's afraid she'll jinx it. I don't even know how tall he is."

"Six one?" Carlotta squinted, shrugging at Sylvia. "Six two?"

"Around there," Sylvia said.

"Blond?" I asked Carlotta. "Dark?"

Carlotta smiled slyly. "He colors it, doesn't he?"

"What makes you think that?" Sylvia said. She was kind of getting into this.

"Come on!" Carlotta said. "Not a bit of gray at his age? Except in the eyebrows, like no one notices those. I mean, not to say he isn't in good shape, and that leather coat was like butter, but he's a good-looking guy. Rinses are tacky. If he's going to go for it, he's gotta really go for it—get some highlights, lowlights."

"I know," Sylvia said. "But I can't say that, not yet."

"No," Carlotta said. "No way. You have to wait for him to bring it up. What does he do?"

"Oh, he's—"

"Let me guess," Carlotta interrupted. "He's either a personal trainer or he works construction. You don't get a build like that by sitting at a desk."

"You really have an eye for details," I said. "I can see why you're a writer." It was a bit of puffery, but I sort of liked her.

Carlotta beamed.

Chapter Eight

Henry was due at Kelly and Dec's by eleven. Normally, I take him over there after school on Friday, but since he'd been away with them for Columbus Day weekend, we'd decided to start this weekend's visit on Saturday.

They have a great house. Like a lot of the immigrant Irish, Declan's father put the money he saved into real estate, buying several rundown properties in Medford and North Cambridge and fixing them up on weekends. Declan took over one of the mortgages when he and Kelly got married. They live on the second and third floors of a Philadelphia-style two-family near Powderhouse Square. His sister Aileen, who got married last year, lives on the first floor with her husband, Alvar, an electrician for Tufts.

Delia and Nell had some kind of digging project going on in the side yard. Being close in age, they tend to argue a lot, but they were united in purpose today. Which was, apparently, to dig as deep a hole as they could. It was my son's brilliant idea to add a hose to the equation. My heart sank, thinking of the thirty-eight dollars I had just plunked down for the new sneakers he was wearing while his rain boots sat idle in the back hall at home. It was my own fault. I should have packed the boots.

Henry was uncoiling the hose.

"Don't turn it on yet," I said.

"Why not?"

I resisted the urge to reply, "Because I said so." Instead, I answered, "You need to check with Daddy."

Delia looked up. Her face was streaked with grime. "He's not here," she said. Delia has the most extraordinary eyes I have ever seen, the palest blue, like ice.

"Where is he?" I asked.

"He went to get a haircut," Nell answered.

"And he's bringing back doughnuts," Delia went on.

"Did he say it was okay? To be digging here?"

"He doesn't care," Delia said, though I noticed she didn't look at me. Clearly, a conversation with Kelly was in order.

That was when Henry squeezed the handle on the nozzle, spraying both Delia and the pile of dirt. She shrieked, dropped the shovel, and scooted away from the water. Nell, apparently delighted that her older sister, who can be on the fastidious side, was now both filthy and furious, screeched with enthusiasm.

"Henry!" I said sharply.

He did it again, this time aiming at the mound of earth with all the watery power he could squeeze. Mud leapt from the pile onto both girls as Nell screamed, "Don't!"

I grabbed the hose from Henry, getting soaked in the process.

"What did I just say?"

"It was on!"

"Girls," I heard Kelly call from the top of the stairs. "Everything okay?"

Kelly offered to put on coffee, but I'd already had too much. She was dressed in cropped yoga pants and a T-shirt and looked as though she was just waiting for Dec to get back so she could go for her run. The kitchen had a Saturday morning feel—the dishwasher was humming, emitting little clouds of steam, and in the air hung the commingled scents of bacon and toast. Crumbs and spots of jelly—grape, it looked like—dotted the tablecloth, and Kelly was folding a load of lights. I watched as she absentmindedly smoothed Declan's boxers into tidy rectangles.

"How are you?" she asked. If she resents or feels sorry for me, she manages not to show it.

"Oh, fine. Thanks again for last weekend. He had a great time."

Kelly smiled. "It's so easy up there. They spent the whole weekend making a fort."

"They did?"

"We could barely get them in at night. They had every flashlight in the house. It was quite the production."

I smiled. Henry's lucky to be part of an extended family with eight or nine kids under twelve. That's not something I could give him. My oldest brother, Joe, is gay, we think, though he has never actually made an announcement. I suppose that doesn't preclude children, at some point, but he and Alan have been living in Portland for three years and they both really like it out there. If and when Joe ever becomes a father—and I hope he does—it will probably happen in the Northwest. My other brother, Jay, lives in Chicago. He and his wife, Louise, who's on the partner track at her law firm, just got a puppy. We'll see how that goes.

We heard a couple of toots; Declan was back. Down in the driveway, the truck door slammed and a lively conversation ensued.

"You're really sure about next weekend?" Kelly asked. "Because my mom's more than happy to—"

"Absolutely!" I said, interrupting. "We can't wait." Some people would find it strange that Kelly and Dec would leave the girls with me, the other woman, while they go off to celebrate their anniversary. But the children are used to spending weekends together, and Henry never gets to have Nell and Delia overnight at our house.

Because he's a little older, and a boy, they're intensely curious about all aspects of his life: Max and Ellie; Homer, the St. Bernard a few doors down, famous for spectacular feats of flatulence; the fact that Henry's allowed to play in the attic, where there is a real sword; the strange foods they sometimes find in our fridge—artichoke hearts and mozzarella floating in brine. Henry's flattered enough by their adoration to overlook the fact that they are girls. As for me, I look forward to being the self-sacrificing one for a change, making it possible for Kelly to spend a romantic weekend at a seaside B and B in Maine with the man whose heart she clearly won—not once, but twice.

"Sorry about the mud," I said as Declan appeared on the stairs.

He just shrugged. The barber had cut his hair a little too short, revealing borders of pale skin at the hairline. He looked kind of goofy. Actually, he looked like his son. I smiled.

"What?" he asked.

"Nothing," I said. Kelly glanced over, her gaze landing on the flat, rectangular doughnut box in his hand.

"You forgot my muffin," she said glumly.

Declan produced a bag from under the box and held it up. Kelly smiled.

"Thank you," she said, and, promising to be in touch with me about the weekend arrangements, she was out the door.

"Want some coffee?" Declan asked.

"No, thanks."

"Doughnut?" He opened the box, which, unfortunately, contained my favorite: cream-filled with chocolate frosting. But there was only one.

"Whose is this?" I asked, pointing.

"Yours," he said, filling the coffeepot with water. "So am I making a full pot here, or a half?"

"Full, I guess."

He poured the water into the coffeemaker and filled a paper cone with the fine, dark powder.

"I talked to a couple of the guys," he said, pushing the On button.

I took a paper napkin from the wrought-iron holder and laid my doughnut on top of it. "Yeah?" I so wanted a bite, but I was going to discipline myself and wait for the coffee, like a mature human being.

"I might have something."

"*Really*? That was quick."

He sat down opposite me and shrugged a funny shrug, a gesture that said, *Hey, I'm good.*

"We're, uh . . . we're working with a fellow," he said.

"What kind of *fellow*?"

He gave me a look.

"The kind I shouldn't ask any questions about?"

"Right you are. Lad's been in and out of Cedar Junction for years. Real slick operator. Been at the art game, one way or another, all his life. Probably knows where the Gardner pieces are, or knows somebody who knows. Anyway, a month or two back, we caught him in a sting—bloody fool; he'd only been out of jail a few weeks. But I suppose he was broke." Declan paused, obviously trying to figure out how little he could tell me. "For a certain . . . sum, he was able to procure a painting for one of our lads."

"Procure, as in *steal*?" I asked.

He shook his head. "No, but he works with the guys that do. The painting was from a home out in Weston, real high-profile case, so he's in a fairly tight spot right now. He's looking at serious time, unless he—"

"Cooperates?"

Declan got up, took two mugs out of the cabinet, and placed one in front of me. He shook a pint of half-and-half and, determining that it was almost empty, located another in the back of the refrigerator. He poured my coffee and casually slipped a plate under my doughnut.

"He'll lend a hand. No choice, poor sod."

"That's really great," I said. "Thanks."

Declan nodded and had a sip of his coffee, black, the way he always takes it. I poured half-and-half into mine, swished it around, and had a sip.

"We had some luck, too," I said.

"Luck?" He grinned. "Your opinion is that I was just lucky?"

I ignored him. "The woman across the hall ran into a guy on Sylvia's landing. He was just coming out of her place."

"No kidding."

"We got a description and everything."

Declan grabbed a pen from the table behind him and the sports section of the *Globe* from a chair. He jotted down the physical particulars I described, penning his notes on a full-page ad the *Globe* had taken out for itself in its own paper. He promised to pay a visit to Carlotta that afternoon, then sat back and sighed.

"Well done," he said.

"Don't act so surprised."

At last, I took a bite of my doughnut. It was heavenly. The volume of cream was generous to the point of obscenity, and only one thing would have made my pleasure more complete: not to have Declan watching me eat it. Which might be the only time in my life I have ever thought, *God, I wish he wasn't here.*

I wiped my mouth. "Are you just going to watch me eat this?"

"I thought I might." He was deadpan.

"Aren't you having one?"

"I'm watching my figure."

"I see."

From the volume of the hooting and squealing outside, where the kids were no doubt wreaking muddy havoc with the hose, I judged that my time alone with Declan would soon be ending. The wet, dirty, joyful hysteria we were overhearing couldn't go on much longer without dissolving into a crisis of tears and bitter recriminations.

The morning sun had thrown a wide swath of rainbow against the far wall. I glanced around, trying to locate a prism or a crystal that would have split the light that way, creating this glimpse of such fleeting and singular beauty, but I couldn't. I pointed it out to Declan, and he smiled.

Two hours later, I was sitting across from Sylvia at a cozy upstairs table in Café Algiers in Harvard Square. I had called to tell her of Declan's progress as soon as I got home, and she answered immediately, as though she had been sitting by the phone. She'd finally been able to make contact with Sam. As we'd suspected, he'd been invited by all his British colleagues and friends at Harvard to join in the weekend's festivities. He couldn't get out of attending a morning lecture on the plays of Denis Johnston, several of whose original typescripts were among Lady Barnes's gifts to Houghton Library, but he could meet Sylvia for lunch. She asked if I wanted to come. Given that my afternoon would otherwise have involved laundry, utility bills, and an hour or two with fairly ineffectual "green" cleaning products, I was happy to say yes.

I haven't lived in Cambridge long enough to miss the "old" Harvard Square, but I've heard my share of melancholy rhapsodies about the lost lunch counters and cafeterias, the dark little taverns and folk clubs and quirky bookstores and curio shops that are lodged in the memories of generations of Harvard students. Little of that place remains. At street level now are the locked and empty lobbies of banks and cell phone companies, spilling their harsh fluorescent lighting brightly onto the evening sidewalks and offering passersby all the charm of operating rooms. Creepy, gazeless mannequins haunt the windows of trendy clothing boutiques. Urgent new merchants riding one wave or another surf grandly into town and back out just as quickly, which is probably of cold comfort to the shopkeepers their landlords displaced, genteel old eccentrics who tended their businesses like petunias.

Café Algiers—like Casablanca, the Brattle Theatre, and Club Passim—has been around for a long time. It was a little too chilly to sit on the patio, so we chose a table on the second floor, tucked in under the steeply sloping wooden ceiling. I ordered a beer and perused the menu, which was studded with tantalizing North African pastes and tagines. We decided to get some hummus with cucumbers to tide us over until Sam arrived.

"What's this guy's name?" Sylvia asked, squeezing lemon into her iced tea. "This . . . crook?"

I shrugged, scooping hummus onto a cucumber slice.

"Does Declan think he did it? How does he know?"

I shook my head. My mouth was full. I was used to the murky ways in which Declan and his fellow detectives went about their jobs, whispering quietly to friends and felons, dangling favors and pardons, prosecutions and plea bargains, but I could see that it was going to take some explaining.

"They caught him in a sting," I finally managed to say. "He delivered a stolen painting to an undercover cop. But he couldn't have taken your manuscript himself because he's still in custody."

Sylvia looked befuddled.

"They've got him on conspiracy, possession of stolen property, and trafficking. He's facing jail time, but if he's willing to work with the police on this—and probably on some other things— they might be able to—"

"Get him off?" she asked, her eyes widening.

"No, not totally. Maybe get the charges reduced, or arrange for a plea."

She sat back in her chair and took a deep breath. "What makes them think he knows anything?"

I sipped my beer, and it was very strange. I'd been intrigued by the description, but the beer itself reminded me of the Christmas pomanders we used to make in Brownies, by sticking dozens of pin-sharp cloves into an unsuspecting orange.

"They know he's really connected. They're pretty sure he's behind a whole string of robberies from college museums all over New England. They even think he knows where the Gardner paintings are, or knows somebody who knows."

"*Really?*" she said.

I nodded. Visiting Boston's Gardner Museum, formerly the home of art collector Isabella Stewart Gardner, is like stepping into a cool, Venetian palace. The air is heavy with floral fragrance from a glorious indoor courtyard.

In 1980, security guards let two Boston policemen into the museum in the middle of the night. The cops said they were responding to an alarm that indicated a fire in one of the upper galleries. Once inside, their true identities were revealed: they weren't cops; they were art thieves. They tied up the security guys and made off with $300 million worth of uninsured paintings and drawings, works by artists like Rembrandt, Degas, and Manet. Not one of the stolen pieces has ever been found and nobody's ever been caught.

"What would this guy do?" Sylvia asked.

"I'm not sure. Maybe he'd put the word out that he'd been contacted by somebody, a person who knew that the manuscript had been stolen and would pay a lot of money to get it. But I'm just guessing. Dec didn't get into that."

Suddenly Sylvia's expression brightened and she half stood up. She was blocked in by the table, though, so she quickly sat back down. A man I took to be Sam was approaching us, and he seemed to have brought a friend.

"Good morning," Sam said cheerfully.

It was afternoon, but never mind.

"You're looking lovely, as usual," he went on, kissing Sylvia on the cheek. *"This,"* he said, emphasizing the word in a way that held a meaning I didn't understand, "is Julian Rowan."

"Nice to meet you," I said.

"Pleasure," he responded.

"Sylvia Cremaldi," Sylvia said, extending her hand. "And this is my friend Anza O'Malley. She's . . . doing some work with me at the Athenaeum."

The name *Julian Rowan* sounded familiar, but I couldn't recall from where. He was tall and about my age, with hair the color of wet hay and paws big enough to palm a basketball, and he was wearing a long silk scarf that had fluttered in his wake, like overly feminine aftershave. Sam, on the other hand, brought to mind the kindly, distracted professors who made up my college's English department, daffy devotees of Milton and Chaucer and bow ties and Scotch.

Julian folded himself into a chair and Sam squeezed in beside Sylvia.

"Julian's here from London for the fall semester," Sam explained.

"Teaching at Boston College," Julian went on.

"And . . . ?" Sam urged, like a parent prompting a child to add "please" to the end of a sentence.

"And collaborating on a book with a professor at Harvard."

"Wow!" I said. "You've got your work cut out for you."

"Indeed," Julian said. "I thought I'd be exploring the Berkshires and popping off to Martha's Vineyard—or 'the Vineyard,' as they say—but . . ." He trailed off, shrugging. "Not so far."

"Julian's collaborator, Rory Concannon, is an old friend of mine," Sam offered. "He's brilliant, but also a little—"

"Crazy?" Julian offered.

"Well, I was going to say eccentric, or unconventional."

Rory Concannon, I thought. Another familiar name. What was wrong with me? Why couldn't I remember where I'd heard these names? Was I getting early-onset Alzheimer's?

"No," Julian said. "He *is* crazy, but in the best possible way."

It slowly came back to me as we ordered our lunches and chatted about Professor Concannon and Julian's work. Julian was one of the two people with whom James Wescott, whose letter Sylvia had just received and whom we had apparently missed in Cambridge, had conferred with about what I now thought of as "our" manuscript.

Julian and a Dr. Something-or-Other, a woman whose name I (naturally) couldn't recall, had agreed with Wescott that there was no such thing as a Book of Kildare. All three believed that the "lost" manuscript was actually the Book of Kells, which had simply been *seen* by Gerald of Wales *in* Kildare and had been safe for centuries in the library at Trinity College, Dublin.

As for Professor Concannon, I suspected I would like him. He couldn't be that crazy if he was a Harvard professor with a book contract, though I suppose there are people who would disagree with that. With a name like Concannon, he was probably also Irish, another check mark in my plus column. In her letter to Finny and Sylvia, Paola Moretti had implored them to take the manuscript to Concannon. This all added up to my feeling that he was probably one of the good guys.

I took a sip of Christmas Past and tried to get my head around all of this. Sylvia had read the letters to Sam over the phone. This I knew. Sam happened to know that one of the people mentioned in one of the letters—James Wescott's—was here in town. Okay, fair enough. But for Julian to be working on a book with someone we had heard of from an entirely different source: For me, this strained probability. More puzzlingly, at least on the subject of *our* manuscript, Julian Rowan and Rory Concannon would radically disagree.

This seemed . . . too connected somehow. Was it all a coincidence? An act of otherworldly engineering? A week ago, I hadn't heard of Julian Rowan or Rory Concannon or Sam or Wescott. But it now appeared that they all knew one another. Was it like that phenomenon in which you are introduced to someone you've never met before and you then start seeing them every time you turn around?

"Let me just ask a question," I said. People looked up from their salads and plates of falafel and couscous.

"How do you guys all know each other? Sam, did you know every person mentioned in those two letters?"

"Oh, no," Sam said. "I don't know Susan McCasson, though I *do* know the person she replaced. But James Wescott was at the National Gallery when I worked at the Library of Congress. And, let's see, I met Rory when he had a Mellon Fellowship at Notre Dame, and he came to the Athenaeum to do research for a couple of weeks."

"And I had a Mellon three years later," Julian explained. "My research overlapped with Rory's, so when I went back to London, we stayed in touch."

"When he was at Stanford?" Sam asked Julian.

"No, before that."

"Oh, right, he had that appointment at the Beinecke. I forgot about that. How long was that for?" Sam asked.

"Just a year," Julian responded.

"And then he came to Harvard," Sam said.

"Right."

They both nodded and smiled. Okay, I got it. The world isn't exactly overrun with people who are fanatical about rare manuscripts, and when you live in a place like Boston, or Cambridge, many of the roads pass through here. I suppose if you were the tuba player for the Boston Symphony, you might have at least a passing relationship with the tuba players at the Metropolitan Opera and in the New York Philharmonic.

"Did you see James Wescott at the conference?" Sylvia asked.

"He was at the opening dinner at the faculty club," Sam said. "But he hasn't been around for a day or two."

"He mentioned going to Vermont," I said.

"That's right," Sam responded, "he did. He just made the trip as a courtesy to Annabel Barnes, who's been very good to the British Library. This collection belonged to her late husband, who went to Harvard, which is why it ended up here. But James is keeping an eye on an important benefactor, as he should. They've got a capital campaign coming up."

Over dessert and coffee, we brought Sam and Julian up to date on the robbery of the manuscript, and on Declan's preliminary investigation. We made it sound as though the entire Boston Police Department was on the case. Which I suppose they actually were, though informally. At least for two more days.

Julian confirmed that he did, in fact, doubt the existence of a so-called Book of Kildare. But there was no question that Sylvia had been in possession of an important text. He was happy to enlist the services of his colleagues at the RFIM to help figure out what it was and what ought to be done with it.

"But first we have to find it," Sylvia said glumly.

"Yes," said Julian.

A gloomy silence descended over the table.

"Who even knew that you had it?" Sam asked.

"No one," Sylvia said glumly.

"Someone must have known," Sam pressed.

"Or else they just got lucky," Julian offered. "What else did they take?"

"Nothing."

"Hmmm," Julian said, glancing at Sam. "That's . . . odd."

"I'm such an idiot," Sylvia said, to no one in particular. "I can't believe I let this happen."

We all traded glances. Finally Sam spoke.

"Now, now, dear. You made a promise to someone you loved. You were only trying to keep it."

———

I did not expect to spend Saturday evening with Julian Rowan. The phone rang at about five, just as I was about to sit down and face the sorry state of my financial empire, which I try to do as infrequently as possible. We always get by, and I know I could borrow money from Dad, or even Joe or Jay, if I had to, but so far I haven't had to.

Declan and I keep things simple. Henry's covered on Dec's health insurance, which is a godsend, and rather than my asking Dec to pay child support, we agreed at the beginning that he would start a college fund for Henry. He puts money into it every week, saving me eighteen years of that particular anxiety. So far, I've been able to handle everything else.

I didn't recognize the number that came up on my phone.

"Hello?"

"Anza? This is Julian."

When I didn't respond immediately, he went on.

"Julian Rowan. We met earlier."

"Oh, hi, Julian. Sure. How are you?"

"Very well, thanks, and you?"

"Great," I said.

Either he'd been gearing himself up for the past hour, or British art historians are among the more direct men on the planet.

"I was wondering," he said, "if you happen to be free this evening?"

I used to be the kind of person who felt that if you didn't have an actual conflict, you were obliged to say yes to anything anyone invited you to do. Nat cured me of that. She pointed out, like a wise and sophisticated aunt, that it was okay to have plans with yourself. To do nothing.

Much to my surprise, though, I realized that, at least tonight, I would prefer Julian's company to my own. I also liked the fact that he hadn't prefaced his question with an awkward inquiry about my current romantic status.

"Yes," I answered, just as directly. "I am."

Which is how I came to be seated next to him at the Brattle Theatre, watching what turned out to be a painfully unfunny French movie about four friends who share a huge, gorgeous apartment in Paris that they could not possibly afford on their incomes. For example, one of the women was a beautician who did the hair and makeup of dead people for their funerals. There were a lot of bad jokes about making corpses look peaceful. I gave up on the plot, what there was of one, about a third of the way in, just as they all piled into a teeny Renault to go for Sunday dinner in the country with one of their families. Once movies get to Sunday in the country with a French family, they're all the same, anyway.

I tried not to be acutely conscious that Julian's leg, which was far too long for the shallow space in front of our seats, had drifted to the left and was leaning against mine. I doubted he was aware of it, but if I pulled my leg away suddenly, not only would he realize he'd been leaning on me, but he might think I was annoyed about this, which I most certainly was not. But the warmth of his calf kept my mind on one of the other particulars of his nearness: a faint scent of shaving cream, mixed with warm, wet wool. It had been raining when he met me in front of the theater, and though he had an umbrella, his gray heather jacket must have gotten damp.

Since I couldn't stay focused on the movie and couldn't stop focusing on our legs touching and Julian smelling, uh, nice, in kind of a farmy way, I tried to put my mind to work on the problem of the ghostly butler, John Grady. Why, I asked myself, did I keep not mentioning him to Sylvia? I could have told her about the lonely old ghost's appearance right after we left the house on Commonwealth Avenue. I could have mentioned him at any point in the past few days. It would be far easier to gain access to the house with Sylvia's help than to engineer a way of doing so on my own, but for some reason, I didn't want her in on it. Even pulling this puzzle to the front of my mind and asking myself the question directly—*Why don't you want Sylvia to know about your encounter with the ghost of John Grady?*—I was left with little more than, *I don't know. I just don't.*

So how was I going to get into the house? I would have to lie, which, fortunately, I happen to be pretty good at. I'm not proud of this, but it's a useful skill. I had been invited to have Sunday dinner tomorrow in the North End with Nat and her family, so I would be going into Boston. Maybe I could take the bus to Commonwealth at eleven or twelve and just stroll on down toward the Public Garden. See if it looked as though anyone were home at the Winslow manse, maybe have a ramble down the back alley that ran the length of the block, behind the houses.

I could even ring the bell; if anyone was there on a Sunday morning, it would probably be Mrs. Martin. She'd certainly remember me, and I could tell her that I thought I had lost an earring when I was there with Sylvia. If an earring didn't turn up after a few minutes of our retracing my footsteps, then we would both conclude that I'd lost the earring somewhere else.

Before leaving, I could ask to use the upstairs bathroom, hoping that John Grady would appear to me as he had earlier in the week. And if it ever got back to Sylvia that I'd stopped by on my own, I'd just explain that I was on my way to a dinner (true) in the neighborhood (sort of true) and on the spur of the moment (not) I had decided to pop in.

My attention was drawn to the image on the screen: an argument was breaking out in the backseat of the Renault, where the funeral-parlor beautician was lighting the next in a continuous chain of cigarettes, much to the annoyance of the roommate squeezed in beside her. From the way they were bickering, you just knew they were going to fall in love by the end of the movie. I was really hoping there wouldn't be a lot of steamy sex at the country house. There's nothing more embarrassing than watching sex in a movie with someone you barely know sitting beside you.

Suddenly, Julian turned to me.

"Are you enjoying this?" he whispered.

I shrugged. He had picked the movie, so I didn't want to make him feel bad.

"It's not very good, is it?" he whispered.

I shook my head.

He stood up. "Shall we?" he asked, with a refreshing lack of ambivalence.

I scrambled to my feet.

We decided to head over to Charlie's Kitchen, just around the corner, for a burger and a beer. As usual, the place was packed, and it didn't take us long to figure out that most of the customers were rowers in town for the Head Of The Charles Regatta, whole teams of strapping young men and women who would normally have been putting away beers with their burgers, but who were loyally forgoing the booze.

We had to share an upstairs table with the coxswain and two members of the men's eight from Northwestern. The other six rowers were at the table right beside us, and I do mean *right* beside us. When it came out that Julian had rowed at Cambridge, we were effectively anointed the tenth and eleventh members of the team. Great fun was made of Julian's accent. We raved about the flavor of the microbrews only we were able to drink.

And when Julian walked me to the T and ended our evening with an uncomplicated kiss on the cheek, I felt both relieved and happy. I'd actually had fun. With an eligible academic. Who was cute. And nice.

How unbelievable was that?

Chapter Nine

THE RAT THAT had stopped dead in its tracks six feet in front of me, in the alley behind Finny's house, was almost a foot long, not counting the tail, which was revoltingly, sickeningly hairless. The rat was fat. It was black. I mean, the thing looked like a beaver with a snake attached to its rear.

I was afraid to turn and run, in case it chased me and ran up the back of my leg and into my hair. I was afraid to move toward it, in case it charged. So there we stood, staring at each other, the blood pounding audibly through my heart: *pa-poom, pa-poom, pa-poom, pa-poom.* And then, obviously concluding that I was a spineless, hapless coward, the rat sauntered lazily over to a nearby Dumpster and disappeared beneath it.

That was when I started running, and I didn't stop until I got to Dartmouth Street. I had so much adrenaline coursing through me that I could have set some kind of record for the hundred-yard dash. And the stupid thing was, I hadn't taken the back way to the house for reasons having to do with John Grady. I had chosen the back-alley route because I wanted to scope out the trash behind the multimillion-dollar brownstones.

You wouldn't believe what some people in this neighborhood throw away. Not people from the families who've been here forever, but condo-dwelling entrepreneurs running lucrative start-ups, and wealthy international students whose parents have leased them a luxurious apartment, and who are so anxious to get out of town after graduation that they throw things away rather than pack them up for shipping. I've seen rugs, antique chairs in need of a bit of repair, sets of dishes, framed posters and paintings.

I hit the jackpot a couple of times, and I was now like one of those people who can't resist buying scratch tickets, having won twenty-five dollars a decade or two ago. I suppose I was even a bit like my furry, opportunistic little friend. Though I do draw a distinction between scavenging leftover Thai take-out and rescuing from the trash two sterling silver candelabra from Firestone and Parsons. There had to be a story behind that particular find. Somebody must have been furious at someone else—their mother-in-law? a two-faced friend?—and in a grand, irrevocable gesture, had put a wedding gift or a family heirloom into the trash. I just happened to be in the right place at the right time.

It turned out to be lucky, my taking the back alley, because I didn't even have to make up a lie to get in the front door. I had no sooner crossed Dartmouth Street than I caught sight of the man himself, or rather, the ghost himself. He was halfway down the next block of the alley, probably right behind Finny's house. I walked toward him, but he didn't notice me approaching. To my right and left, where the household help might once have sat outside on the shady brick stoops, escaping the heat of the basement kitchens and greeting those who were not welcome to use the buildings' front entrances, were massive Mercedeses and BMWs squeezed into tiny parking spaces.

"Mr. Grady," I said softly.

He looked up, startled. "Oh, my," he said.

I smiled. "Do you remember me? My name is Anza. I was here the other day with Sylvia."

"I do," he said, bowing slightly.

He looked bewildered, but otherwise just as he had five days ago: benevolent, disheveled, lost.

"I was hoping to find you," I said.

"And I hoped that you would," he responded. His brogue was rich and dulcet.

I glanced down at the box at his feet; it contained books that were obviously being discarded in preparation for the sale of the house.

"You were looking for your document," I guessed.

He nodded.

"Can I help?" He wouldn't have been able to lift the books out of the box. He wouldn't have had the strength.

"I'd be most grateful," he said.

I slid the box toward the house and sat down on a low wall. A set of stairs led down into an enclosed rear courtyard, where a shed on the right ran the depth of the space. It was unusual to see one of these structures as it had always existed, from the time when horse-drawn wagons hauled coal through these alleyways and downstairs servants shoveled the weekly delivery into sheds off the kitchens. Few of the structures remained; most had been scrapped to make room for valuable off-street parking spaces or restored to add footage to ground-floor condos. Depending on who bought the Winslow house, this historical relic might be headed for a similar fate.

"Please, sit down," I said.

He came over and sat down near me on the wall. I began taking books out of the box: mildewy old novels, disintegrating paperbacks offering tips for low-cost travel, a picture book about boats, a commemorative volume published on the 250th anniversary of

Trinity Church. I had a hopeful moment when I glimpsed a couple of children's books in the bottom of the box, but neither turned out to be *The Butterfly's Ball*.

He looked crestfallen.

"I'm sorry," I said.

"Esther may have it. She always loved it."

"Esther?" I tried to remember which sister was Esther—the artist, or the one who was into yoga.

"The youngest. She was our pet. Always underfoot. She knew every word of that poem, too, God bless her."

"Do you remember it?" I asked.

"Oh, yes," he said, and without further prompting began to recite.

> *Come, take up your Hats and away let us haste*
> *To the Butterfly's Ball, and the Grasshopper's Feast!*
> *The Trumpeter, Gad-fly, has summon'd the crew,*
> *And the Revels are now only waiting for you.*
> *And on the smooth Grass, by the side of a Wood,*
> *Beneath a broad Oak that for Ages had stood,*
> *Saw the children of Earth, and the Tenants of air,*
> *For an evening's Amusement together repair.*

He paused, beaming.

"Is that the end?" I asked.

"Oh, dear, no. It goes on for a couple of pages. Esther knew every word of it by heart."

"Where did it come from? The book itself?"

"It belonged to Gwennie. Our daughter. We lost her, when she was five. She and Miss Edlyn were like sisters."

I must have looked puzzled, because he went on to clarify the facts.

"His Lordship and Her Ladyship had just the one daughter, Edlyn. She was born two months after Mairead and I had our little Gwendolyn. My wife was Miss Edlyn's nursemaid, and the two little girls were inseparable. Rupert and Percy, Edlyn's older brothers, were already boarding at St. Clement's by the time she was born, so if not for our Gwennie, there wouldn't have been a playmate in the household. It was Percy who introduced Miss Edlyn to Mr. Winslow. They were at Harvard together, though Percy was older than Phineas. Percy brought him to the house in Brighton, the summer Miss Edlyn was nineteen. By the next Christmas, they were married."

"And you and your wife came here, to live with her, after she married Mr. Winslow."

He smiled. "You have a fine memory."

"How did you come to be working for the family?" I asked.

He gazed at me for several moments, then took a deep breath.

"I'm from Galway, but I was living in London. I'd gotten a job as a houseman for the Shand-Thompsons. Mairead's aunt Una was a cook for the family. She'd been with them for forty years. She brought Mairead down from Salthill when I had been working in the household for, oh, just about a year. We were married a year later. Gwennie was born in 1937, and two months after that, Her Ladyship gave birth to Miss Edlyn."

I saw him struggle to contain his emotions, remembering so much more than the bare facts he was relating to me.

"You see, it wasn't the usual situation: this was wartime. The government expected the Germans to bomb London at any time, so they drew up a plan to round up all the children and the pregnant women and get them to safety in the countryside before the bombs fell. Whole schools of children went together. I remember it like it was yesterday, the mothers and the kiddoes walking along streets toward the train station, everybody crying, the children wearing name tags pinned to their jackets, toting their little gas masks and not much more than a change of clothes and a sandwich or two.

"I'd been sent out on an errand, and when I got back to the house, I was asked to come into the parlor, which tells you right there how upside down everything was. You wouldn't be invited into the parlor, unless you were being dismissed. His Lordship and Her Ladyship were there, and Mairead had Gwennie on her lap. Miss Edlyn was crawling around on the floor. Mairead and I were told to pack our things as quickly as we were able and take the babies up to Brighton, to the summer home the family had there, by the sea. There was a car waiting to take us."

"You and your wife? Take your own daughter and Edlyn out of London?"

"Yes, ma'am. Her Ladyship intended to come along after us, but she was on the frail side, just getting her strength back after a bout with pleurisy. His Lordship wouldn't let her make the journey. Miss Edlyn was with my wife all day long, as it was, so she was well used to her. It was no hardship on the children, really, them being so young, so off we went to Brighton in the car."

"Just the four of you?"

"And Edmund, the driver. But he turned right around and went back to London. We stayed in Brighton through the holidays and into the spring. Then in May, when Hitler invaded France, it wasn't safe to stay right there on the coast any longer. If the wind was on your side, you could practically fling a stone across the channel and hit a lad standing on the beach in France. We were able to get a train out of Brighton headed to South Wales, a place called Swansea. His Lordship sent us money and the train tickets and arranged for the use of a wee cottage right in from the water."

"Just the four of you? You and your wife and *your* daughter and your employer's daughter, who later became Mrs. Winslow?"

"Yes, ma'am."

"And then, when the war was over, you all came back to London?"

He paused before speaking. "Not all of us," he said quietly. "Not Gwennie."

I didn't have the heart to ask what had happened to his daughter.

"No wonder they sent you to live with Edlyn," I said, anxious to change the subject. "You practically raised her."

"In the early years, I suppose you could say. His Lordship was involved in the war effort and couldn't leave London, and Her Ladyship was never strong enough to travel."

I had been so absorbed in our conversation that I hadn't noticed a car make the turn from Dartmouth Street into the alley. But from my low and fairly sheltered perch, I could now recognize the driver: Tad Winslow. He was driving toward us and the house. If I didn't duck away quickly, I was going to have to explain what I was doing in the alley behind his family home, pawing through boxes of his rejects.

I stood up quickly and walked in the direction of Clarendon Street.

"Come with me," I said aloud. It couldn't hurt to keep talking to a ghost only I could see. No one, including Tad, was likely to want to tangle with a person who seemed to be hearing voices and was carrying on a lively conversation with them. Then again, these days you see a lot of people walking down the street, apparently talking to themselves. They're wearing Bluetooth headsets for their cell phones.

Mr. Grady floated along beside me.

"Please, don't go," he pleaded. "I must find that deed."

"I know." I was walking briskly. Though I'd been stung, the other day, by Tad's utter disinterest in me, I was now counting my lucky stars that I hadn't registered on his radar.

"Was that the last of the books?" I asked.

"No."

"Where are the rest?"

"Upstairs in the hall. They're being sent to the Bryn Mawr Book Store. Josie went to Bryn Mawr."

I knew the store. It was a warm and inviting little haven for book lovers, in a Cambridge neighborhood known for its tantalizing food boutiques and astronomical house prices. Proceeds from the sale of secondhand books went to fund scholarships at Bryn Mawr College.

"Is someone picking them up?" I asked.

"I suppose so, yes."

"When?"

"That I don't know."

I paused when we reached Clarendon Street. "Is there any way I can get into the house? Is there any time when no one's around?"

"Mrs. Martin goes home at six," he said.

"But I'm sure she locks everything up tight. Doesn't she?"

He paused to think. Hollywood's got it all wrong when it comes to the amount of power ghosts actually have. They can't open windows. They can't turn keys in locks and let you in. They *can* interfere with electronic alarm systems, though, just by standing next to them. I was about to ask whether the Winslows had one when he said, "One of the windows was broken last week. They were taking apart the brass bed in Josie's old room and one of side rails slipped and went right through the glass. It was old glass, rounded, with a lavender tint. They'll not be able to replace it, really, but they've something on order from out of state."

"Is the window accessible?"

"By the back fire escape, yes. It's on the fourth floor."

"And they didn't . . . board it up or anything?" (asked the

person who was relieved of her mother's engagement ring because she couldn't be bothered to install a reliable lock).

"Oh, they've got a piece of plywood across it," he answered,
"but it isn't a bang-up job. And who would dare to climb that old
fire escape?"

He glanced at me sort of sideways, then looked away.

Would I? Could I? And if so, when? I was on my way to Nat's
family for dinner, which never took less than five hours. And
Henry was due home at seven.

Oh, yeah. Henry.

No, I was not going to climb four stories in the dark on what
had appeared to be a hundred-year-old fire escape. There was a
time when I wouldn't have thought twice about it, and there
might yet be a time when I wouldn't hesitate to take on the chal-
lenge, but it certainly wasn't now. Besides not wanting to end up
flat in the alley being sniffed at, or worse, by the rat and all his
cousins, there was that inconvenient little law against breaking
and entering.

Mr. Grady could tell what I was thinking. Not because ghosts
can read minds—they can't—but because I have never been very
good at hiding what I'm feeling. "I'll think of something," I said.
"I promise."

He smiled a little sadly, bowed, and was gone.

Chapter Ten

A s i accepted a slice of lemon-ricotta pie, dessert I was far too full for but would probably eat anyway, I tried to trace what had brought us onto the unlikely subject of the Great Molasses Flood. I think it grew out of Pasquina's simmering displeasure at seeing cans of Diet Coke on her Sunday dinner table, contraband brought upstairs from the second-floor apartment of Nat's aunt Marcella.

Pasquina despised the consumption of soda, and *diet* soda, especially at Sunday dinner, was beneath her contempt. Having grown up on a grape farm in the Mazara valley, just outside of Palermo, she believed that the human body had not been designed to consume anything that hadn't once walked the earth, grown in soil, swum the seas, or hung from a branch. Somehow, a conversation about artificial sweeteners had led us onto the subjects of sugar, then honey, then molasses.

I'm ashamed to admit it, now that I understand what a tragedy it really was, but the whole idea of a molasses tank exploding and flooding the street just below us waist-high with bubbling brown goo had always struck me as sort of . . . comical, like something out of a Tex Avery cartoon. Not to mention implausible. I mean, really—how could that have happened?

"Lifted a train right off the tracks," insisted Nat's brother, Franco. "Buildings flattened, people and horses smothered. It was like . . . lava coming down a mountain."

"When was this?" I asked.

"Winter, 1919," Pasquina piped up. Think what you want about her dietary theories; at eighty-one, the woman has the energy of a jackrabbit and a better memory than anyone else at the table.

"You weren't even here then, Nana!" Nat said.

"No, no, but Papa talked about it."

Papa, Pasquina's late father-in-law, had run a barbershop, Alonso's, on Salem Street for decades. Like his son, Pasquina's late husband, he'd paid the ultimate price for his love of a good smoke. Or forty.

"All the old-timers talk about it," Pasquina went on, shaking her head. "It took months and months to clean it all up. The water in the harbor all that summer: still brown."

I glanced down the table at Nat's new "friend," Rocco, who was wedged in between Marcella and Nat's mom. Rocco was a bartender Nat had met recently at one of the clubs she was always trying to drag me to. In the dim, crowded dining room, he looked a little too . . . good, especially for someone who had probably worked until two or three this morning.

What was it? Man makeup? Multiple hair products? He caught my glance and sent a smirky little nod in my direction, one I couldn't help but interpret as meaning, *Yeah, I know. I don't blame you for staring. Everybody does.*

Marcella was one of the more successful Realtors working in the area of the North End and the Waterfront. She was wearing a low-cut blouse with red lace peeking out. Though she had to be nearing sixty, she walked five miles a day and was rigorous about her diet and salon procedures, enabling her to dress like a woman half her age. This was not lost on Rocco. Faced with the choice of spending the afternoon chatting up the steamy, perfumed Marcella or Nat's mom, Regina, a kindly nurse-practitioner at Brigham and Women's Hospital, Rocco had thrown his lot in with the City Mouse.

In doing so, though, he had probably sealed his fate with Franco. Franco didn't like the fact that the unctuous Rocco had spent his entire meal showering attention on the sexy Marcella, barely giving their mother the time of day. Rocco was no sooner out the door, Marcella's business card in his pocket, than Franco rose to Regina's defense.

"I don't know what you see in that guy," he said to Nat, shaking his head.

Nat was clearing the table. Pasquina had gone to have a little lie-down, and the men had stretched out in the living room with cigars and Italian soccer on Digital TV.

Nat glanced up quickly. "What do you mean?"

"He's a bonehead," Franco observed delicately.

"Franco!" Regina said softly.

Marcella stood up and brushed crumbs off her short, chestnut skirt. "He's very successful, Franco. He wants to buy a building with a couple of his friends."

"And do what with it?" Franco sneered.

"Open his own club. You could learn a few things, you know, if you put down your fork every once in a while and participated in the conversation at the table."

"Ow!" said Nat's cousin Gennaro, grinning.

"What's that supposed to mean?" Franco sat up, perhaps to minimize the slouch that might have led his aunt to draw the wrong conclusion: that he was packing on some pounds.

Marcella pursed her lips and glanced at her sister, who shook her head slightly. Marcella reached for the remains of the pie and filled a glass with dirty cutlery. She headed into the kitchen.

"Well *I* think he's very nice," Regina said to Nat. "He was very polite. It's an awful lot of people to meet at one time."

"He's a bonehead," said Franco.

Nat walked me to the train.

"I liked him," I lied. "I mean, I didn't really get to talk to him much but he seemed pretty nice. Franco's just—"

Nat reached into her pocket and pulled out a box of Marlboro Lights.

"He's a fine one to talk," Nat sniffed, cradling the flame of her lighter from a chill wind that had suddenly blown in from the water. It made me want to be home, right now, with Henry.

"You remember that girl he brought to Ma's sixtieth?" Nat went on, inhaling a chestful of smoke.

I didn't, but Franco's girlfriends were always kind of the same: blond fans of tanning parlors, French pedicures, and fur.

"She's in jail! She embezzled over a hundred thousand dollars from the company where she worked."

"Wow," I said, trying to call up a particular face. I couldn't.

"I mean, cut the guy some slack," Nat continued. "He even brought flowers for Nana!"

I put my arm around her shoulder. "Forget about Franco," I said. "He's just . . . overprotective."

"Of me?"

"Of you; of your mom. I'm sure he didn't mean it the way it sounded."

Nat stopped short and gave me a look. There weren't too many ways to parse the meaning of Franco's judgment.

"Anyway," I said, looping my arm through hers, "guess who has a new job, starting tomorrow?"

I filled her in on the events that had transpired since her call to me a week ago this evening; in fact, this very hour. She was fascinated to hear about my encounter with the monks and horrified to learn that their precious manuscript had vanished from Sylvia's apartment.

I remembered another important matter just as we reached the end of Hanover Street. From there, I would continue on alone across the disappointingly slight swath of green space that had replaced the Central Artery when the "Big Dig" took cross-city traffic underground.

For years, beleaguered commuters had endured traffic jams and weekly changes in the direction of one-way streets by dreaming of a regular Central Park reconnecting the North End with the rest of the city. When the towers supporting the Central Artery came down, though, the "Rose Kennedy Greenway" was revealed to be not much more than a string of little green parcels, bisected by traffic moving at highway speeds. Already, interest groups were lining up with proposals to erect commemorative monuments on the measly patches of green and build more structures to replace the ones that had just been dismantled.

"Speaking of guys who are crazy about you," I said.

Nat frowned, puzzled.

"The one I live with would really love a movie date."

"Awww," Nat said. "That's sweet! I'll take him anytime."

"Thanks," I said. "I'll call you."

Nat nodded, dropped her cigarette onto the sidewalk and crushed it with the toe of a brown suede boot. We embraced, and then, taking my life into my hands, I headed into the traffic, toward Haymarket.

Nona had called from Cleveland while I was out, so I picked up the phone while waiting for Henry and Dec.

"*Cucciola mia!*" she said when she heard my voice. "Where *were* you?"

"Pasquina's." Anticipating the next few questions, I answered them before she asked.

"She served a great dinner: stuffed artichokes, pea soup with croutons, baked eggplant with capers and tomatoes, and rabbit."

"Cooked how?" Nona asked. A tone of suspicion had crept into her voice.

"Braised, with red and yellow peppers."

"Red and *yellow?*" she said disapprovingly.

Nona would never use two sweet peppers in a braise. Red and green, yellow and green, orange and green—all fine. But red and yellow? Much too similar, sweet and mild; the dish would lack depth. A variation like this was as unimaginable to my grandmother as my making lasagna "English" style, with béchamel sauce, an experiment I tried when I was fifteen. I guess I was rebelling. She still brings it up occasionally.

"Was it tough?"

"The rabbit? No."

"Gamy?" Another reason to lean on green peppers.

"Not really, no."

"Hmmm," she said, sounding a little disappointed. It probably felt unfair, her childhood friend's being fortunate enough not only to turn out a flawless dinner, despite using the wrong peppers, but also to be spending Sunday afternoon surrounded by her entire extended family. Plus me. Whereas Nona probably went to eight o'clock Mass, then had dinner with someone else's family or spent the day alone. Dad wasn't far away, but she wasn't *his* mother. He'd be there in a blink if she needed her screens mended or her driveway shoveled, but he wasn't going to hang around her hot little house all afternoon.

I feel awfully guilty about the two of them being alone. I wonder if Joe and Jay ever feel this way, and somehow I doubt it. Men are expected to go off into the world and make their way, but for a woman, it's different. You feel . . . selfish. Disloyal. And Joe and Jay weren't nearly as tied to Nona as I was, between the ghost business—my brothers did not inherit the gift—and my being the only girl.

I had wanted, and needed, to get away on my own for a while after college. I just couldn't bring myself to move back home and resume a version of the life I had led from the time I was a little girl until I went away to school. Dad was never all that crazy about my being involved in the world of the spirits. Nona, on the other hand, just loved the drama of the phone ringing, especially in the middle of the night, and of our being summoned—we usually went together—to a stranger's house or a funeral home or the office of a private detective. She still answers the calls whenever they come, but now, she goes alone.

"How's my boy?" she asked.

"He's great. He'll be home any minute."

"Oh. Where is he?"

"He was at his dad's for the weekend."

"Ah." Her tone was a little smug. She knows Henry goes to Dec's on the weekends, and I think she gets just a tiny bit of satisfaction from knowing that I, too, am often alone on Sundays. *Chi la fa l'aspetti,* she always used to say. What goes around comes around.

Nona has never met Declan, but her tone turns chilly every time his name is mentioned. The irony is, she would love him.

But it's easier for her to blame him than me for the fact that I will probably never move back home. If he hadn't gotten me pregnant, after all, I wouldn't have to stay in Boston for the foreseeable future, if not for the rest of my life, so that Henry can be near his father. Then again, Nona wouldn't have a great-grandson who sends her drawings for her refrigerator and tells her jokes over the phone and falls asleep in her lap on Christmas Day.

I considered telling her that Nell and Delia were coming here next weekend, but I stopped myself. What was the point? No matter how hard I try to paint my situation as that of a regular mom with a regular family life—laundry, cooking, sleepovers, birthday parties—she is never going to accept it completely. I might do a perfectly commendable job in my unfortunate situation, but in her mind, the fact will always remain that I gave birth to a child out of *wedlock*.

A word that doesn't exactly fill me with a sense of hopeful abandon.

Complicating matters, she really can't disapprove of the choice Declan made to go back to Kelly. What she wishes will happen, she has often told me, is that I will meet a "nice young man" who will marry me and adopt Henry, so my son can have a "real father." *Easier said than done*, I always think, and besides, he *has* a real father. A great one.

What always reassures her that I am still "her girl," though, are tales of the ghosts with whom I am presently communicating.

"Monks?" she said. "How old?"

"Oh, close to a thousand, I think."

"Where are they from?"

"Ireland."

"If they want a bishop," she went on, "you call Monsignor Dolan. He knows everybody. And you helped him a lot."

I'd met the sprightly cleric in my late teens, when Nona was sidelined with a case of sciatica. A successful local contractor had died suddenly, just months after making a new will in which he left a valuable piece of lakeside property to the Diocese of Cleveland. But the will could not be found. The lawyer had skipped town, under a cloud of conflict-of-interest charges. And while the contractor's wife remembered seeing an envelope that she believed contained the revised will, no one could find it in the days following the man's death.

That's where I came in, and Monsignor Dolan was in the room when the spirit of the contractor told me where the document was filed. Or rather, misfiled. There's a summer camp now on the edge of the lake, and in fall and spring, the buildings are used for conferences. It's much in demand as a location for weddings, and that's easy money for the diocese. Monsignor Dolan gives me all the credit for this, and having been in the room when the conversation happened, he no longer doubts the existence of ghosts. He's always happy to help me when I call.

I glanced at the clock: six twenty. Where were the guys?

"I have something to tell you," Nona went on. I snapped to, fearing the worst: cancer.

"I met someone," Nona said.

I waited for her to go on, but she didn't.

"What do you mean?" I asked.

"I *met* someone."

"Like ... a man?" I asked. If she were my age, I wouldn't feel comfortable voicing this assumption, especially in Cambridge. But this was Nona.

"Of course, a *man*," she said.

"Really?" Wow. "Well, who *is* he? What's his name?"

"Paul," Nona answered. "His wife died a year ago."

"How did you meet him?"

"At church. He invited me out for coffee."

"When was this?"

"Oh, I don't know. A while ago."

"Have you seen him again? Since this coffee?"

"Every day," she said cheerfully.

"Nona, that's so great!" I said. "That's really ... great," I added, unable, in my shock, to think of anything else to say.

What followed was even more shocking.

My grandmother giggled.

Henry was in a philosophical mood. The church Declan and Kelly take the kids to, St. Ambrose's, can be a little on the old-school side, depending on who says the Mass. When Henry's very tired, which he often is on Sunday nights, he can get fretful over things he's heard in the sermon, words or concepts that unsettled him in the moment, dispersed like phantoms when he hit the fresh air, and now have returned to hover over his bed.

"Mama," he said after I'd kissed him and tucked him in and gotten him a second glass of water and promised for the third time that I would firm up his movie date with Nat.

I gave him a stern look. The preliminaries were now officially over. It was bedtime.

"Is your mama in heaven?"

Oh, okay. So he wasn't just stalling. I sat back down on his bed and took a minute. "I hope so," I finally said, thinking, *Whatever heaven is.*

"Don't you *know*?"

I shook my head. "Nobody knows, sweetie, not for sure. Nobody ever came back to tell us."

He thought about this for a minute.

"But you *think* she is, right?"

I wondered how truthful I should be. On the spectrum of

confidence in the existence of the exact version of heaven I was raised to spend my life earning admission to, I fall somewhere in the middle. I am absolutely certain that a person's existence doesn't end with their last heartbeat; I've seen plenty of evidence of that. But I suspect that what lies on the other side of the white light is something far, far grander and more magnificent than the heaven depicted in my grade school catechism, and Henry's, books that feature images of angels floating around on clouds. Anything is possible, really. I mean, think how unlikely it is that we are alive at all, held on by gravity to an enormous ball turning majestically through space.

"Right?" Henry said, with a little more urgency. Clearly I hadn't answered fast enough.

He was five, he was tired, he was scared. The time for a nuanced examination of faith and doubt was not now.

"Right," I said. I hoped it would end there, with a sigh of relief and Henry snuggling deep under the covers, but it didn't.

"She died when you were little. Littler than me."

I nodded. He'd heard the story before but he often asked me to repeat it, as though familiarity would eventually rub off its awful edges.

"We were walking to Nona's," I began, as I always begin.

"Nona's same house?" he asked.

"Yup. Uncle Joe and Uncle Jay were at Nona's and Mama and I were walking over to Nona's to pick them up."

"From Pop's."

"Well, it's Pop's house now, but everybody lived there then. Mama and Pop and me, and Uncle Joe and Uncle Jay."

"I *know!*"

I smiled. "I know you know. You know the whole story. So why don't you tell it to *me* for a change?"

He dove under the covers. When he peeked out he was grinning nervously and shaking his head. He scurried back under the comforter.

"Come on," I said.

Silence.

"I thought you knew the story," I said.

"I do!"

"You must not remember it, then, because—"

From under the covers, I heard him say, "Your mama got hit by a car. And she died. But you didn't."

"That's right," I said. "She pushed the stroller out of the way, so I was safe."

He peeked out, and he was no longer grinning.

"But if you got hit, too, you'd be in heaven with your mama."

"May-*be*," I said, trying to lighten the conversation with a singsongy tone.

I finally had an inkling of what this might be about. I wrapped his comforter around him and dragged him onto my lap.

"Are you afraid I might die?" I asked quietly.

He looked at me and gave a tentative little nod. Given the hour and how tired he was, there was only one way to handle this.

"Well I'm *not* going to," I said. "Not today, not tomorrow, not ever."

He gave me a suspicious look. Was I pulling his leg? Or could what he most wished for possibly be true? Bravely, he said, "Everybody dies, Ma. You have to die sometime."

I shook my head. "Nope. Not me. I'm the only person who ever lived who is never, ever, *ever* going to die."

He was starting to smile. "You will, too!"

"Nope. No way! I'm going to hang around and *bug* you and drive you crazy until I'm a thousand years old and have no teeth and have white hair down to the ground! And I'll make you wait on me and I'll scare away all your friends."

I stood up and slung him down onto the bed. He was giggling now and trying to pull away from me. I threw in a tickle or two, stealth-style.

"And if they won't go away," I continued, "I'll fry them up and eat them! And I'll fry you up and eat you, too! Rrrrrrr!" I tackled him and rustled the covers and tickled his squirming form.

"Noooo!" he said, "I'll eat *you!* I'll fry *you* up and eat *you!!!*" He made gobbling sounds and tried to tickle me.

"And then what?" I said, in my meanest, witchiest voice.

"I'll go live with Daddy!" he shouted, triumphantly.

Chapter Eleven

As usual, this morning, I had been early. I hadn't wanted to be late on my first day of work, so I'd allowed for an extra forty-five minutes of travel time, in case there were problems on the Red Line. There weren't. With time to spare, I got off at Charles Street, bought a grapefruit juice at Savenor's, and made my way over to Beacon, then up the hill toward the Athenaeum.

The air was cool. It was drizzling steadily and the streets were alive with both the living and the dead. I see them all, all the time, side by side, but I am able to tune out earthbound spirits the same way we all tune out other people, every day of our lives. Say you go to a store or a park, or any place that's filled with people. You might take particular notice of an individual or two, but unless you make contact with that person by speaking to them or by staring at them until they look at you or by hitting them with a Frisbee or something, they probably won't notice you. We're all just a face in a sea of faces. I suppose we couldn't get through life without the ability to ignore 99 percent of what crosses our field of vision, competing for our attention.

Fortunately, the same rules applied to the ghosts I saw this morning. There was the sad young woman in Colonial dress, sitting on one of the benches in the Public Garden. There was the ghost of a man I took to be a slave, possibly captured and murdered as he moved between safe houses on the Underground Railroad. There were the emaciated spirits of a father and his little girl, and while I knew nothing for certain, I guessed that they had been passengers on one of the "coffin ships" that brought the sickly victims of Ireland's Great Famine to New York and New England. There was the ghost of a hollow-eyed young man in his late teens or early twenties. He seemed surprised to be in the realm of the spirits, and I guessed that he had recently died in an accident or from a drug overdose. None of the ghosts noticed me, though, because I didn't make eye contact with them or speak to them. They assumed I couldn't see them, so they ignored me the same way they ignored all the other people on the street. And because earthbound spirits can't pass through the bodies of living people, despite what you might see in the movies, they politely, and in a few cases, impolitely, shared the sidewalks with the rest of us, weaving in and out of the commuters scurrying for their offices, stepping aside for the mothers hurrying children to school, and darting out of the way, ironically, since they were already dead, of killer cyclists.

I had walked past the old Granary Burying Ground countless times when I lived in Back Bay but I had never taken the time to pause, climb its limestone steps, and pass through its monumental gateway to the small, quiet cemetery within. Today, I did.

Because in the movies cemeteries are always filled with ghosts, you're probably assuming that it was another earthbound spirit that lured me into the quiet garden, yet one more lost soul with something urgent on its mind. But that's another Hollywood myth. It doesn't work that way. Ghosts need energy, human energy, in order to survive, and they're not going to get it from dead people, so they don't tend to hang around in cemeteries. You might see the occasional departed fussbudget checking up on the maintenance of her grave, but that's usually it. This morning, there wasn't a ghost to be seen within the cool, damp walls of the burial ground.

There were, however, the final resting places of some serious historical personages: three signers of the Declaration of Independence, eight Massachusetts governors, and Paul Revere himself. And Mother Goose. *The real Mother Goose?* I'd wondered. (*Was there* a real Mother Goose?) I didn't know. But I did know there was a real Benjamin Franklin, and both his parents were buried there, under a curiously modern granite obelisk about twenty feet tall.

The trees had lost almost all of their leaves, and a cool, gray mist hovered over the ground. Some of the tombstones had sunk so deeply into the earth that it was impossible to read their full inscriptions.

Two hours later, though, as I gazed down from the windows in Sylvia's office, the very same spot no longer seemed somber and melancholy, as it had earlier, but full of energy and life. The sun had broken through the layer of cloud and burned off all the morning mist, and tourists in bright rain slickers and baseball caps were now wandering the paths, taking photographs of notable headstones. Dozens of grammar school children, probably on a Freedom Trail field trip, were chasing one another up and down the soggy grass aisles.

It was nearly eleven, and I was waiting for Sylvia, who had been summoned to an unscheduled meeting by her boss, Amanda Perkins. I use the word *boss,* but really, Sylvia is her own boss. Still, because she is working under this roof on books that now belong to the Athenaeum, she's in fairly close contact with the powers-that-be. The phone had rung just minutes after I'd arrived, and Amanda had asked to see her. Immediately.

"Oh, my God," Sylvia had said. "She knows!"

"Knows what?"

"About the book! About the fact that I took it home and it—"

"There's no way," I said, interrupting what appeared to be a panic attack in the making. "How could she know?"

"She never calls me. Why would she be calling me?"

"You *do* work here. I'm sure it's something . . . ordinary."

Sylvia stood up and started to pace.

"Look," I continued, "don't you think that if she knew about the book, you'd have heard about it by now?"

"Not necessarily." She was not in the mood to be reassured.

"As far as they know, it doesn't exist, remember?" I said.

She was frowning and shaking her head; fear was overtaking reason.

"You hid it inside that cover," I reminded her. "What was the book?"

"Hoeffler," she answered softly. *"Mysterium Musicum."*

"Right. So if they're looking for anything, they're looking for that."

"Great," she said sharply. "First I get a message from Tad, and now this."

"Tad?" My stomach did a little swoop. So he *had* seen me in the alley behind his house! He'd recognized me after all, and now he was going to demand an explanation.

"What did *he* want?" I asked nervously.

"No idea," she answered. "I tried him back, but it went to voice mail."

"He's probably just checking up on those books," I said, not believing this for a minute.

"Maybe," she'd said.

She'd been gone for over an hour now, though, and I must have been getting more and more nervous myself, because when I heard a noise behind me, I surprised myself by letting out a little shriek. I wheeled around.

It was the monk. The young one.

"I beg your pardon," he said.

"That's all right," I answered.

"I've been forbidden to speak to you," he said anxiously, glancing back at the door to be sure that his volatile abbot had not appeared, "but I had to come."

"Is it the Book of Kildare?" I blurted out, afraid he might vanish at any moment.

He seemed puzzled. "Cill-Dara was our abbey," he said quietly.

I thought for a minute. The Book of Kildare was probably given that name later, by art historians. To this monk, it would have been just one—although maybe a very important one—of the many manuscripts transcribed or created in their scriptorium.

"Were you killed?" I asked.

He nodded. "The abbey was burned to the ground. But please, I must hurry."

"How can I help you?" I asked.

"He will *only* speak to a man of the Church."

"A priest?"

He shook his head firmly. "A *cardinal!*"

I smiled. "I seriously doubt that I can—"

"Or a bishop," he added quickly.

"I can try," I said. "I mean, I *will* try, but what about a monsignor? That might be easier to pull off."

"It's urgent!" he said loudly, apparently annoyed that I didn't seem to be taking this seriously enough. "It's being destroyed."

I felt a chill. "*What?* What do you mean?"

From the look on his face, I gathered that he felt he had already said too much. He and his abbot might be dead, but he still felt bound by the vow of absolute obedience that he had taken in life.

"The manuscript's being destroyed?"

He pursed his lips, squeezed his eyes tightly shut, and allowed himself to make one tiny nod in the affirmative.

"How?" I demanded. "Who's destroying it?"

He shook his head. He would say no more.

"Who? *Tell me!* The person who stole it?"

His eyes flew open. "*Stole* it?" he whispered. "It's been stolen?"

"It was taken from Sylvia's place," I informed him quietly.

"Oh, no," he said, shaking his head. "No! Dear God, please . . ."

And then he vanished.

———

Chandler had taken a personal day, so we had the bindery to our-selves. About ten minutes after the monk disappeared, Sylvia had come back upstairs to get me, to take me through the first-day formalities of tax forms and keys and introductions. I was curious to have a conversation with Amanda, but when we got back around to her office, it was locked. I hadn't yet heard the details of their meeting; Sylvia said she'd tell me everything once we were alone and settled in downstairs.

One nice thing about bookbinding is that it really can't be rushed. The process is methodical, and each little step takes as much time as it takes. You might wish the glue would dry more quickly, but it dries when it dries, depending on how humid the air happens to be, how porous the papers are, how fine the leather is, and half a dozen other factors. You have no alternative but to slow yourself down.

Sylvia offered me a choice of books to work on, and I chose a three-volume set of Cicero's essays. These weren't among the valuable books waiting to be rebound; they were probably just college texts retained by Finny or someone in his family for sentimental reasons. But that was all right. I was happy to leave the high-profile manuscripts to Sylvia.

The introduction was in French and the text was in Latin, so I wouldn't be tempted to read any of it, which, for me, is an occupational hazard. In a way, it was a shame to rebind them; they were so evocative and beautiful in their falling-apart way. They had been published in Paris in 1923, with a paperback cover that was now a soft, faded shade of pumpkin. The weight of the typesetter's keys on the paper had embossed each page with an imprint of the text on the opposite side. The paper itself was supple and worn, as though the volumes had been carried around for years in a leather bag or a generous pocket. In the margins of the pages were notes written in pencil, in Latin and English, in neat, tiny script. An index card was tucked into one of the chapters. It looked as old as the book, and whoever had written the margin notes had written just one sentence on the card, in Latin. I wondered if that person was Finny.

The books were held together by packing tape: eight neat pieces, themselves now yellow and brittle, crossing the spine of each volume. I wouldn't be able to replicate the engraving of Lupa, the wolf who nursed the founders of Rome, Romulus and Remus, or the simple, elegant logo of the publisher, La Société des Belles Lettres, which, along with "7 francs," was the only text printed on the back cover. But I could preserve the pages themselves, and with them, the evidence of one human being to whom the essays had once spoken.

I set to work. Sylvia was resewing chapters of a book of botanical plates, so we established ourselves at the big central table and settled in.

She let out a doleful sigh. "I'm in way over my head," she said. "I think I'd better just come clean to everybody, let them call the police, and be done with it. And resign, if they don't fire me first. Which they definitely will."

"What happened?"

"She's onto something. I know she suspects there's something going on."

"What did she say?" I pressed.

"She asked me point-blank."

"Asked you *what*?"

"Whether there was ever an illuminated manuscript in the Winslow Collection. And if so, where it was right now. Because it's clearly not at the Athenaeum, it hasn't been bought or sold at auction in the past year, according to her *extensive* sources in the field, and she happens to know for a fact that such a manuscript was quite recently in Finny's possession."

"Yikes," I said. "How does she know that?"

"She got a call about a month ago from someone she would only identify as 'a curator in New York.' It has to be Paola Moretti at The Cloisters. Tad was in touch with both Paola Moretti and James Wescott after he got their letters, the ones he gave to us. He told them both that his father had died and that the whole collection had come here. Don't you remember how excited Moretti was in her letter? She was sure we had our hands on the Book of Kildare. I'll bet you anything she called Amanda."

I nodded. It made sense so far.

"Amanda apparently went through all the records, and obviously—"

"She didn't find anything."

"Right. I don't know why she didn't just ask me about it, but she didn't. She claims she sort of forgot about it, assumed it was just a mistake, but then, over the weekend, she was at a dinner at Harvard, something to do with that symposium. She was seated near James Wescott, who *also* mentioned the book. He might not have believed that there was any such thing as a Book of Kildare, but we still had an illuminated manuscript. Amanda said that Wescott congratulated her on 'landing the Winslow Collection' and specifically asked about the book."

I let out a sigh. This was bad.

"What did you say?"

"What could I say? I lied. I said I knew about the book, that Finny *had* had it and it was beautiful and probably very valuable, but that I wasn't privy to everything he did, every decision he made. Especially toward the end. When the manuscript wasn't among the ones that got packed up to come over here, I told her, I just assumed that Finny had done something else with it—given it to one of his children, sold it privately, I don't know. He didn't have to answer to me. I was just someone he hired to bind his books."

"So she has no idea how close you were, you and Finny." I was fishing here.

"No," she said. "None at all. No one did, really."

I thought so.

"Do you think she believed you?" I asked.

"I have no idea," Sylvia said. "For all I know, she thinks *I* stole it."

"No! Why would she think that? What you said makes perfect sense."

Sylvia sat back and shook her head. We were startled by the ringing of her cell phone. She glanced at the screen on her phone.

"Oh, no," she groaned. "It's Tad."

Tad's call, like Amanda's, was more of a summons. It had nothing to do with the books he'd asked Sylvia to appraise; he seemed to have forgotten all about those. It concerned a phone call he'd gotten on Friday from Amanda. She was trying to solve a puzzle, she'd told him, and there were a couple of missing pieces. She was hoping he'd be able to help.

Tad asked Sylvia how soon he could see her; he was leaving in the morning for a trip to London and wanted to straighten this out before he left. Could he take her to lunch? No, she replied, that wasn't possible today. But she could leave work around three and meet him at the house at three thirty.

"Will you come with me?" she pleaded.

The timing wasn't ideal—I had to pick up Henry at five—but accompanying Sylvia would solve one problem: getting me back into that house so that I could try to help John Grady.

"Please?" she asked. "Just for a half hour?"

"All right," I said.

The Boston Common felt strangely forsaken as we walked slowly toward Arlington Street. The recently refurbished wading pool, which doubled as a skating rink in winter, had the lonesome, soulful look of beach houses boarded up off-season. Soggy leaves had accumulated around the recessed drains, and a girl of about three, wearing rain boots with glandular-looking froggy eyes, was trying to kick the leaves across the aqua concrete. Nearby, a bored young mother talked on her cell phone, smoking and dropping ashes into the empty pool.

"I have to tell him the truth," Sylvia announced.

I didn't say anything for a moment, as a cascade of potential consequences unfolded in my mind. She'd lose her job. I'd lose mine. Charges would be filed. Declan would be reprimanded, maybe even demoted, for handling the theft "unofficially." And no matter how it turned out in the end, Sylvia would have a hard time ever getting hired again, after a vague, cloudy incident that left people in the book world whispering, something to do with fraud and theft. I started to feel angry at this prospect. It wasn't right. She was a good person. She was just trying to honor a promise to a dying man she'd obviously loved.

"Which truth?" I finally asked.

She looked up quickly.

"The fact," I said, "that his father didn't trust him enough to let him in on a secret he shared with *you*? That his own dad thought he was so shallow and greedy that he would never be able to appreciate the meaning of what he had? That all Tad would want to do would be to sell it to the highest bidder? Even if that meant the book would be locked away forever in somebody's private collection?"

"Finny didn't want that," Sylvia said, looking more and more upset. "It's the one thing he *didn't* want."

"I know."

"He was on a mission," she said, with feeling. "It meant so much to him. It was like a parting gift he wanted to give to the world."

I nodded. Tears were gathering in her eyes. She paused and sat down on a bench. I sat down beside her. The bench was wet, but it was too late now. She pulled a Kleenex out of her purse and dabbed at her eyes.

"He just didn't live long enough," she whispered, as the tears spilled over.

"I know," I said softly.

I glanced at my watch. Three twenty.

"Look," I said, "if you come clean now, the whole thing's going to blow sky-high. Between him and Amanda, it'll be all over the papers. Plus, whoever took the book will probably decide it's too hot to handle right now and they'll go underground with it, so even Declan won't be able to help. If telling the truth would get the book back, that would be one thing. But I don't think it will."

"Me, either."

"And," I added, "I hate to say it, but . . . you'll probably get arrested."

"Oh, I'll definitely get arrested," she said, sniffing. She let out a deep sigh, then turned and looked me in the eye. "What would you do?" she asked.

"I *think* I'd—" I paused. To be honest, I didn't know what I would do in her shoes. Court was court, jail time was jail time, and there was Henry. But I actually don't think I would ever have had the idea—or the guts—to make the false cover in the first place, setting this whole thing in motion. I don't mind the occasional white lie, or even the occasional whopper, but in this case, I think the goody-goody in me probably would have won out.

Did that make me a better person than Sylvia, who was risking everything—her job, her livelihood, her future—to honor a promise, and to try to shepherd Finny's gift into the world?

No. I didn't think it did. The world was full of mean, selfish cowards who hid behind the letter of the law when it served their ends. If this *was* the precious Book of Kildare, and it was stolen, then hidden away from the world for the narcissistic pleasure of one person, or a small group of people, this was wrong. Finny was right: it should be in a place where everyone who wanted to could see it and appreciate it and be inspired by it.

"I think I'd try to stall," I finally said. "If you can. Maybe by the time Tad gets back from London, Dec will have made some progress. Maybe we'll even have gotten the book back." I doubted this, but I said it anyway. "And you can return it to him and at least explain what you were trying to do. He might still be mad, but at least he'll have the book."

"What about Amanda?" Sylvia said.

"She's got no right to it. Would Finny have wanted them to have it? Probably not. Would Tad have given away a book that's probably worth millions of dollars?"

"No," Sylvia said firmly. "Definitely not."

"Right," I said. "Of course she's sniffing around, but that book doesn't belong to them and it never did. And it was never meant to."

She nodded, a little uncertainly.

"Of course she's desperate for it," I hammered on. "Who wouldn't be, in her position? It'd be a coup to bring it in."

"She's just doing her job," Sylvia said, with more kindness than I thought was called for. Then she sighed, stood up, and motioned for me to come along. We didn't speak for the rest of the way.

Chapter Twelve

FINNY'S HOUSE SEEMED gloomier than ever. Tad opened the door himself, and he looked surprised to see me by Sylvia's side. I could practically hear him thinking, *What are you two, joined at the hip?*

He was dressed in a navy polo shirt and pants the shade of ripe persimmons. I had learned last year, when Henry and I took a day trip to Nantucket, that wearing pants like these signified that you were a Nantucket person. They were in all the shops, marked down that day because it was the end of September, the color identified on the tag as "Nantucket red." Henry had wanted a pair, and one of the canvas belts embroidered with whales. He settled for the belt.

We followed Tad across the foyer and into the living room. We sat down on a threadbare sofa, and Tad established himself in a black wooden Harvard chair. It was still a beautiful room, but it had seen more impressive days. A grand piano stood in the bay of windows that faced Commonwealth Avenue, and a massive fireplace of black marble dominated the far wall. Mahogany bookcases, crowned with intricately carved moldings, ran floor to ceiling for the length of the room. A plaster frieze of grapes, flowers, and leaves drew my eye toward the twenty-foot ceiling.

And there he was, the ghost of John Grady, up in the corner of the room. Once he caught my eye, he floated down to the floor and stood at attention behind a tatty gold armchair. I winked at him to let him know that I saw him, and he smiled and bowed gratefully.

"Thank you for coming," said Tad, in the irritated tone of a busy executive who has been forced to make time for something he considers beneath him.

"Sure," said Sylvia.

He glanced at me and appeared to hesitate. "Are you two . . . roommates?" he asked. What I think he meant was, *Are you two . . . girlfriends?*

"Oh no," I said, hopping in quickly. "I live in Cambridge. With my son."

This had the dual purpose of clearing up the roommate business and establishing that the woman who looked exactly like me, whom he might have seen rummaging through his family's trash yesterday, was not likely to have been me. I would have been in Cambridge, with my son.

"And I'm in Brookline," said Sylvia. "Near Cleveland Circle."

If what he was actually wondering about was our personal relationship, we hadn't really answered his question. But maybe that was just as well; it might keep him a little off balance, confused and distracted, so Sylvia would have an easier time pulling the wool over his eyes.

Tad nodded, glancing from Sylvia to me, and then back.

"I'm a little confused," he said, in a tone that suggested he wasn't confused at all, but was going to pretend to be, so that Sylvia could hang herself with lies and evasions.

"I'm hoping you can help me straighten something out."

"Be glad to," Sylvia chirped. "If I can." She seemed like a different person than the one who had sat beside me weeping on a park bench not fifteen minutes ago. She seemed downright . . . perky. If she was able to keep up this bright and cheery facade, she just might pull this off.

"A manuscript seems to be missing," said Tad, imperially.

I looked over; there was a slight tightness to Sylvia's smile, but she seemed to be holding steady.

"Really? From where?" she asked.

Good answer, I thought.

"From here?" she went on quickly.

"Uh, no," said Tad. "Well, not exactly. I mean, I'm not quite sure." He suddenly sounded even more annoyed. Apparently, he didn't like being asked questions to which he didn't have the answers.

"From the Athenaeum?" Sylvia asked. I wondered if she was beginning to sense an advantage. "You mentioned that Amanda had called you."

"Yes, she did." Of this fact, at least, he *was* sure.

"On Friday," Sylvia continued briskly, shooting me a glance.

I held my breath, just praying that Tad had not heard from Amanda again today. If the only conversation they'd had was the one on Friday, he wouldn't know that a couple of hours ago, Sylvia had admitted to Amanda that she was familiar with the manuscript.

"Yes," he said.

I looked over. Relief was evident on her face.

"So it was about . . . one of the books you gave them?" Sylvia continued, frowning and looking puzzled.

Excellent choice of pronoun, I thought. *You.*

"Well, yes," he said. "At least, I'm fairly certain I did. There were so many books."

That were so unimportant to you, I thought. Sylvia had described to me the dispensation of the collection. Tad had declared that he had no room in his home for all these old books. What he meant was, books were not his style. He and his second wife lived in an ultramodern house in Wayland. It had recently been featured in the Sunday magazine section of the *Globe,* lately devoted almost entirely, it seemed to me, to home makeovers and the residential work of local architects and interior designers.

Sylvia had showed me a copy of the article. One perfect pear had sat on a black square plate in the middle of a poured-concrete dining table, beside a slim black vase holding exactly one calla lily. A jumble of old books would have really messed things up.

Esther, Tad's younger sister, had chosen several volumes from her father's collection. She had already taken what she wanted from the various bookcases scattered throughout the house when she moved to the Berkshires a few years ago. She insisted that she didn't want any more books, valuable or not. She barely had room for the books she already owned, and her basement out there was damp, so she couldn't even store things without worrying about mold and mildew. She was fine with whatever Tad wanted to do with their father's books and thought that making a gift of them to the Athenaeum was a great idea.

Tad and Josie, his older sister, had not been on speaking terms—something to do with a boat—when all the decisions were being made. Tad had apparently sent her a registered letter giving her a deadline to claim anything she wanted from the family manse. When she blew it off, Tad moved forward as executor. He hired a Harvard student to pack up the boxes of books and drop them off at the Athenaeum.

At the moment, Sylvia appeared to have a slight advantage: Tad seemed kind of fuzzy on which books he had actually given away.

"I logged in all the volumes myself," Sylvia said. "Did Amanda go through my list?"

"It wasn't there," Tad said curtly.

"What was the book?" Sylvia asked.

"Something on . . ." Tad stumbled. "A book on . . . illuminating."

I bit the inside of my cheek to keep from smiling.

"You mean, like . . . lighting?" Sylvia asked. "Like stage lighting, or lighting design?"

"I'm really not sure," Tad went on. "All I know is that it's a very valuable book and it's missing."

"And it was on lighting," Sylvia said, seeming to rack her brain for anything she could remember on the subject.

"What about Gorham's history of the Tiffany lamp," I suggested. "Or that treatise on Caravaggio—what was that called? *Shadow and Light*? Did he have anything like that?"

Sylvia shook her head.

"No, no," Tad broke in. "It was something to do with the Catholic Church. And old. Really old."

"There was that book on Brunelleschi churches," I said.

"No," he said angrily, springing to his feet.

"Do *you* remember anything like that?" Sylvia asked.

"Of course I don't," he snapped. "If I did, I wouldn't have had to call you, would I?"

Sylvia didn't rise to the bait. "I definitely didn't log in anything on lighting or lamps or the use of light in the design of Catholic churches—nothing like that."

"Did ever *see* a book like that?" he demanded. "When you were working for my father?"

"No," she answered. "But then again, I only came in contact with a small fraction of the books your father owned—just the ones he wanted re-bound. You'd have a better idea than I do of whether he ever owned . . . something like that."

"How the hell would I know?" he barked, his patience expiring.

Sylvia and I exchanged glances.

"Well," she said, slowly and carefully. "You *are* the person who donated the books."

He looked flushed and angry. If he had been in a cartoon, two cones of steam would have been whistling out of his ears.

The cell phone in his pocket began to ring. He fished it out and glanced at the name that came up on the screen. "I have to take this," he said curtly. "Thank you for coming. I'll figure it out when I get back from Europe."

I smiled and nodded.

"Have a good trip," Sylvia said as Tad stood up and hurried out of the room.

I had an almost uncontrollable urge to bolt. I imagined us walking calmly to the front door, closing it behind us, and then hightailing it down the steps and up Commonwealth Avenue, two of the Three Stooges in one of those "Yip, yip, yip!" moments, tripping over each other trying to scramble away from the scene of a fiasco.

Sylvia let out a sigh of relief.

"Not bad," I said.

"I was shaking. Could you tell?"

I shook my head.

"I just want to say hi to Mrs. Martin," she continued. "I know you have to go, so . . . Thanks for coming."

"No problem. I'll see you tomorrow."

John Grady had not moved in the past ten minutes. I glanced over to let him know that I had not forgotten my promise.

"I'll just use the ladies' room before I go," I said.

"There's one down the hall," Sylvia replied.

"I have an idea," I whispered as I approached the ghost of the butler. I opened the heavy mahogany door to the bathroom, stepped inside, and waited for him to follow. He didn't; his posture remained rigid and his gaze downcast. He shook his head slowly.

"We can't talk out there," I said quietly. "Tad or Mrs. Martin might hear us. Or rather, hear me."

"No, no, I . . . I couldn't, ma'am," he said shyly.

I understood his embarrassment at the prospect of coming into the bathroom with me. But something much larger was at stake. This just wasn't the time for butlery propriety.

"Please," I said. "I really want to help you find that deed. But I have to leave in a minute. I have to go pick up my son."

He looked up at me, took a deep breath, and appeared to steel himself. He stepped gingerly inside, and I closed the door softly behind him. I leaned against the edge of the marble sink. He could barely meet my gaze.

"You said that Mrs. Martin leaves at six," I began.

"She does," the ghost replied.

"Every day?"

"Every day," he answered.

"I assume that the house has an alarm system."

He nodded. "Mrs. Martin puts in the code before she leaves at night."

"Is there anyone else besides Tad who's in and out?"

"No, Miss . . ."

"My name is Anza. Please—it feels really weird to be called 'Miss' or 'ma'am.'"

"I beg your pardon," he said politely. "Then you must call me Johnny."

"All right," I said, *"Johnny."*

"Anza," he said sweetly, bowing. "Pleasure."

"You know that Tad is going to London?" I asked. "I was thinking that if you could disable the alarm system, I could come back some night and try to help you find your book."

Ghosts, being comprised of pure energy, can really muck up an electronic burglar alarm. He would only have to stand right beside or in front of the primary control panel for the signal waves to be completely disrupted, effectively disabling the system.

He frowned slightly. "I don't know if I can."

"You can, trust me."

"Now, I wouldn't want to be putting you in any danger," he said. "That wouldn't be right."

"You wouldn't be," I said. "As long as nobody's here."

He nodded vaguely. Something about this plan made him uneasy.

"Look, you're not doing anything wrong. That deed is yours. It's just . . . lost."

He looked up searchingly.

"And if you don't find it now——" I broke off.

"I never will," he concluded sadly. "I know that."

"I'm afraid you're right."

There was a moment of companionable silence. We could hear Mrs. Martin and Sylvia talking in the kitchen, but through the centuries-old walls, their words were just a low rumble. Tad's leather soles were clunking back and forth on the floorboards just above us, and a road crew somewhere within hearing distance seemed to be jack hammering up concrete.

"I can't come tomorrow night," I offered, "but I could come on Wednesday. We should probably wait until after dark, say nine thirty or so. I'll come in the back way."

He nodded.

"The alarm. What do I do?"

"Do you know where the main control panel is?"

He nodded.

"At nine thirty, you go and stand as close to it as you can. Right up in front of it. You'll see—the little red light will go off, or turn green, depending on what type of system it is. I'll wait a few minutes and then I'll come in the back way. I'll figure out the lock somehow."

What I meant was, I would figure out a way to break in.

"You come down and get me. All right?"

"What will you tell your husband?" Johnny asked.

"I don't have one. Only a son." I smiled.

"How old is he?"

"Five."

"What's his name?" Johnny inquired.

"Henry. Henry Owen O'Malley."

"Owen was my father's name," Johnny said softly.

"And mine," I replied.

"You know it's the Irish for John," he continued. "As is Sean, of course."

"I do," I said.

The social event of the fall, in Henry's kindergarten class, was to be the marriage of *Q* and *U*.

"You'll get a letter," my son informed me, crumbling a stack of Ritz crackers into his cream of tomato soup. He brushed the crumbs off his palms and stirred the crackers into a thick, tomato mush. I hoped he would eventually eat some of this, and some of the grilled cheese sandwich that was getting cold beside his bowl, but with Henry, you never knew. He might finish it all and ask for seconds or eat three bites and beg to be excused.

"It's a real wedding," he insisted. "With a cake. It'll come in the mail."

"The cake?" I was teasing.

"The *letter*," he said.

"Who's it from?" I asked.

"Me. And Miss O. And the other kids."

I nodded. Henry took a bite of tomato mush. And then another. I decided to add some Ritz to my soup.

"When is this?" I asked.

"I don't know."

"Soon? Or in a while?"

"In a while," Henry said.

Details of the event emerged at a glacial pace. They were doing two letters a week. This week's letters were *m* and *n*. Didn't I remember? He *told* me they had had mmmmmuffins on Monday. That was because *mmmmmuffin* was an *m*-word. Miss O. had made the muffins. Blueberry, but Melanie couldn't have one, because she was allergic to blueberries. And peanuts. If she ate one peanut she would die. So Miss O. had a needle for a shot. In case by mistake she ate a peanut. Melanie, not Miss O. Miss O. wasn't allergic to peanuts, but she didn't like them, so she didn't ever eat them.

My eyes were beginning to glaze over. I had to break into this stream of consciousness or we would be here until midnight.

"What are you doing for *n*?" I asked.

Friday was going to be Nnnnnnight Day, Henry informed me. Didn't I think that was funny? Night Day?

"*Very* funny," I said, falsely cheerful.

"But not knight like a knight in shining armor," he informed me, biting into his sandwich and pulling it away to create a long loopy string of mozzarella. "*That's* a *k* word, but you don't say the *k*, like 'kuh-night'—you just say 'night.'"

"Hmm," I said. "There's a *k* in *knight*? I never knew that."

Henry nodded, pleased with his superior knowledge.

"What are you doing for Night Day?" I asked. "Going to school in your pajamas?"

"No! But after lunch it's going to be Night. Miss O.'s going to turn off all the lights and pull down the shades and she's going to read us two books with a flashlight."

"Which books? Do you know?"

"*In the Night Kitchen,*" Henry answered. "Which she said is a little scary. And *Goodnight Moon.*"

"Which isn't."

"No," Henry said. "But I wouldn't be scared anyway."

"Not you," I said. "You're not the type to get scared."

"Nope," he said, concentrating now on his sandwich. The information stream had apparently trickled into a dry bed.

"Sweetie," I said. "I'm sorry, but I don't quite get the *wedding* part."

He gave me a look I expected I would see a lot in his teenage years, a look that said, *How can you possibly be so dense?*

He took a deep breath and pushed his bowl aside. This was serious.

"Okay. You know letters make up words, right?"

I nodded.

"Do you know what a vowel is?"

"I do."

"*A,*" Henry said, refreshing my memory, or educating me, in case I was bluffing, "*e . . . i . . . o . . . u . . .*"

"And sometimes *y,*" I sang.

He looked relieved to learn that I wasn't completely illiterate. Channeling Miss O., he continued. "Why do we need vowels?"

I shrugged. He had a definite answer in mind, so I let him go for it.

"Because otherwise," he explained patiently, "words would sound like this: nklprtstrlkdtrplmpwxlpthk!"

"Mlpktrbxlpdyrtszmlpywt?" I asked.

"Yeah," he said, grinning now and adding more loudly, "LMNPKLTRBZKHTRGY!!!"

"*That's* a mouthful."

"Yes," he said triumphantly. "So you put a vowel next to a constement so you can say it!"

"I see," I said seriously. "I always wondered about that."

"But the *tricky* part is, there's only one vowel you can ever put with *q!*"

"Really?"

"Yeah! *U!*"

He sat back with a swagger, flush with confidence.

"Never *a*?" I said.

"Nope."

"*E?*"

"Unh-unh," he said firmly, shaking his head. "Or no *i*. Or no *o*. Or no *u*. I mean, *yes u*."

"But no *y*," I said.

"Yeah, so that's why we're having a wedding, so we'll always re-member. Dylan's going to be *U* and Katie R.'s going to be *Q*. And Miss O. will marry them."

"Katie R.?"

"Yeah. There's Katie M. and Katie R."

"And you're absolutely sure there's going to be cake? Because it isn't really a wedding without cake."

"Yup," he said proudly. "Vanilla. We took a vote."

"Then count me in," I said.

Chapter Thirteen

Henry had just fallen asleep when the phone rang. I lunged for it before the ringing could wake him and sentence me to another half hour of his stalling and claiming to be unable to fall back to sleep.

"Hello?"

"Hey, it's Dec."

This was a surprise. "Hi! Where are you?"

"Down in the driveway. You busy?"

"Nope; I just got him down." I glanced out the window and sure enough, there was Declan's truck. "You want to come up?"

"Yeah, if that's okay."

Oh yeah, it was okay. It was always okay.

I speed-cleaned the kitchen for forty-five seconds, throwing our dishes into the sink and wiping off the table, stuffing the newspapers and junk mail into the recycling bin, straightening the rag rug. I opened the door at the top of the stairs so Declan wouldn't wake Henry by knocking and raced into my bedroom to pull a sweater over my black T-shirt, which had gotten wrecked with bleach. Dec was pulling out a kitchen chair when I came back into the kitchen.

"Howdy," he said.

"Hi. You working?"

"Just got off."

"You want a beer?"

He pondered this for a moment. "Ah, why not?" he said.

I always keep his favorite—Smithwick's—in the fridge, but he hardly ever has one. There are some problems with "the drink" in his extended family, so he's thoughtful about alcohol. It surprised me that he said yes.

I reached into the fridge, pulled out a beer, opened it, and handed it to him. I poured myself an inch or two of zinfandel and sat down.

"Have you eaten?" I asked.

"I have, thanks."

"Cheers," I said, and we clinked bottle and glass.

"So, I paid a visit to your pal Carlotta," he began. "She's a piece of work."

"Aw, she seemed sweet."

He made a face and shook his head. "She asked if she could call me about some *screenplay* she's writing. Get 'the cop stuff' right, she said. *Jay-sus*, that's all I need."

I laughed. "Did you get any more information?"

He shook his head. "Not much. I did blow the bit about the boyfriend, though, and the bike, so you might want to give Sylvia a heads-up."

"What do you mean?"

Dec had a sip of his beer. "Well, I wouldn't be asking Carlotta to tell me about Sylvia's boyfriend, now, would I? I'd be asking Sylvia herself. I told Carlotta straight up that the place had been broken into and that something valuable had been stolen. I just didn't mention what."

I nodded.

"There was one interesting bit, though," he went on. "She told me the lad spoke with an accent. I said, What, like me? She said no, and not British, either, and not Italian or Polish, she would have recognized those on account of her grandparents. Perfect English, it was, though, so I asked her, could the accent have been Dutch?"

"*Dutch?* Where'd you come up with that?"

"Scully." Dec raised his bottle in a toast and had a sip of beer.

"The guy who agreed to help you?"

Declan nodded. "He's cooperating. Gotten downright chatty, he has."

"*Really?*"

"Yeah, well, it's that or a decade or two of Christmas Eves at Cedar Junction."

"I guess I'd pick Door Number One," I said.

"There you go. I had some time alone with him before Bowen and Darrah came in to question him. I told him I needed a special favor, just between me and himself. Poor bastard; I like the guy. I told him I was the one who broke the Loughlin case, so I had a very special relationship with Judge Weinstein. You scratch my back, I told him, and I'll scratch yours. On the QT, though—he wasn't to breathe a word to Darrah or Bowen, or the deal was off. And I'd deny to the death that we'd ever had the conversation."

Dec had broken the Loughlin case with a little help from me. It was a horrible murder—a public defender named Rick Loughlin had been gunned down in front of his son and half the boy's Little League team after Loughlin defended a Cambodian gang member charged with rape and aggravated assault. Loughlin had gotten his client off, and a week or so later, three members of a rival gang came after the lawyer one evening at a local ice cream stand, where he was buying cones for the kids.

I offered to try to help, and it turned out I could. I located the ghost of Rick Loughlin at one of several locations I tried: the West Concord ball field, watching his son's team compete for the city championship, in a game that was dedicated to him. Loughlin's ghost, anxious to see his killer behind bars, told me everything I needed—or rather, Dec needed—to crack the case. In doing so, Dec earned the respect of a powerful judge, Judge Weinstein, who'd been a public defender with Loughlin before being appointed to the bench. When the time came for Scully's fate to be determined, a whisper from Declan into the good judge's ear wouldn't hurt a bit.

"Right off the bat, he had an idea," Declan went on.

"How would he know?" I asked, incredulous. "He's been in custody! You sure he's not just throwing you a dead end?"

"And why would he do that?"

"To get in your good graces. Make it seem like he's eager to help."

Declan laughed, a laugh that indicated he was choosing to tolerate good-naturedly my serious underestimation of his shrewdness.

"Well, there *were* some helpful details," Dec said.

"Like what?"

"Bastard picked the lock, for starters. That's not everybody's MO, not in this day and age. No question it was a high-end job; fellow was probably paid a tidy sum to go after the one thing, and he went in, found it, and got the hell out. Didn't even help himself to the emerald earrings, which tells you we're dealing with a class act. As felons go, I mean. The emeralds would have been a snap to fence. Easy. Or at the very least, a real decent gift for his girlfriend."

He paused and smiled, and I was suddenly embarrassed. Had I ever been his *girlfriend*? Would he ever have thought to apply that affectionate term to me?

Probably sensing the awkwardness of the moment, he went on. "He's also got to be smooth enough to handle a complication like Carlotta. Runs into her on the landing with the book in his knapsack and doesn't so much as break a sweat. Just launches right in, cool as trout on a plate. That takes a certain level of skill."

"So Scully thought of this guy . . ."

"Immediately," Declan said. "Dutch lad, Jannus Van Vleck. Probably involved in that Van Gogh heist. Maybe not the lifter himself, but definitely in the mix. No question. If somebody with money to burn wants to get their hands on a specific painting or something like, say, your manuscript, Van Vleck's name would be on the short list. And Scully knows for certain that he's been in the area."

"No kidding," I said. "So what do we do? Find the person with money to burn?"

Dec had a sip. "I'm thinking on that. I've gotta be really careful. They'll have me by the—sorry! It'll be hell to pay if it comes out that I'm cuttin' deals on the side."

"I know."

"Yeah, well, you let me worry about that."

"Thanks." I love it when Dec says things like this. He's such a guy's guy.

He nodded. "But what I'm asking myself here is much more basic. Who knew about the book? Not that she had it at her flat, I'm not talking about that. Just—who even knew that the book existed?"

"Well, Finny, obviously."

"Yeah, but he's dead," Declan said. "Isn't he?"

I nodded. "There's Sam Blake, Sylvia's old boss, but she really trusts him."

Declan gave me a sly look.

"I don't see it," I said. "I really don't. I had lunch with him. He's just not the type."

"There is no type, darlin'."

"Plus, I doubt he has any money. I could ask Sylvia, though."

"Do that."

"They wrote to some people in the field," I continued. "Finny and Sylvia did. But these folks are world-renowned curators at huge museums. They wouldn't hire an art thief because . . . they wouldn't have to. If they found out about something they wanted, they'd just buy it. Besides, one of them didn't even think the book was all that important. Old, rare, beautiful, yeah, but not the discovery of the decade."

"Hmmm," Declan said. "Well there's no gettin' around the fact that *somebody* knew—or made a lucky guess—that she had it. They found out where she lived—easy enough to do; nowadays you can Google anybody—and they waited till she left and went in. My money's on this lad Van Vleck."

"And someone really rich is behind it," I said. "You're sure about that."

"Oh, yeah. Dead sure. Guys like Van Vleck don't work for the love of it."

"Well," I said, a little nervously, "Finny's son Tad's got reams of dough. And he's getting kind of suspicious. So is Sylvia's boss, Amanda. But at this point they're just confused. They have a hunch there's some kind of valuable book floating around but they don't really know what it is. Or where."

"How'd *they* get to talking?" Declan asked. "Assuming they are."

I nodded. "Amanda got a call from a woman named Paola Moretti. At least we *think* it was Paola Moretti who called. Amanda didn't identify the person by name, but it has to have been her."

"How did *she* know about it, this Moretti dame?" Declan asked.

"She's at the Met, the medieval part of it, The Cloisters."

"I'm familiar with The Cloisters, Anz—"

"Sorry." I sometimes forget that he went to Northeastern, and lived in a dorm near the Museum of Fine Arts. I forget how he loved walking over there and drifting through the galleries on Monday nights, when admission was free.

"Paola was one of the curators that Sylvia and Finny wrote to, just before Finny died. By the time she wrote back, Finny had passed away, and Tad, being the executor, got the letter. He told her that the whole book collection had gone to the Athenaeum, and that if she wanted more information, she'd have to be in touch with Amanda."

Declan nodded and finished off his beer. I pointed to the empty bottle. *Another?* He shook his head.

"Amanda went through the list of all the books in the Winslow Collection and didn't find anything like it."

"Why not?"

"Because," I said, "Sylvia didn't log it in. She'd promised Finny that'd she'd keep trying to authenticate it, or at least trace the provenance. She knew he wouldn't have wanted the book at the Athenaeum."

Dec shot me a puzzled glance. "No? It's a library."

I shrugged. "I guess he had something nobler in mind. Like giving it back to the people it was taken from."

"Right," said Dec. "And this Amanda called—what's his name? Thad?"

"Tad. Who's a jerk. He's only gotten interested because he smells money."

We sat for a couple of moments without speaking. Declan glanced at his watch, and I guessed he might be wondering whether he'd get home in time to see Nell and Delia before they fell asleep. Just then, as though sibling rivalry had registered in his dreams, Henry appeared sleepily in the kitchen doorway.

"Hi, Daddy," he said, half awake. He padded over and crawled into Declan's lap.

"Hey, pal," Declan said, smoothing down a cowlick in Henry's sandy brown hair. "What are you doing up?"

"I heard you," Henry said.

"Sorry about that."

I was touched by the lovely ordinariness of this moment, the kind of intimate scene that happened almost never in our lives. But I wasn't going to let myself go all mushy.

"Daddy," Henry said, barely able to keep his eyes open. "Can you come to the wedding of Q and U?"

Declan shot me a glance that said, *Huh?*

I smiled and nodded, which I knew Declan would take to mean, *I'll tell you later.*

"Sure, buddy," Declan answered quietly. With any luck, Henry would fall right back to sleep and Dec could carry him back to bed.

"Everybody's a letter," Henry mumbled.

"Yeah?" Declan said softly.

"I'm *h*," said Henry. "I have to make a costume."

Costume? I thought. Shit.

Chapter Fourteen

I WAS GLAD I had chosen the Cicero pamphlets to work on first. I get a certain satisfaction out of doing really simple jobs perfectly: folding towels and sheets so that their corners are exact, straightening up the linen closet so it looks like a page out of *Martha Stewart Living*. Don't get me wrong, though: these are small, serene pockets of order in a vast sea of comfortable chaos. I like that our home feels lived-in.

The *Essays* I could rebind simply and almost perfectly. There was nothing remotely complicated about the job. Modest and quiet among the flashier and more exciting titles, they were the literary equivalents of well-worn linen dish towels, ironed into tidy rectangles and tied with a grosgrain ribbon.

Bookbinders sharing a bindery sometimes converse throughout the day, but Chandler didn't encourage chitchat, and that was putting it mildly. Every so often he'd look up from his drafting table, only to discover to his renewed discontent that I was still sitting there, working away on my stool at the tall central table. Today, Sylvia was spending as much time in her office as she was downstairs with the two of us, so if it hadn't been for the companionship of WBUR, Boston University's public radio station, I would have had a long and silent morning. I wouldn't have dared to turn on the radio myself, but Chandler had it on when I arrived.

As I cut, glued, and sewed, Tom Ashbrook interviewed a handful of doctors, some military and some civilian, about the medical and emotional care of returning soldiers. Veterans called in to the program, telling heartbreaking tales of their thwarted efforts to reenter the flow of normal life: to get treatment, claim benefits, find a job. *On Point* was followed by news at noon: embassy bombings, flood relief efforts following Typhoon Fengshen, and a doping scandal involving cyclists in the Tour de France. This afternoon, *Fresh Air* was going to be rebroadcasting an old interview Terry Gross had done with the film director Anthony Minghella, whose recent death had stunned and saddened the film community. I hoped to be able to listen to that, but I wasn't in control of the dial.

Sylvia popped her head in at about twelve thirty to see if I wanted anything out in the world: she was going to DeLuca's to pick up a sandwich. I had packed my lunch this morning when I packed Henry's, and while I wasn't overly excited about PB&J on whole wheat, a peach YoBaby, and a Granny Smith apple, I couldn't let myself get into the habit of spending eight or ten dollars a day on lunch.

I followed Sylvia into the hall. "Can I use your office?" I whispered. "I'm going to try to reach Monsignor Dolan."

"Sure," she said. "Just dial nine, then the number."

This morning, before she'd brought me downstairs to the bindery, we'd spent close to an hour talking in her office. I'd brought her up to date on Declan's progress.

"So he's not going to the police?" she'd asked me anxiously. "I mean, he's not going to file an official report?"

"Not yet. He hasn't spoken to anyone but this guy Scully, and as long as he's making progress, he won't."

Sylvia glanced out the window and nodded, trying to take everything in.

"He wanted me to ask you something, though."

She looked over.

I knew that the questions I was about to put to her would bring Sylvia up short, but if she balked, I was just going to have to remind her that Declan was doing *us* the favor. He didn't have to be helping us, at some real risk to himself professionally, but he was.

"What's Sam's background?" I asked.

Her features arranged themselves into a puzzled frown. "He doesn't think Sam's involved, does he? Because there's no way. Not in a million years."

"Oh, no, I don't think so," I said, trying to make light of the subject. I shared her opinion, but I'd learned to leave the detecting to Dec. "He's just trying to get a feel for everybody. We're throwing all these names at him and he's still trying to figure out who's who."

This seemed to satisfy her.

"Is he married?" I asked. That wouldn't tell me much, but I had to start somewhere.

"He was, but he got divorced a while ago."

"Any kids?"

"One son, Ben. He's twenty-two, twenty-three."

"Is he in school?"

Sylvia shook her head. She smiled vaguely but didn't offer any more information.

"What does he do?" I asked.

She seemed to hesitate. "Um, I'm not actually sure what he's doing right now. I think he—has a job."

"Doing what?"

"I don't know," she snapped, then let out a sigh and closed her eyes.

There was something she wasn't telling me. I waited for her to go on. The silence grew heavier and more awkward as the seconds ticked by, but I wasn't going to let her off the hook.

"Okay, he's had a few problems," she finally said, diplomatically.

"What kind of problems?" I asked.

"He's a great kid," she insisted. "Last time Sam told me about him, he was doing really well."

She seemed reluctant to divulge any further details, and while I had to admire her loyalty, I found myself getting impatient. Loyalty to Finny had gotten her into this situation, and now I was in it with her. And so was Declan. If she wanted to find her missing manuscript, she was going to have to be just a little less loyal.

"Sylvia," I started in. The tone of my voice must have tipped her off to my growing irritation because she opened right up.

"All right, all right. Ben got into drugs," she responded. "They sent him away to boarding school while they were going through the divorce. They thought it would be easier on him not to be around while the settlement was being worked out, but, well, he fell in with kind of a fast crowd and he got hooked on coke."

"Just coke?" I asked. "Or other things."

She shrugged. "I don't really know. All I know is that he's been in and out of rehab for five or six years. Sam's been through hell with him. He even got Ben a job here, but it didn't work out. He only lasted a couple of weeks."

"What did he do here?"

"Oh, nothing too taxing. Worked in the mail room, did some painting, errands, odd jobs. Then one day he just didn't show up.

He was back on the streets. Sam didn't hear from him for almost a month."

"How sad," I said.

She nodded. "And Sam's such a sweetheart. If there's anybody who doesn't deserve it—"

"No parent deserves it," I said.

I didn't want to ask the next question, but if I didn't, I'd only have to come back and ask it later, after I reported back to Dec.

"Does Sam have a key to your apartment?"

"No," she said.

"You never left a key with him? Or left your keys at his place long enough for—"

"Someone to make a copy?" she asked.

I nodded.

"I don't think so," she said. "I can't think of when I would have."

This felt a little spongy to me, like maybe she wasn't telling me the truth, the whole truth, and nothing but the truth. But I couldn't be sure. Dec would have to take it from here.

"Is he from a wealthy family?" Given what I suspected he made professionally, not to mention the cost of residential rehab programs, he wouldn't have much extra cash floating around unless he'd inherited it or gotten a big chunk some other way.

"Who? Sam? No."

"Well, you mentioned boarding school."

"Sam's father taught in the English department at St. Paul's. In fact, I think he was the head of the department. There's a room named after him in the school library. That's where they sent Ben."

"So they probably didn't have to pay too much, given the grandfather."

"Probably not," Sylvia said.

"What about his ex-wife?" I asked. I suspected it was rare for men to get rich in a divorce settlement, but I supposed it could happen.

"She moved to Vermont," Sylvia answered. "She lives in a commune."

I didn't know there *were* communes anymore. I thought they fell out of fashion around the time granola became available at every Store 24.

"She fell in love with a guy," Sylvia continued.

Ah, I thought, *the beginning, or the end, of many a good story.*

Monsignor Dolan was "unavailable."

"May I ask who's calling?" said his secretary in a terse, impatient tone.

"Anza O'Malley," I replied.

After a minute, I heard an annoyed little grunt. My name alone had not answered her question, but it would be all Monsignor Dolan would need to hear. Besides, what was I supposed to add? Any mention of ghosts would immediately brand me as a nutcase. I could see Miss Katy Gibbs crumpling up the little pink While You Were Out slip and tossing it into the wastebasket as soon as she hung up. Should I say I was an *old friend*? That could raise an eyebrow or two, which, given the assistant's prissy attitude, might be kind of fun. Or I could say I was someone *from his past.*

"May I inquire what this is in reference to?" she went on coolly. *Inquire.* That said it all.

"Oh, he'll know," I answered cheerfully, then started to feel a little mean. The poor woman probably just needed her lunch.

"We worked together a few years ago," I said, "on the acquisition of the—where the Holy Family Center is now. That land."

"Yes?" she said, waiting for me to go on.

"And I'd like to speak to him as soon as possible. Is he in the office?"

"He's in meetings all day," she answered briskly. She'd been dying to say it since the beginning of the conversation. "In fact," she went on, "all week."

"It'll only take a minute," I pressed. "I just have a quick question."

There was silence on the other end of the line. "The monsignor has a very full schedule. But if you'll give me your contact information, we'll have someone get back to you."

I'd expected this, but it still annoyed me. "All right," I said. "The name is Anza O'Malley."

"I got that," she snapped, as though I'd insulted her secretarial skills.

I took a deep breath. What was this woman's problem? I gave her my cell phone number.

"Eight three five four?" she asked.

"Nine four," I corrected her. "Eight three *nine* four."

"Eight three nine four."

"Right," I said. "Thanks very much."

"You're wel—" She'd disconnected the call.

I hung up the receiver, and seconds later, the monks appeared before me.

"You were eavesdropping!" I said. The young monk glanced nervously at his superior, and I thought I detected the hint of a smile from the abbot. That would have been a first.

"My blessing upon you," said the old ghost grandly.

It wasn't exactly, *Sorry I was so rude and obnoxious,* but I supposed we were on the right path. Given that the abbot was thinking in Irish, though, the blessing was actually more like *May the Blessed Virgin Mary, Holy Mother of God Almighty, sanctify the road beneath your feet and lead you to the seat nearest the fire.*

"Thank you," I said. "Now. Can we please start over?"

The abbot gave me a quizzical stare. He had so much hair! Eyebrows that curled up and around, a furry beard that seemed to start just under his hazel eyes, and I won't even get into the spiky tendrils jutting out of his nose and ears.

"No more crashing around," I said sternly. "No more breaking things. And most important, no more scaring Sylvia! I know you're upset, and I don't blame you, but all that does is make things worse."

The abbot nodded almost imperceptibly.

"I'm trying to help, here," I continued.

"For which we are most grateful," said the young monk, glancing anxiously at his abbot, who remained impassive. The Irish was something like *Your bounty is as the plenty of the fish of the sea*, but I got the general idea.

"Why don't we sit down," I suggested, trying to gauge just how friendly things were going to get. I had my answer when I saw the abbot pull himself up to a sterner and more erect posture. The young monk sucked in a deep breath, obviously fearing the worst.

"All right," I said. "I get it. You don't want to deal with me. That's fine. I hope I'll hear back from a friend of mine soon, and then maybe—"

"Who is he?" the abbot demanded.

"The person you called," the young monk explained.

"He's a monsignor," I said proudly. "Monsignor Francis Xavier Dolan of the Diocese of Cleveland. We're old friends."

The abbot looked suspicious. He probably found it hard to believe that any legitimate member of the Church's Royal Family would have much to do with the likes of me. Apart from forgiving my sins, that is, of which I'm sure he assumed I had many.

Well, I do. Who doesn't?

Like the answer to a heavenly petition I hadn't yet had time to compose, my cell phone rang.

So there, I thought, letting it ring a second time for effect. *Ha!*

"Anza!" came the voice of my old pal, the now-monsignor. "What a nice surprise!"

I activated the speakerphone and tried, but not too hard, to wipe the smug expression off my face.

"Father Fran," I said warmly. People call him Monsignor Dolan now, but to me he'll always be Father Fran. I'd tried to call him Monsignor once, just after he got the promotion, but he swatted that away like a pesky fly.

"How are you, dear?" he asked. "And how's the young man? What is he now, three? Four?"

"Five," I said. "We're great. Really great. Anyway, I know you're busy."

"Not for you, my dear," he said. "I'm never too busy for you. What's on your mind?"

I took a deep breath and glanced at the monks. "I'm here with a couple of . . . friends. An abbot and a monk. From the twelfth century."

"More ghosts?" asked Father Fran.

That got their attention.

"How did you know?" I asked.

"Because it's the only time you ever call me."

"I know. I'm awful. I'm sorry!" I said. "But do you have a couple of minutes?"

"I have exactly twelve minutes before I have to get onto a conference call with Bishop Zuchowski. Fire away."

"Okay," I said. "First of all, since I called you 'Father Fran,' I'm not sure they believe that I really am talking to a monsignor. Could you clear that up for me?"

"Have you got me on speaker?" he asked.

"Yeah," I said.

He launched in, in Latin. He couldn't hear the monks, but they could certainly hear him. Within minutes they were answering him in Latin, joined across the centuries in some kind of conversation, followed by an antiphonal prayer that was as familiar to the monks as it was to the monsignor in Cleveland. There were bobbings and bowings and eyes closing and a few soft knocks with fists over their hearts. Their eyes were damp and their expression faraway when silence returned to the room.

"How was that?" Father Fran asked.

"Great," I answered.

"Good," he said. "Is that all?"

"No. The thing is, they don't want to deal with me."

"Well, it would be hard for them," he explained kindly. "That kind of thing—a straightforward relationship between a young woman and a monk, much less an abbot—it just wouldn't have been done. They probably entered the order as young boys."

"I know," I said, "and I understand all that, but the thing is, we've got something pretty big going on here, and they'll only share what they know with . . . someone like you. Or someone *above* you. You're not going to be in Boston anytime soon, are you?"

"Unfortunately not."

"Do you know anyone here? Somebody I could call?"

"Hmmm," he said. "Let me give that some thought. I'll have Rosemary get back to you."

"Is that your assistant?" I asked, and when he replied that it was, out slipped, "Oh, joy."

I was mortified, but he burst out laughing. "I know, I know," he said. "But she's a good soul. Besides, you wouldn't believe how many calls I get now. I couldn't have someone like *you* answering the phone!"

This made me laugh, because he was right. I'd have his waiting room filled to bursting with sad sacks and hopeless causes, all wanting to bend his ear about something or other. In other words, people like me.

"Thanks so much," I said. "I really appreciate this."

"Anytime, dear. Can they still hear me?"

I looked at the monks. They nodded. "Yes," I said.

"Now you listen to me, you two," said Father Fran. "This young woman has a heart of gold. She's been awfully good to me, and even better to Holy Mother Church."

I thought he was gilding the lily a bit, but I wasn't about to interrupt.

"So I don't want to hear about any more nonsense. I know I can rely on you to treat her with the respect she deserves. She's a person you can trust."

I was embarrassed now and staring at the floor. Father Fran and I said our good-byes and ended the call. I looked up.

Rather than treat me with the respect I deserved, much less trust me, the monks had flown the coop. And in the spot where they had just been standing stood Sylvia.

I was surprised that their hasty departure hadn't at least messed up her hair. Sensing that she had just missed an occurrence of some importance, she asked, "What's going on?"

"Oh," I whispered wearily, "nothing much."

Chapter Fifteen

Voices and low laughter spilled out of the bindery and into the basement hall. Sylvia shot me a puzzled glance. I shrugged. We stepped inside to discover Chandler at the central table, showcasing his current work in progress: an early-edition piano score by Rachmaninoff, with handwritten notes by the composer in the margins. Sam was peering at something Chandler was pointing out on the manuscript.

With him was a man I didn't recognize. He was on the tall side, in his late fifties or early sixties, and he wore a suit so beautifully tailored that it had to have been made for him. His shirt was of the whitest white and his tie an elegant stripe of silver and cranberry. The silver matched his hair, which was fairly long, and his cheeks boasted a tinge of the tie's cranberry, which I decided to attribute to a brisk, recent walk through the cool autumn air, and not a fondness for gin with his noonday meal.

"Sylvia!" Sam said. "We were wondering where you were!"

Chandler, deflated by our sudden appearance, didn't seem to have been wondering. He looked as though he wished we would just go back to wherever we came from.

A flush rose to Sylvia's cheeks, and I would have liked to have been able to say: *No*, Sam has no way of knowing that we were just talking about him and *no*, you did not betray him by telling me about Ben.

"What are you doing here?" she asked. I'm sure she meant to convey delight and warmth, but it didn't come out that way.

"Well, we had to have our annual lunch at Locke-Ober's," Sam explained. "It wouldn't be a trip to Boston without a bowl of JFK's lobster stew, would it, Jim?"

"Certainly not," the man said amiably. He had a posh British accent.

"James Wescott," he went on, extending his hand warmly, first to Sylvia, and then to me.

"Oh!" replied Sylvia. It came out like a strangled little cry. As she glanced anxiously between Wescott, Sam, and Chandler, I tried to provide her with a little time to collect herself.

I introduced myself and asked, "How was Vermont?"

This appeared to startle the well-dressed man. He didn't respond immediately.

"Oh, maybe I've got the wrong person," I said, feigning confusion. "I'm sorry." I glanced at Sam for help. "When we all had lunch on Saturday, with Julian . . ."

"Julian Rowan," Sam clarified, apparently for James.

"Oh!" James said, smiling. "That's right! Julian *is* here, isn't he?"

"Boston College," Sam said.

"Yes, of course!" This seemed to delight the Brit. My, he was a chipper fellow.

"We were talking," I went on, "about someone—I *thought* his name was James—who was at the British Museum."

"That's right," Sam confirmed. "You've got it right; that's this James."

Beside him, the handsome Brit beamed and nodded.

At last recovering her footing, Sylvia stepped in.

"You mentioned in your letter," she said, addressing Wescott, "that you might go up to Vermont. After you were finished with the Harvard conference. I used to work with Finny Winslow. We wrote to you last winter about that illuminated manuscript that he had."

Miraculously, I thought, Chandler's phone began to ring, and he stepped away to answer it. I wondered if the monks were trying to give us a hand by stirring up a little electrical distraction, but no, we'd just gotten lucky. Chandler sunk into a sullen conversation with the person on the other end.

"Yes, yes, of course! I remember now!" James said, nodding. "Did you ever get to the bottom of that?"

"Not yet," Sylvia responded.

"It's not *here*, is it?" James asked, his eyes widening. "I would just love to have a look at it."

Sylvia cleared her throat and then said firmly, "No. To tell you the truth, I'm not sure *where* it is these days."

No! I thought. *Don't tell him it's missing!*

But on she went, calmly. "The executor's not exactly—how should I put it?—well, books just aren't his thing. There was some *confusion*, after he took over, about whether that particular title was one of the ones he sent over here with the rest of Finny's collection. I assumed it would be, naturally, but when the time came for me to log it in . . ." She paused and shrugged.

Wow. That was good. She hadn't even lied.

"So, you work for the Athenaeum?" James asked her. "I'm a little confused."

"I'm a freelancer. I'm rebinding much of the Winslow Collection. Anza's a bookbinder, too. She's helping me. There's a dedicated fund; it was established before Mr. Winslow died. I'm just working out of here until the job is done."

"I see," James said. "A shame about that manuscript, though. Is there a chance he might have sold it?"

"I suppose he could have," Sylvia responded. "And one of his daughters, who lives out in the Berkshires, took some of the books. I mean, he gave them to her. I wasn't close to his children, and toward the end, when he was very ill, there were a lot of family members in and out. You know what happens, when things get to that point."

"The vultures descend," Sam said sharply.

Sylvia nodded sadly.

I wondered what Sam was making of all this. He knew that the book had been stolen, and he knew that Sylvia was if not exactly *lying* to his old friend James Wescott, then at least obscuring the truth.

But what was she supposed to do, with Chandler right here? It was Sam who'd put her in this difficult position. Then again, he probably just missed the companionship of his former colleagues, and the familiarity of the bindery, where he'd spent much of his professional life. They'd been just down the street having lunch at Locke-Ober, we'd been talking about James during our lunch on Saturday, and probably on impulse, Sam had decided to bring him by. He probably didn't stop to think it all through.

"Oh well, I imagine it'll resurface one of these days," James said reassuringly. "They always do."

Not always, I thought.

There was a moment of awkward silence. Turning to me, James skillfully restarted the conversation.

"To answer your question, Vermont was magnificent! They tell me the leaves were a little dull this year, but from what was still left on the trees, I can't imagine their being any more spectacular."

"Where were you?" I asked, grateful that we were now onto a

neutral subject. I suddenly pictured James Wescott in a Vermont commune, beginning to remove his remarkable suit.

"Near Woodstock," he replied, and to the strange, spontaneous commune image, my brain now added mud, a beard, The Who, and a bong.

Not that *Woodstock,* I said to myself.

There was a message from Julian on my machine. He'd come to realize, following our lunch on Saturday, that he had no one but himself to blame for his failure to see a little bit of New England. The next few weekends were fraught with complications—visitors coming and going, college events that he couldn't miss—so he was thinking about taking a drive out to the Berkshires later in the week, maybe Thursday or Friday. He knew it was short notice, and on top of that, a weekday, but he wondered if by chance I had any time. If so, might I be interested in coming along?

I thought of his leg pressed unself-consciously against mine in the movie theater and immediately decided I would. Just as immediately, I concluded that I couldn't, because, unbeknownst to Julian—and I would have to mention this sometime soon, if we ever got together again—I had a little boy. *Damn!* I mean, not damn about Henry, just damn about no date.

A moment later, I had an inspiration. Friday wouldn't work, because Delia and Nell were coming here right after Henry got out of school, but if I could get Nat to take Henry to the movies on Thursday night, and if she could also pick him up from after-school and also feed him a slice of pizza at some point and also hang around the apartment until I got back, which I would try to do on the early side, then maybe I could go! If Thursday worked for Julian, that is.

It was the first of two inspired thoughts that came to me as

I folded laundry, relishing the fact that Henry was occupied quietly in his room. I'd been stressing about the costume. For all my craftiness when it comes to books, I'm not good at costumes. At Halloween, when better mothers than I are sewing and stapling and making helmets and tiaras, we're at Target buying the cheesy kind in the box.

I think costumes are stupid. I hate costume parties. Masks, especially Mardi Gras masks, give me the creeps.

Henry was already getting on my case about *needing* to get going on his costume, which we *needed* to finish in time for the Q and U wedding. He had no idea when this was, of course. *Didn't you get the invitation?* he'd asked accusingly, as though not yet having received the all-important letter constituted a failure of some kind on my part.

As for the costume itself, it had to have everything to do with the letter *h*. A guessing game with all of his classmates, each of whom had been assigned a letter, was going to precede the wedding.

First he had announced that he wanted to be a Hunter with a raccoon Hat. I nixed that right away, because you can't be a hunter without a gun, and to have a five-year-old carrying a fake rifle into a kindergarten party, especially here in Cambridge, well, it just wasn't going to happen. With a slaughtered raccoon on his head? Not a chance.

Because I'd said no to the hunter idea, Henry acted as though I had used up the one and only no to which I was entitled. But I surprised him. I said no again—this time to a devil costume, which would be all red, he'd told me excitedly, with horns and a pitchfork and a curly tail that pointed up to the ceiling, a tail with a spike on the end. What did that have to do with *h*? I'd asked him. That was the joke! he'd explained, fairly bursting with pride at his own subtle wit. He was Hot.

Again, I'd had to disappoint him. The devil doesn't get much airtime, as far as I can tell, in current theological instruction, at least at the kindergarten level; I suspected that this idea had more to do with the books of Maurice Sendak than those of the Old Testament. But a couple of older nuns were still at work in the school, running the one-room library and helping struggling students master their letters and numbers. I'd met them both—one was a rabid Red Sox fan—and I doubted that either of them would be offended by Henry's sashaying up the aisle in red tights and pointy red slippers, which, by the way, I was going to be expected to make. Still, it *was* a Catholic school. Why take a chance?

Henry was fit to be tied. He thought my ideas were inane. He could be Handsome, I'd teased him. We'd make him up like a movie star and he'd get all the girls. He didn't see the Humor. How about Humpty Dumpty? Or a Horse? Harry Potter! He rejected each of these ideas on principle, the principle being: they weren't his.

Then I had a brainstorm. Ellie! She loved stuff like this! And she could sew! She was always bemoaning the fact that she didn't get to participate in Halloween with her grandchildren. Pictures of them in their costumes, carrying orange plastic jack-o-lanterns presumably filled with candy, just made her want to cry.

And not only that, we'd be killing two birds with one stone. With Halloween just around the corner, the costume might be able to serve double duty, sparing me the annual torture of the trip to Target, where Henry always got wound up into a frenzied panic, searching madly, and usually in vain, for the *perfect* costume. The good ones sell out early. Better mothers than I am keep track of when they go on sale, which I gather must be sometime in the summer.

I finished folding the laundry. Now I felt guilty. He wouldn't be little forever, and I should be thanking my lucky stars that he was excited and passionate and full of ideas and imagination. And I did. I adored this about him, even when it got us into trouble.

But tonight, I was tired, hungry, and in need of a helping hand to get to the end of the week. To my great good fortune, I could probably count on four.

Chapter Sixteen

I LUCKED INTO a visitor parking place near the corner of Marlborough and Clarendon. At night, most of the metered spots in Back Bay revert to being reserved for the use of the people who live around here and have residential stickers on their cars. Miss the fine print explaining this on the parking signs, and you'll come back to discover a hundred-dollar ticket on your windshield. Near the corners of some of the blocks, though, are one or two coveted spots marked "Visitor." I'd never actually scored one of these before, so I thought this might be a good omen. Tonight, I was going to be lucky.

Come to think of it, I already had *been* lucky. Thanks to an exhausting after-school walking trip to the playground on the Cambridge Common, nearly a mile away from St. Enda's, Henry had practically fallen asleep into his plate of franks and beans. He'd dawdled lazily in the bathtub, had gotten into his Spider-Man pj's as I ran down to the basement to throw a load of towels into the wash, and by the time I made it back up to his room, ready to usher him into dreamland with the next chapter of *Redwall,* he was out.

He didn't even wake up when I took the book out of his

hands, lifted him off his quilt, and got him settled in under the covers. Max and Ellie, who were babysitting, were going to be disappointed tonight. There'd be no calls for reassuring drinks of water and no need to rock him back to sleep in their upstairs den.

The skies had been unsettled all day, with occasional bolts of sunshine breaking through. But now, the gray heavens hung low. You don't see stars in Boston, not often anyway—there's too much light on the ground for them to be visible—but tonight, behind a somber ceiling of dense, gloomy mist, there wasn't even the hint of a moon. The air, for the first time this fall, was actually cold. It was drizzling steadily, the wind gusting angrily and auras of fog surrounded the streetlights, all of this reminding me that before I knew it, Thanksgiving would be here.

It was a little too late—nine fifteen—for one of my favorite bad habits: peering through the windows of other people's houses. The best time to do this is right around dusk, when the occupants of a house first start to realize that it's getting dark out and switch on their interior lights. Most folks don't close their curtains right away, though, so in the fleeting minutes during which it's brighter in the rooms than it is outside on the street, someone as curious as I am can catch thrilling, normally forbidden glimpses of chandeliers and paintings and wallpapered walls. As true darkness descends, though, people usually close their curtains. Tonight, possibly owing to the wintry dampness that was driving away autumn, most of the curtains had been closed.

I paused at the beginning of the alley. The thought of sneaking around after dark in Finny's house, assuming I could actually get inside the house, didn't bother me at all. But the prospect of encountering that rat again or one of his scavenging pals in the dark, deserted alley behind the house filled me with absolute dread.

It was all I'd thought about in the past two days. Not the possibility that in my desire to ease the distress of a restless old ghost, I could get myself arrested for breaking and entering. No, that thought barely crossed my mind. What haunted me instead, in the moments before I fell asleep, and in those just before I woke up, were the several hundred feet of shadowy alleyway— the dim, Dumpster-filled picnic ground for the shifty nocturnal set—that lay between a bright, well-traveled block of Dartmouth Street and the back entrance to the Winslow home.

I'd taken precautions. I'd worn heavy rubber rain boots, the better for kicking the rats away, and my thickest pair of jeans over dense cotton leggings, in case I didn't see one of them coming and it managed to scramble up the back of my leg.

I belted my raincoat and tied it tight, so that if one of them did manage to get up my leg, he wouldn't get past my waist. I'd brought a flashlight and Henry's baseball bat. The bat would probably be useless, as it was made of aluminum and sized and weighted for a five-year-old playing T-ball, but I figured it was better than nothing.

I glanced at my watch—nine twenty-eight. I had to go. Now. I took a deep breath and headed into the alley, my gaze darting right and left. Sure enough, there was a heart-stopping rustle as I passed the first Dumpster, and I caught the nauseating flick of a long, fat tail disappearing behind a nearby can. Fighting the urge to scream and run, I walked as quickly as I could toward the small, reassuring structure onto which I'd now fastened my gaze—the little shed behind the house. In a minute, with my blood rushing loudly through my ears, I was there.

Now what? I thought, trying to take in a decent breath. Had Johnny been able to deactivate the alarm? I had no way of knowing. We should have agreed upon a signal. I should have instructed him to appear to me in one of the windows to let me know the coast was clear, or to come outside and meet me on the stoop. I hadn't really thought this through when I hatched the plan with him on Monday. I'd made it all up on the spot. And now I had a problem.

If the alarm system was the modern kind, the kind lots of people are putting in nowadays, the whole thing would be electronic. Like when you press that button on your car key as you cross a parking lot, and when you get to your car, the doors are all unlocked. If the house had a system like this, and if Johnny had been able to shut it all down, the back door might already be open.

But I didn't peg Finny Winslow for the kind of guy who'd spring for a flashy, ultra-high-tech system. Tad, yes: in its sleek, impersonal efficiency, it would neatly satisfy the sensibility that savored the sight of a lone pear on a square plate on Tad's concrete dining table. Finny, on the other hand, struck me as the sort of person who might enjoy the feel of keys in his pocket. I could see him bowing to the need for some kind of alarm system, probably years ago, but I couldn't see him updating it every year, not from the looks of rest of the house. In his world, you bought something good in the first place, and then you made it last.

In other words, alarm or no alarm, the door probably still locked with a key. The problem was, I didn't have a key. Nor did I have a set of lock picks, and even if I had, I don't know how to use them. I'd once used a bobby pin to open a door that blew shut unexpectedly, but the lock was old and loose. And tonight, I didn't have a bobby pin. All I had was a credit card, which might be a little thick, and a driver's license, which was a little thinner. I do know how to slide a credit card down between a door and the doorframe, which is sometimes successful at pushing the bolt conveniently aside. Sometimes, but not always.

It wasn't much of a plan, but it was the only one I had.

I scanned the upper windows one last time for a glimpse of ghostly Johnny. Nothing. My hands were shaking, either from the cold or from the adrenaline that had been released by my near-encounters with the rats. I stepped up to the door, looked around to make sure I wasn't being observed, and held my breath. I prepared myself mentally to run, because if Johnny had let me down, or had simply been unable to disable the alarm, and I started messing around with the back-door lock, I was going to set it off. I'd know that if I stepped inside and the little red light was blinking.

I peered closely at the lock, trying to gauge what I was up against before touching anything. Just at that moment, a freezing gust of rainy wind swept in from behind me and I heard a squeal that made my heart leap into my throat. I jumped back, sick with fear, my gaze plummeting to the ground, where I expected to see a squadron of rodents shimmering toward my feet. I flicked on the flashlight. Nothing.

A second blast of wintry air drew my attention back up to the door. The squeal had not come from a rat, but from a pair of old hinges.

The gust had blown open the door.

Inside, the ghost of Johnny was nowhere to be seen. I didn't dare close the door behind me: I didn't want to make any noise, I didn't want to risk leaving fingerprints, and I sure didn't want to activate the alarm again, if closing the door might do that. It would then be impossible for me to make my escape without drawing the attention of the rent-a-cops on duty at the security company. On the other hand, neighbors parking their cars in the alley spots would be quick to call the police if they noticed the back door of their late neighbor's home wide open, flapping and banging in the wind. I nudged the door almost closed with the toe of my boot.

I now found myself in the downstairs back hall, which led to rooms that were probably the building's original laundry room, drying room, and kitchen. I wouldn't have known this if I hadn't once taken a tour of the Gibson House over on Beacon Street, a Victorian mansion perfectly preserved and turned into a museum by its final owner, a visionary man described in their literature as an "improper Bostonian" and a "colorful bon vivant" with an "eccentric lifestyle." I had a hunch these were euphemisms for *gay*, but I wasn't sure.

The fact that the rooms I was now tiptoeing quietly through were restful and hollow—big, empty, unused spaces in one of the priciest areas of the city in which to live—told me just how comfortable the Winslows were. This space was valuable (a basement apartment with a separate entrance?), and they'd never once in all these years had to utilize it for cash. I suspected this would change soon. With Tad in charge, I doubted the space would remain undeveloped for long.

I crept quietly across the old kitchen and paused in the back corner. The wind and rain were picking up, and the house, like all old houses, was alive with creaks, groans, and rattles that made me catch my breath, but which had probably gone unnoticed by the folks who lived here. I flicked on my flashlight and shined it around the space. Where was Johnny? Should I cut bait and leave? I was more than happy to help the old fellow out, but really, this was rude. He hadn't struck me as the kind of ghost who wouldn't keep up his end of the bargain. After all, what was it to me if the precious deed was never located? Nothing. But to the ghost of John Grady, it apparently meant the world.

The beam of my light illuminated the entrance to the back stairwell, paneled in dark wainscoting. I crossed the space quietly and listened, then placed one foot tentatively in the center of the first tread. It creaked piteously. I tried the area of the tread nearest the outside wall, figuring that part might be the sturdiest and quietest. I was right. There was barely a sound as I transferred my whole weight onto my foot.

Emboldened, I decided to go for it. I quickly climbed up to the first landing, pausing at the bend in the stairs to see if I could hear anything. An ancient velvet curtain, once maroon and now a plummy mud color, partially hid the landing from view, sparing people on the first floor an accidental glimpse of a servant scurrying up or down.

It was then that the paralyzing sound reached me: the chilling smash of glass being shattered. I heard it again, and then again. Someone—or something—was on a rampage not twenty-five feet away from me, in the front hall, or possibly the living room.

I froze. A sour wave of nausea swept through me as I tried to control my own breathing so as to remain totally, utterly silent. Some function in my brain kicked into gear—my subconscious, I guess, or whatever primeval mechanism it is that guides imperiled humans and animals toward survival. With my mind's eye, I calmly watched a short film of myself racing back down the stairs, not caring how much noise I made, just scrambling as fast as I could through the deserted basement rooms and out the back door. *Fly! Now! Go!* I was urged. The message was crystal clear.

But I couldn't. My legs wouldn't listen. I was in one of those horrible dreams in which I was desperately trying to run, but my legs were heavy, heavy, so very heavy that I felt I was up to my knees in quicksand.

Then I heard Johnny's voice. "No, no! Stop this immediately!" It took me a moment to realize that it *was* his voice. His tone was stern and commanding, not the gentle, dulcet murmurings of a beloved butler, but the sharp, authoritarian bark of a cavalry sergeant. The shattering of glass ceased, only to be followed a moment later by the rhythmic thud of wood being splintered. Whoever was doing this was oblivious to Johnny's orders, confirming what I already knew: the maniac was a real, live person who couldn't see or hear the ghost hovering nearby, bearing witness to the destruction.

I pulled back into the shadows, trying to make myself as flat as possible against the landing's back wall. I was in the shallow corner behind the curtain, barely daring to breathe, when the shattering of wood abruptly ceased and I heard the sounds of footsteps approaching. Nearer and nearer they came until I knew for certain that only five or six feet and a whole lot of luck—more than I'd dreamed of when I pulled into the Visitor spot—lay between me and imminent disclosure, followed by arrest, humiliation, and jail. And that was the best-case scenario. I could also get killed.

Who is going to raise Henry? I thought in a panic. Oh, yeah, Declan.

"I hate you!" I heard a woman hiss. "I hate you!" she said more loudly, and then I heard another smash of glass. This was followed by the loudest wail I have ever been five feet from. It sounded like a banshee keening in the wind. Then I heard the thud of someone collapsing on the floor, and I almost couldn't keep myself from peeking around the curtain. But I held steady. It didn't sound like a collapse, as in someone fainting dead away; it was more like a person thumping herself down to a sitting position against a wall. The wall being the other side of the one I was leaning against.

Hence commenced the most woeful bout of weeping and wailing I think I've ever heard. It was a dam breaking. It was the Grand Cooley Dam breaking. The waters rushed and thundered like the falls at Niagara until the woman crying eventually wore herself out, winding down and down until all that could be heard was the occasional hiccup of a pathetic little sob. Whoever she was slowly got up.

"Bastard," she spat, then the footsteps clacked away. I took the first real breath I'd had in what had probably been five minutes, but what had felt like ten or fifteen.

I caught a glimpse of her as she hurried back to the kitchen, a slim, tall woman not much older than I am. She was carrying a huge box when she came back out, a box so big she could barely get her arms around it or see over it, which was a good thing, or I'm certain she would have noticed me.

I heard her footsteps recede down the hall and clump slowly down the main stairs toward the basement. In another minute, I heard the back door slam shut. The engine of a car was started, just outside the door. Come to think of it, there had been a car parked back there—some kind of light-colored SUV. A bumper sticker, which I was far too preoccupied at the time to focus on, had nevertheless been registered by my peripheral vision and stored in my brain for later examination. It offered itself to me now.

Each of the letters comprising the word was a version of a symbol of one of the world's great religions. "COEXIST," the letters had spelled.

Alone now, I hoped, drained by my terror and drenched with sweat, I stepped out of the stairwell. There was Johnny, standing helplessly over the wreckage of the rampage: the smashed remnants of a number of framed black-and-white eight-by-ten photographs. From under the shattered glass, in a series of professional shots, beamed the smiling faces of three children playing on the beach, toasting marshmallows around a seaside campfire, tucking into corn on the cob at a well-used picnic table. There was one of a young boy about eight—probably Tad—holding up a lobster, and another of two young girls in a battered dinghy, freckled and sunburned in too-big life jackets.

"It was Josie," Johnny said quietly. "She knew Tad left for London today. Otherwise, she wouldn't have come around."

So *that's* why the back door had been open.

"What's her problem?" I asked, unbelting my raincoat and peeling it off. Johnny led me into the living room, where a beautiful wooden model of an antique sailboat—a painstakingly built replica, I guessed, of a beloved family vessel—lay in splinters on the floor.

"He sold the family sailboat without her permission," Johnny explained. "Oh, the arguments they had." He shook his head. "Awful. She demanded that he get it back, but he said he couldn't: he'd signed the papers and the sailboat was gone. She claimed it was the only thing she cared about at all, of all the things they were divvying up. They haven't spoken in months. She's always been on the . . . dramatic side, Josie has."

"I'd say so," I offered. "She sure gave me a fright."

"I'm very sorry. I'm so grateful that you came."

Johnny led me to the third-floor hallway, where the boxes of books lay waiting for pickup. It must have been so frustrating to him, all this time, not being able to search through the boxes himself, but ghosts can lift only the very lightest of objects. A book is far too heavy.

Slowly, I made my way through the volumes, pausing as the butler recounted stories occasioned by the sight of one book or another. There was the time Miss Edlyn broke her collarbone trying to get to a nest in an apple tree, occasioning three weeks in bed with *The Adventures of Polly Flanders* and *Polly Flanders on the High Seas*.

There was the book of Shelley verse from the bloke they were afraid she might marry, until he was unceremoniously swept aside, to their great relief, by the appearance on the scene of Finny Winslow. There were travel books and picture books, cheap, paperback copies of Shakespeare plays and a complete boxed set, circa 1958, of the *Encyclopaedia Britannica*. The Bryn Mawr Book Store was going to be thrilled with that.

Nowhere, though, was *The Butterfly's Ball*.

"I was afraid not," Johnny said sadly. "I believe Miss Esther has it."

"Where does she live again?" I asked.

"West Stockbridge," he answered. "She has a farmhouse out there. And a studio. A sculptor she is, and a fine one, though it's a different ball of wax these days. Not like Bernini."

"Abstract?" I guessed.

He nodded. "She does . . . eggs and such."

"Oh."

"Yes." He was too polite to say more.

"Maybe I'll pay her a visit," I said, then immediately wished I had paused to think about this. "The Berkshires" cover a lot of ground, and Julian might not be keen on an unexpected detour from whatever kind of trip he had in mind. Still, we'd have to eat. West Stockbridge was quaint, New Englandy, and home to one or two pretty nice places to have a meal.

Johnny looked so eager and hopeful that I instantly knew I couldn't disappoint him.

"I'm going to be out in that area tomorrow."

"You're not!"

"I am. I'm going out there with a . . . friend. He's here from England, and well, he wanted to do a bit of sightseeing."

"What will you tell her?" he asked, a worried frown now wrinkling his forehead.

"Well, what's she like? Could I tell her the truth?"

His expression brightened. "Oh, certainly! Esther? Yes, yes, of course you could! She believes in ghosts. Has all her life. And me always insisting there was no such thing!"

He shook his head at the irony, then glanced up at me hopefully.

"All right," I said. "I'll do it."

Chapter Seventeen

Julian picked me up in a car so old-fashioned it could only be called a "roadster." Not the poky kind you sometimes see ferrying women in bonnets and men in dorky outfits, on their way to Sunday-afternoon gatherings of antique car clubs. More like a zippy convertible from an old black-and-white film, the kind of car that necessitated a woman's wearing Jackie O. sunglasses and protecting her hairdo with a scarf as her handsome companion drove way too fast along the coast of the Italian Riviera.

I have some scarves, all gifts, but I think of them as being sort of, well, middle-aged. I know that a chic French woman can work wonders with a silk scarf from Hermès, draping it casually over a shoulder, tying it into a necklace of knots, wearing it as a belt around her waspish waist, or using it to adorn the strap of her handbag. But I'm neither chic nor French, so when Julian said, "You might need a scarf," my heart sank. It was that or a baseball cap, though, which felt completely out of keeping with the cool old car, so I went digging through one of my drawers and pulled out the least offensive scarf I owned, a navy polyester knockoff featuring horses and bridles.

Of course I can pull it off, I thought with bravado, experimenting in front of the mirror while Julian used what he referred to as the "gents." Hey, I'd read *Vogue,* many times; that's where I'd learned about scarves so treasured and so valuable that women inherited them—officially, in wills—from their mothers. Besides, I had been a "gypsy" once or twice for Halloween, a costume that consisted primarily of a scarf and lots of fake jewelry.

I decided to tie the scarf in the back, rather than under my chin, the latter being a style that made me look disturbingly like my grandmother and all her friends, women who never got used to going to Mass without a hat, or at least a small doily or a clean piece of Kleenex bobby-pinned to the tops of their heads. Come to think of it, though, Nona had probably been wearing a scarf when she attracted the attention of her new gentleman friend. Then again, he probably voted for Eisenhower and saw the black-and-white roadster film when it was first in theaters. I pulled some strands of hair down all around, and when Julian appeared, he gave me an approving nod. He was definitely being polite.

The car, which belonged to a friend of his, a BC professor, didn't have seat belts, and Julian wanted to drive with the top down, so we decided to take the slow, scenic route across the top of the state rather than the Mass. Pike, which would have swept us swiftly and blandly west. This would add another hour, each way, to the trip, but I was game. It was only nine in the morning; we'd be there by noon. Even if we left at nine tonight and got home at midnight or one, we'd be fine.

Nat, true blue and probably secretly hoping that the opportunity for a little hanky-panky would present itself to me, had offered to spend the night with Henry and get him off to school. I did have to work in the morning, though, making up for taking today off, and I was seriously behind on my other job, the

Sherwood Glen coffee-table books, so a motel interlude wasn't part of the plan. At least my plan.

The morning's weather, juxtaposed with last night's, offered an illustration of the local adage "If you don't like the weather in New England, wait five minutes." We were headed, the forecaster had announced this morning, into a period of "Indian summer," an annual heat wave that inevitably arrived a day or two after you'd finally given up on there being an Indian summer that year, packed away all your warm-weather clothing, and hauled out the wooly sweaters and socks. Its wintry cousin was the snowstorm in May.

It was already warm as we got into the car and headed toward Fresh Pond Parkway. Later, it was going to be almost summery: in the high seventies in some places. Last night I'd been brooding moodily on the imminence of Thanksgiving, and this morning, I was zipping along in a convertible, wearing a short-sleeved shirt.

The plan was to mosey on out to Lenox, stopping anywhere we felt like stopping. Julian was interested in touring The Mount, Edith Wharton's old estate, and in finding somewhere to have a great dinner. That was all. Driving out there and taking in the scenery along the way seemed to be the point, not visiting all the area's tourist attractions. This sounded good to me. I asked if we could make a quick detour to West Stockbridge, five or six miles from Lenox, and Julian was more than accommodating.

"I'm just picking up something for a friend," I explained vaguely. "It won't take long."

"Of course," he said pleasantly.

I decided to tackle the subject of Henry right away. There was no way that Julian, having come inside to use the bathroom, could not have noticed the toys and children's books all over the place. Remembering how straightforward he'd been when he asked me to the movies, when we left the movies, and when he kissed me good night, I decided to follow suit.

"Just so you know," I began, "I have a son. His name is Henry. He's five."

Julian glanced over. *"Evidently."* He smiled, then returned his gaze to the road.

I waited for him to go on. He didn't.

"Meaning . . . ?" I prompted.

"Little blue trainers? Snoopy toothbrush?"

I wasn't sure what to say next, because I didn't know if this was a date, in which case my having a child might be a fact of some importance, or not a date, in which case it wouldn't.

"I have a daughter," he said.

"You *do*?" I was shocked.

He nodded. "She's eight. She lives with her mother in Sussex, boards at Brambletye. I have her in the summers, though, in London."

"Wow."

"So I take it you're not with . . . your son's father," he went on.

"Nope," I said. "We're friendly, though."

"We're not," Julian said. "In point of fact, we despise each other."

"That can't be easy."

"Oh, it's easy enough," he said. "She's quite despicable, really."

"I meant, with your daughter . . ."

"We do all right, Ruby and me. It's all rather grand, life with Mummy and Lord Heathsby, so London's quite amusing for her. Carryout curries and all that."

"I'm sure she loves it."

"She seems to. Like camp, I suppose. Sleeping under the eaves, in a room half the size of a maid's room at Moors End."

"Moors End?" I asked.

"Moors End House," he answered, and smiled. "That's what it's called today. It's sort of a . . . castle."

———※◆※———

The Mount was magnificent. As we approached Edith Wharton's elegant, Palladian forty-two-room summer "cottage," I resisted the urge to ask Julian how it shaped up beside the castle in which his daughter apparently lived. I decided it would be more polite to Google *Moors End House* when I got home.

We were just in time for a tour, so we spent more than an hour wandering through buildings and gardens constructed according to the design principles in Wharton's *The Decoration of Houses.* Reacting against the dark, heavy, fussy style of the Victorians, our tour guide informed us, the author had argued that simplicity, symmetry, and architectural proportion made rooms pleasant to be in. I immediately resolved to rearrange our furniture as soon as I got home, get rid of the heavy green drapes in our living room (hand-me-downs from a friend of Ellie's), and paint our entire apartment in shades of peach and sky blue.

Later, after touring the formal flower garden, the rock garden, the Italian walled garden, and the grass terraces, I vowed to talk to Ellie and Max about how much nicer we could make our back and side yards, which were overrun with lilacs and violets. It wasn't a matter of spending much money, it was just a matter of a little elbow grease, which, in my newly inspired state, I decided I would be glad to provide. I could make a grass terrace. How complicated could that be? Clip our overgrown hedges into some topiaries, get the hostas all lined up in crisp, military rows. True, I wouldn't be able to replicate The Mount's breathtaking view of Laurel Lake, but we had Fresh Pond nearby and it was pretty nice.

Exhausted by the renovations I had already planned and carried out, bringing our little family's aesthetic experience into line with Edith Wharton's design principles, I slumped into a chair at The Mount's Terrace Café and ordered a huge lunch.

Across from me, Julian grinned.

"And a bottle of the Graves," he added.

Over lunch, we chatted easily, talking about the kids, and about Declan and Tilda, Ruby's mother, whom Julian had known "at university" but never married. When Ruby made her surprise appearance, Tilda had been incensed to discover that Julian had no intention of disappearing conveniently from both their lives, leaving Tilda free to find her daughter a new daddy. As we finished off the crisp white wine, we traded tales of the journeys that had brought us into the world of old books.

I glanced up at The Mount as we sipped our coffee and suddenly felt a little sad. I wished I hadn't learned quite so much during our tour, for despite the feeling of permanence conveyed by the buildings and grounds, the aura they exuded of having been here forever, gracefully overlooking Laurel Lake for as long as Moors End House had overlooked whatever it overlooks—the moors, probably—Edith Wharton had lived here for just ten years. For all the care that she'd lavished on the gardens and the plasterwork, the greenhouse and the oak-paneled library, not to mention the writing that she did while she lived here—working in her simple, spare bedroom until noon every day—the house was only briefly a home.

A decade after she moved in, she was gone, living in Paris, her marriage dissolved. The Mount became a girls' school, later a theater company, and at various points it lay vacant, falling into ruin. Even as we sat here sipping our coffee in the unseasonable warmth, it was teetering on the brink of financial collapse. Funds were needed for preservation. Its future was lurching from one restoration grant to the next.

"Sort of sad, don't you think?" I asked.

"What?"

"How short a time she was here, after everything she put into it."

Julian shrugged. "She'd been unhappy, a society matron who only dabbled in writing. The happier she got, and the more successful, the better Paris looked. I mean, who doesn't love Paris?"

"I suppose."

"Really, Anza, be serious. Where would *you* rather be when you're fifty? Stuck out here in the middle of nowhere, with a crazy husband embezzling your money? Or free as a bird in Paris, in the arms of a dashing young rake who's unlocked your *repressed desire?*"

I smiled at Julian. He really was charming, with those little crinkles of amusement at the corners of his eyes. I glanced back at Laurel Lake, glittering in the sunlight.

I didn't know, really. I honestly couldn't say. I think I would have kicked the husband out and kept the house.

I had printed out directions to Esther's, starting on Main Street in West Stockbridge. It didn't take us long to find the place. It looked like something out of a Beatrix Potter book, a full-scale version of a cozy snug that a family of happy rabbits might live in. It was set way back from the road, on a foundation of massive fieldstones. Hardy nasturtiums were still blooming in their summer pots, throwing out final, doomed, radiant bursts of buttercup and tangerine.

"Before we go in," I said, placing my hand on Julian's knee, "there's something I should tell you." The having-a-kid conversation had worked out so well, and our time at The Mount had been so comfortable and easy, that I'd decided to take a trusting leap with that other little secret I had on my chest.

Under different circumstances, I might have waited a while, tested the waters. But I was really starting to like Julian, and there was no point in letting that go on, no point whatsoever, if the ghost business was eventually going to be a deal breaker. That's me, though: dive right in. Faced with the choice of pulling off a Band-Aid slowly and gently or in one quick, searing yank, I always opt for speed.

He looked over. I took a deep breath, then hesitated. *No, I* thought, anxiety rising, *this isn't the time.* I'd just ask him to wait in the car. *No!* I immediately told myself, *I can't do that!* It might take a while to explain everything to Esther and then to look for the book; I couldn't just leave him sitting out here in the driveway, wondering what in the world I was up to in there. I'd just end up feeding him a big song and dance when I came back out, and what was the point of that?

Besides, people sometimes surprise me, often when I least expect it. I'll psych myself up for the big revelation, and the matter-of-fact response will be, "Oh, yeah? I saw a ghost once."

"What?" he said, squeezing my hand.

"Um." Yikes.

"What is it?" he asked kindly.

"Okay, okay." I took a deep breath. "There's something I should tell you about myself. You see, I . . ."

I immediately knew that I shouldn't have opened my mouth. This was a very bad idea. I shook my head. "Never mind," I said.

"What?" he pressed. "What is it?"

I sighed. "It's nothing, really."

"If it's nothing, then why won't you tell me?"

"Because—"

"Because why?" he asked.

"Because . . . you'll think I'm crazy."

"No I won't."

"You will. Trust me."

He smiled. "Let me guess. You . . . are secretly . . . a . . . spy!"

"No."

"You are not really . . . a girl."

[177]

I smiled. "Arrgh!" I said, mad at myself for having cracked opened the door. "All right, all right." I took one more deep breath before I whispered, "I can see ghosts. And talk to them. Always could. Since I was . . . little."

There. It was out. He gave me a wry, tilted look, one indicating that he might be waiting for the punch line of this queer little joke.

I shrugged. "That's it. The woman who lives here isn't really a friend of mine, she's a friend of . . . this ghost I know."

"This ghost you know," he said dryly.

I nodded. "He's—was—a butler. He hasn't crossed over yet—because he wants to find the deed to a house in Wales. It's in a book that this woman might have. I'm trying to help find it."

Not elegant, my explanation, but as simple and clear as I could make it. Those were the facts.

He looked dazed and puzzled, as though he knew he was intellectually capable of filling in the missing piece here, he just couldn't get the facts to line up.

So I threw some more at him, hoping his frown would begin to loosen up.

"His name was John Grady. He was Irish."

"Who?" Julian asked.

"The ghost."

His expression said, *I was afraid of that.*

"He and his wife—," I started.

"This . . . *ghost's* wife?"

I nodded, but I could already hear disbelief in his voice. Which is fine, really. It doesn't offend me. People either believe me or they don't. I don't care one way or the other, frankly. I'm not sure *I* would believe me if I were in their shoes. Someone points to a purple elephant in the sky, and you can't see it? For you, it's not there—it doesn't exist. That's how we're taught to make sense of the physical world: playing peekaboo with our mothers, learning that our stuffed bear hasn't really vanished into thin air. What's *real* can't become invisible—it's just hidden behind Mama's back. Can't find your other shoe? Keep looking. It exists. It's somewhere. What's actual doesn't just vanish.

The converse, of course, we also learn: if you can't see it, or touch it, or hear it yourself, it isn't real.

I can easily pull a ghost, like a well-loved teddy bear, from behind my back, if someone is open-minded and will give me a chance. But most people close right down: they're threatened, they're scared, what I say just flips them out. I understand that, and experience has taught me I have to respect it. When I see that steel door coming down behind someone's eyes, it's usually best for me to back off.

But today, I didn't want to back off. I wanted Julian to find this fascinating. I wanted him to think it was the most interesting thing he'd ever heard, and that I was the most captivating woman he had ever met, so I persisted.

"Come in with me," I said. "There's no reason to be afraid."

"I'm not *afraid*," he scoffed. There was a tone in his voice that I hadn't heard before. A dismissive edge, as though he were thinking he *should have known* something was wrong with me.

"It'll make more sense inside. I can show you—"

"No." He cut me off. His expression had hardened. "I'll wait here, if it's all the same to you." He tried to soften the effect of his words with a smile, but it was a cool, distant smile. "Have a walk around, perhaps."

For now, anyway, it appeared that the subject was closed.

"Sure; great!" I said, way too cheerfully. "I won't be long."

"Suit yourself," he said.

As Johnny had predicted, Esther had no trouble believing the story I told her. I had not telephoned ahead, both because I hadn't had time and because I hadn't wanted to give Esther the chance to blow me off over the phone. Winning her confidence as I stood on her doorstep was going to be the trickiest part, I knew, so I'd asked Johnny for some details I could use to gain Esther's trust, facts I couldn't possibly know unless they'd been imparted to me by someone in the household. Or the ghost of someone in the household.

I did a quick tap dance when she answered my knock. She was tall and lanky like her sister, but the skin on her face and hands was roughened by sun and country living. Before she could gather her wits—or slam the door in my face—I launched into the story of how she had broken her mother's Limoges sugar bowl in the bathtub, where it was sailing Lulu, Esther's stuffed chick, to China. I identified her favorite flavor of ice cream, at least her childhood favorite—peppermint stick. I reminded her of how she'd broken her wrist at her first riding lesson, after she kicked the chestnut mare into a trot while the instructor's back was turned. And all through her childhood, I said, she'd had an "imaginary playmate" named Millie.

Imaginary playmates are ghosts. They're usually the ghosts of children who have died, and who remain connected to the homes in which other children now live.

At the mention of Millie, Esther's eyes filled up with tears and she swept me quickly into her kitchen.

Millie, she explained as she put on the kettle for tea, was a little girl who'd lived in their house on Commonwealth Avenue and died in the influenza epidemic of 1918. Esther's bedroom had once belonged to Millie, who'd just turned eight when she succumbed to the flu. Esther had only pieced this together a few years ago, when she'd done some research on the previous owners of her former home.

It was Millie who'd taught Esther to tie her shoes, and not Josie, who took the credit. Millie had been central to Esther's life for as long as Esther could remember; she even remembered looking through the bars of her crib and seeing Millie rocking in the chair.

"I'm sure you did," I said. "That's not unusual."

"No one believed me," she said.

"That's not unusual, either, unfortunately," I responded.

"One day when I was—I think I was seven—she just disappeared. By then I had figured out that she was a . . . spirit of some kind, because as I got older, she stayed the same age. We began to argue as we got closer and closer in age, the way sisters do. Then one day, when I came home from school, she was gone. Just *gone*. We'd had a silly fight that morning and, well, I never saw her again. I was devastated. It was like having a sister die." She looked at me appealingly. "Do you know why she left?" she asked. "Do you know where she is?"

I shook my head.

"You can't . . . talk to her?"

"I don't have that gift," I admitted. "I'm not a medium. Once a spirit crosses over, they're lost to me, too."

She nodded sadly. "But you *can* talk to Mr. Grady."

"Yes, because he's still here. He says he's sorry, by the way."

"For what?" she asked.

"For not believing you. About Millie."

A fond, faraway look came over her face. "Oh, it's not his fault. He was always a sweetheart."

"He still is," I said.

We quickly combed the shelves and boxes holding Esther's

books. Fifteen or twenty minutes after I'd left him sitting in the car, I stepped outside to inform Julian that I was nearly finished, but he wasn't anywhere to be seen. With any luck, he was having a lovely ramble around the spacious grounds, forgetting he'd just decided I had a screw loose.

As we descended the stairs from the attic, where we had just gone through the last of the boxes, Esther said, "I can picture it so clearly. The cover had children playing ring-around-the-rosy under an apple tree. And all around the tree were butterflies." She smiled at the memory. "Josie must have it. Of the two of us, she was more of a reader. I was the one with Play-Doh and pastels."

"Why would he think *you* had it?" I asked.

"I don't know. I did love it." She paused, lost in thought for a moment. "I think I reminded him of my mother—I have her hair and eyes."

"That makes sense," I said.

"And he's sure the deed is in there?"

"He seems to think so."

"Funny place to put it. And why in the world would he have bought a cottage in Wales?"

"I'm not sure." I paused on the front porch, glancing around to see if Julian had returned. I saw him coming over a rise in the distance, slowly making his way toward the house.

"I'll call Josie," Esther said.

Better you than me, I thought, remembering the tantrum I'd witnessed last night.

"That would be great," I said. "Do you think there's a chance she has it?"

"Oh, sure. There's a good chance. Of the three of us, she's the most sentimental about . . . certain things."

I could believe this. I'd seen frightening evidence of her sentimental attachments.

"Can I ask you one thing?" Esther said.

"Sure."

"If I do find it, can I come with you? When you give it to Mr. Grady. I'd give anything in the world to talk to him again."

"Oh yeah, sure," I said. "You won't to able to . . . talk to him yourself."

"Oh I *know*. But I could just—"

"He'll be able to hear you, and I can tell you what he says."

Esther's eyes immediately filled up. "Thank you," she whispered.

"You're welcome," I said, and we embraced. She was shaking with emotion, but she quickly pulled herself together and smiled.

"Tell him it wasn't me who broke the sugar bowl," she said. "It was Millie."

Dinner was . . . weird. Had Esther and I managed to turn up the deed, I might have been able to show it to Julian as some kind of proof. Not proof, certainly, that I could communicate with earthbound spirits, much less evidence that ghosts exist. But merely as a concrete object to lend veracity to my claim that I'd come here with a simple, specific goal: to pick up something for a friend.

"We couldn't find it," I'd explained.

"Ah," Julian had said, concentrating on his driving. "That's too bad."

"Before he died, he tucked it into a book of poems, and, well, the book has disappeared." I immediately regretted using the world *disappeared*, which edged us uncomfortably close to the language of the supernatural. I'd intended to steer the conversation clear of anything to do with the realm of the mystical, but I tend to jump in to end awkward silences.

"Not *disappeared*," I went on self-consciously, drawing even more attention to the very territory I had hoped to avoid. "It's probably at her sister's. Esther's sister's." Then, because Julian was showing no interest whatsoever in following my narrative, I sputtered on nervously, like a car running out of gas.

"The woman who lives here. The artist."

"Yes. The egg sculptures. I saw one of them."

Phew! I thought, grateful for the prospect of another subject of conversation.

"How were the grounds?" I asked. "They looked beautiful."

"Very nice."

It went on like this, in fits and awkward starts, until we were well into a bottle of wine and halfway through our steak Diane (Julian) and striped bass with succotash (me).

"You never really told me why you don't believe in a Book of Kildare," I said.

"You never really asked," he answered, but not with this afternoon's sarcasm. He poured me another glass of wine, then drained the bottle into his own goblet. He had a sip and sat back.

"Of course I didn't actually examine it," he began.

"Neither did James Wescott."

"No, right, that's true."

"What do you think of him?" I asked.

"Wescott? I've only worked with him a few times. What I know, I mainly know by reputation."

"Which is?"

Julian shrugged. "Sharp fellow, the rich old widows adore him, good fund-raiser, but, overall, maybe a little disappointing."

"Really? How so?"

"He's missed some opportunities, misplayed his hand a couple of times. Lost out on three or four important acquisitions because he wasn't very strategic. I mean, he's basically competent and well liked, but he was kind of a wunderkind, and he hasn't really lived up to the hype. He's due to retire in the next few years, and there aren't too many rubies in the crown."

I nodded. This made sense. Wescott had been smooth and handsome and charming, and he probably looked great in a tux, mingling with dukes and duchesses, but he'd been awfully quick to dismiss Finny and Sylvia's theory.

"Then he shouldn't have been so dismissive," I said. "Making up his mind so definitively, without even examining Finny's book. If that's how he acts all the time, it's no wonder he misses opportunities."

Julian grinned and shook his head. "Well, in that case, I do think he was right. Look, I would love to believe that there could be a manuscript of that caliber floating around. There's just very little evidence it ever existed. Just that one medieval cleric who claimed to have seen it, the same story cited over and over."

"Have you read the actual story?" I asked. "In the diary he wrote for Henry the Second."

"Can't say that I have."

"There's a new translation—"

"Which you just happen to be familiar with?" He looked vaguely amused.

"*No;* I came across it over the weekend, online. To tell you the truth, I've had my own doubts about Sylvia and her claims."

This seemed to surprise him. "Well, you've done a good job of hiding them."

"Just trying to keep an *open mind.*" This was a little dig, and I think he knew it. I smiled to soften the edge of the comment. "Besides, I love reading this stuff. It was hilarious. And beautiful."

"The writing?"

"Yeah." I took a bite of my bass before elaborating. It was salty and tender, and the corn in my succotash was as sweet as candy. "He was sent to accompany Henry's son John on a trip to Ireland. He took it upon himself to write a diary for the king, describing all kinds of things he saw, people he met. Mini treatises on topography and resentful badgers and fish with golden teeth. Dozens of stories."

"What kind of stories?"

"Oh, about a lion that was in love with a woman. A wolf that conversed with a priest. Deadly poisons in the turf underfoot and scheming animals and an island off the coast where if you left a dead body out in the air, it didn't decompose."

"Appealing."

"And a stone with a hole in it, which refilled itself mysteriously every day with wine. Oh, and bugs! Stories about bugs, like the grasshoppers who sing better after their heads are chopped off, and the shepherds who 'deprive them of their heads'—that was the exact phrase, *deprive them of their heads*—just to hear the beautiful harmonies they made as they expired."

Julian smiled, and said, "And *this* is the man you believe."

"I'm not saying I believe him. It's just fascinating to read. Regarding the creation of the Book of Kildare, he believed it was a miracle. The story was that every night, an angel would come in a dream to the monk who was working on the book and show him a picture inscribed on a tablet. The angel would ask the monk, 'Can you copy this?' And every night the scribe would answer, 'No, I can't. It's too beautiful and too complicated.'"

I had a sip of my wine and continued. "And then the angel would say, 'Well, tonight, you should pray to your patroness, Saint Brigid, and ask her to speak to Our Lord, ask Him if He'll give you—"

"More talent?" Julian was grinning.

"Basically, yeah. And the next day, the monk would discover he could duplicate *exactly* the picture the angel had showed him in the dream. It went on like this, day after day, until the book was finished."

Julian didn't speak right away, but at least he wasn't giving me the stony stare.

"I suppose you also believe in angels," he finally said.

I shrugged. Let him dig, if he really wanted to know.

Surprisingly, he persisted. "Do you?"

"Not the kind you see in the pictures," I finally said. "Not the kind with wings and a halo."

"What kind, then?" he asked.

I sighed and put down my fork. I really didn't want to answer, just to endure another patronizing smirk. All of a sudden, I was tired of Julian's sly insinuations, and fed up with working so hard to reestablish the easy rapport we'd shared before he got to know me a little better. Sure, he was cute and affable, and he could be charming and downright funny, but he could also be cutting and cold, assuming a stance of bemused superiority.

"Well," I finally said. "You certainly seem to have everything figured out."

He glanced up quickly. *This* he hadn't been expecting.

"Look," I continued. "I'm not trying to convince you of anything. I don't care what you believe or don't believe. But I'm also not going to deny what I've been experiencing my whole life. If you can't deal with it, that's fine, but at least——"

I was shocked to feel a thickness in my throat and tears beginning to gather behind my eyes. I went to finish my sentence, but my words felt tight.

"At least . . ."

Julian's eyes widened. "I'm sorry," he said. "Forgive me, please, I'm——"

"Let's just go," I said.

"No, no, please. Oh God, Anza, I'm really so . . . Let's have dessert. Coffee? Would you like a cappuccino? Let's get you a cappuccino."

I let out a sigh, feeling the prickling of tears at the backs of my eyes. "Okay," I whispered.

Chapter Eighteen

It was well past midnight when I tiptoed up the steps to our apartment. Julian and I had retreated to far safer turf during the three-hour drive home, chatting politely about books and research and the few people we knew in common, silently agreeing to pretend that the awkward flare-ups had never happened. I realized, as I unlocked the door and tiptoed inside, that I had no clear idea of how I felt about him. It was confusing, all that charm and wit being turned on me so suddenly. Was I blowing things out of proportion? Maybe, when the dust settled in a day or two or three or four, I would know.

Nat was fast asleep on the foldout couch, and to be honest, I was a little relieved. I just wasn't up for a late-night heart-to-heart.

I switched on the bathroom light and surveyed the day's damage. I was once again sick of my hair, and the scarf and the wind hadn't helped. It occurred to me that Tilda probably had fabulous hair, colored and conditioned and snipped and shaped monthly by hairstylists in London. I wished I were small enough for a chic, short haircut or disciplined enough to grow out loose, sexy layers, but I was neither. A couple of days of frustrating hair would send me flying off to one salon or another, where someone wearing a style I would never, ever consider—and once, those earrings that gradually spread your earlobes into huge, gaping holes—would talk me into trying something "a little different," something that required a PhD in products.

The gullible gambles never lasted very long—I could never remember which product went on when—and a week or two later, bored with fussing around with goos and gels, I would catch a glimpse of myself in a store window and realize that I was once again stranded, hairwise, somewhere between Margaret Thatcher and Tipper Gore, circa 2000.

I brushed my teeth and tiptoed in to check on Henry. Whereas I sleep like a stone, waking up in virtually the same position as that in which I fell asleep, Henry's a thrasher. There's not much point in a top sheet—it quickly gets squeezed into an accordion of wrinkles at his feet—and his comforter ends up on the floor more nights than not. Tonight was no exception, but the room was warm. A dewy film of sweat on his forehead suggested active, exciting dreams, and Henry drew instinctively toward me as I sat down on the side of his bed.

He opened his eyes a little. "Mama," he said, pulling closer, then drifted immediately back to sleep.

I leaned down and kissed him, catching a hint of the warm, sweet perfume that hangs above the beds of sleeping little boys, at least mine. Henry didn't stir, but something in me did. Who cared about hair, and whether it was fabulous and perfect every day? Who cared about Julian, with his smug, sarcastic attitude and those stupid, cute little wrinkles at the corners of his eyes? Who cared about Tilda getting primped and highlighted and Edith Wharton having the perfect gardens, or about all the other ways in which our improvised little life felt down-at-the-heels, or incomplete, or not quite what it could be with a little more effort.

I already had everything. And I was home.

———— ❦ ————

Nat left at about eleven the next morning. I'd stopped by the bakery on my way home from dropping Henry at school and come home to find her in the shower, the foldout couch closed, the sheets and blankets piled neatly on one of the cushions.

"You wanna know what I think?" she asked a little later, stirring sugar into her coffee.

"Let me guess."

She smiled and peered into the box of pastries: two apple Danish, two cinnamon doughnuts, and a croissant the size of New Jersey. Nat thinks men are like melons: sized up too early, they can leave a lot to be desired, but allowed to ripen in their own good time, they're another fruit entirely.

I'm the opposite: I think you know most of what you need to know about a person in the first half hour. Thirty seconds: you're mutually attracted, or not. Five minutes: enough to gauge the intellectual horsepower. Fifteen minutes: likely to be nice to waitresses? Kids? Dogs? Another fifteen minutes and you've got a pretty good idea of whether it's worth taking a chance. Like that first night, when I said to Declan, "Can't complain," and he said, "Sure you can," and I said, "Who would listen?" and he said, "I would." In five minutes, I knew almost everything I needed to know.

Almost. There was that . . . Kelly wrinkle. But I'm not talking about everything working out. I'm talking about the decision to give it a go.

Nat took the croissant out of the box and cut it in half. "So, it was all fine until you got talking about—"

"The ghost stuff, yeah," I said.

"Exactly," concluded Nat.

"Exactly what?"

She put the croissant on her plate and cut it in half again. This is why she can have a wardrobe comprised of ten exquisite items. Her size never changes, because she doesn't do things like eat croissants the size of dessert plates.

"You forget that it's . . . kind of weird, talking to ghosts," she said. "And freaky for some people. I mean, not for you and me, because we've always—"

"I know."

"So cut the guy some slack, all right? He put himself out there to ask you out, twice, so he obviously likes you and wants to spend time with you."

"Want*ed*."

Nat shrugged and had a bite of croissant. What she was saying was true, but the fact remained that I had revealed something pretty personal to Julian, an aspect of myself that I feel vulnerable talking about, and in return, he'd treated me like a smelly sock. And by the way, he was also wrong: ghosts do exist, whether he believes in them or not. I have nothing against the skeptical, but the polite thing would have been to act pleasant and open-minded and keep a lid on the cutting little jibes. But I guess they don't teach manners at Oxford.

"Okay," I said. "I'll give him another chance."

"You will not. You say you will, but you won't."

I smiled and reached for the half-croissant. Pastry in midair, I changed my mind and replaced it with an apple Danish. The doorbell rang as I was pouring us both more coffee.

"Who could that be?" I asked Nat, who of course had no idea.

It was a man from Winston Flowers, with an armful of what,

from the looks of the bundle, I judged could only be a dozen roses.

I was wrong. It was two dozen. Of the most gorgeous salmon-colored roses I had ever seen.

The card read: "I was a beast." It was signed "Julian."

In shock, I handed the card to Nat.

"Well, well, well," she said.

I'd planned to go into the Athenaeum, but around noon, when I was still drifting around the apartment, trying to get myself organized and out of the house, I realized that this made no sense. In less than five hours, two of which would have to be spent commuting into Boston and back, the much-anticipated weekend with Delia and Nell would be upon me, and I was nowhere near ready.

I needed to shop, do laundry, bake chocolate chip cookies, clean the house, blow up air mattresses, and generally ensure that when the girls returned home with tales of their weekend, I wouldn't come off as a slacker semi-mom with an empty fridge and no clean sheets. Shallow, I know, and probably deeply insecure, but Kelly sets a pretty high bar, with campfires and scavenger hunts and beach afternoons and complicated art projects. I didn't want Nell and Delia telling tales of frozen pizza and hours spent zoning out in front of the TV.

I phoned Sylvia, and as I expected, she was fine with my not coming in. Officially, for the purposes of Amanda Perkins and the director of Human Resources and other nonrelevant busybodies, I'm a freelance bookbinder working twenty hours a week. But as Sylvia and I both know, I wasn't really hired to bind books. I was hired to interact with the monks.

Finny Winslow would have been fine with this use of his

money, Sylvia assured me, and whether she was right about that or not, the call was hers to make. And truthfully, there wasn't much point in my being in the bindery today, or any day, until I could appease the persnickety ghosts by showing up with a monsignor or an auxiliary bishop in tow.

I breathed a sigh of relief as I hung up. Not only did I have other things to think about than the concerns of three anxious spirits, which had basically taken over my waking life for nearly two weeks, I had other work to do. And I don't mean baking cookies. There were the tacky Sherwood Glen coffee-table books, to be presented to the lucky new home owners in less than a month. I had four other binding projects in various stages of incompletion, and five or six inquiries to which I had yet to respond—calls and e-mails regarding jobs that might get me through Christmas, *if* I was lucky enough to get them.

One concerned a full-time position that a friend had just heard was going to be opening up at the Boston Public Library. A job with *benefits*! No matter what else I did or didn't get around to doing this afternoon, *that* was a call I had to return.

Then there was my father, with whom I hadn't spoken in two weeks. Nona's seventy-fifth birthday was coming up, and Jay had sent me an e-mail about Thanksgiving plans. What that was all about, I had no idea; every year we do the same thing—converge on Dad and Nona and settle into behaving and being treated like children for three days. I also had to talk to Ellie about the costume, find a new pediatrician for Henry—the one we'd had since Henry was born was taking a staff position at Children's Hospital—and go through the various notices and requests from the school, which had been piling up on the kitchen counter since the beginning of the term.

In other words, I had to deal with Life.

By six o'clock, when Declan and Kelly arrived with the girls,

I'd made real progress. The cookies were cooling, the house was respectable, and I'd responded to all the work inquiries. I hadn't trod the sheeny paths of Sherwood Glen, but I'd lined up two more freelance jobs, placed a call to my friend at the BPL, and left a message on my dad's machine.

I sat down briefly and contemplated what lay just ahead: forty-eight hours of supervising and cooking for and refereeing and entertaining three wildly overexcited children. *Forty-eight hours.* Without a break. Two overnights.

I couldn't do it. I was too tired. No, I wasn't just tired, I was fried.

Delia was bursting with anticipation as she raced up the stairs. She handed me a package she had obviously wrapped herself.

"It's a present," she said, eyes sparkling. "Open it!"

The wrapper was also a card. It read: "I ♥ Anza," followed by lots of *x*'s and *o*'s and a signature fancied up with curlicues. There were rainbows, quite a few, above a picture of a little stick person holding hands (I think) with a big stick person wearing a triangle of a skirt. I noticed there were no other little stick people in the picture.

The gift was a bracelet made of elbow macaroni and string and colored with Magic Markers. I tried to slip it on but it was too small.

"It's beautiful! I love it!" I raved, sweeping her up in a huge hug.

Of course I could do it.

Henry grabbed Kelly by the hand and dragged her in to show her his bedroom. She'd seen it before, many times, but in his excitement over their arrival, he seemed to forget that Kelly had ever stepped foot inside his room.

Declan had good news and bad news. The bad news was, a guy

he described as a "scuzzy lowlife" had been able to post Scully's bail, so Scully had been released late on Thursday.

"No!" I protested. "Couldn't you find a way to hold him?"

Declan smiled. "Afraid it doesn't work that way."

The good news was, Scully seemed genuinely determined to avoid as much jail time as possible, so in the twenty-four hours since he'd hit the street, he'd made a number of fruitful inquiries regarding the recent activities of Jannus Van Vleck.

"And?" I asked.

Declan nodded.

"What?"

"Could well be our man."

My stomach dropped. "How do you know?"

"Well, I don't. Not for sure, anyway, not yet. But he did fly from Amsterdam to New York about a week ago. And he was definitely here in the area between Wednesday and Friday—three of Scully's contacts either saw him or spoke to him."

"Where is he now? Do they know?"

"Possibly Nantucket."

"Does he have the book?"

"Don't know."

I paused and listened to voices and laughter from Henry's room. The regular screech of straining springs told me that someone was bouncing, if not actually jumping, on the bed.

"So what do we do?" I asked.

"Nothing yet."

"Why?"

"*Why?*" Declan asked. "Because no one's reported a crime, Anza. You wanted me to handle everything on the DL, so I can't do anywhere near what I'd be able to do if I could put it up on the board. Remind me again why we can't just treat this like a standard B and E?"

"Because there'll be too many questions: why she had the book in her apartment, who actually owns it—"

"And who does?" he asked.

"No one, really. That's the problem. Tad will feel it belongs to him and his sisters, and he'll probably want to sell it, which was exactly what Finny didn't want. He wanted Sylvia to keep on doing what they had been doing—talking to art historians, trying to prove that their theory was right. She was the only one he trusted with it."

"If he trusted her so goddamned much," Declan said, "he should have left *her* the friggin' book. It would have saved everybody a lot of trouble."

"He probably wasn't thinking straight, Dec. The poor man *was* dying."

Declan let out a sigh and reached for one of the cookies. He nodded approvingly as he took a bite.

"So I was thinking," he said, "that we might try floating a counteroffer. See what kind of bugs crawl out from under the rock. Meantime, we try to get a reliable bead on Van Vleck's whereabouts."

This meant nothing to me: "float a counteroffer."

I must have looked as though he was speaking Japanese, because he said, "I'll have Scully put the word out that a second party, someone besides whoever commissioned this, is aware that the book is . . . available, and is prepared to double Van Vleck's fee."

"Who's going to put up the money?"

"No one, Anza." He was speaking slowly, as though he was explaining a simple concept to one of the girls. "We don't actually need the cash. We show up, demand to inspect the book, and then offer the bastard immunity from prosecution if he tells us who commissioned the theft. I tell you, it'll fry my ass to let that slippery son-of-a-b walk, but you'll have your book, and if we're lucky, we might be able to take some kind of action against whoever put him up to it."

"And if we're not? Lucky?"

"Then at least you'll have your book. And what's-his-name can rest in peace."

I didn't want to ask the question, but I had to. "Is this legal, Dec?"

"Hell, no. I'm breaking every rule in the book."

"Then maybe it isn't such a good idea."

"You got any others?"

I didn't, unfortunately, but I had no time to regret that, nor to bemoan the fact that I had ever dragged Declan into this sorry mess, because a small typhoon comprised of three manic children was roaring in my direction. Actually, it was the cookies they were roaring toward, so I only had a moment to sweep the cooling racks out of reach.

You see, given a few hours to get Life under control, I can be a pretty fair mom, or at least the kind who doesn't let famished children tuck into racks of warm chocolate chip cookies before they're almost filled up with chicken and mashed potatoes and green beans.

I smiled, though, when Declan snagged a couple more cookies for the road. For the journey to the inn where he was about to spend an enviable weekend romancing his wife, he could take as many of my cookies as he liked.

Chapter Nineteen

I HAD AN unexpected break on Saturday afternoon. As I cleaned
up the kitchen following our first group activity, the surprisingly
messy project of making homemade waffles, the kids started
working on a hideout in the backyard, in the sheltered space between our overgrown holly hedge and the fence that our neighbors had recently put up.

I'd tried to steer them toward another location—the points on
those holly leaves are as sharp as pins—but the foliage there was
dense and opaque, which I guess was why they liked the spot. They
settled themselves in under the pine-green canopy, at first with just
a painting tarp to make the ground beneath them sittable, but then
with an ever-expanding cache of creature comforts—cups of juice,
flashlights, cheese Goldfish crackers, books.

The hubbub attracted Homer, the flatulent St. Bernard from a
few houses over. Homer's excited barking brought Ellie into the
backyard, and as it turned out, she had just come home with half
a dozen pumpkins. She wondered if the kids wanted to help her
carve them. Beginning to tire of being pricked by the holly leaves,
they jumped at the chance. They hurried into her kitchen, where

the woodstove was crackling with an unnecessary fire, black bean soup was bubbling on the burner, and a pan of crusty corn bread sat cooling on the sill.

Had she been planning to try to lure them into an afternoon of grandmotherly delights? I can't be sure, though black bean soup just happens to be one of Henry's favorites. But carving the pumpkins? This early? By Halloween, they would surely sag into soft, toothless caricatures of the witchy and the ancient. Still, there'd be no complaints from me—the kids were happy, Ellie and Max sure seemed happy, and I was overjoyed. That only left poor, abandoned Homer, moping on the steps.

I drifted in and out of Max and Ellie's as the afternoon wore on, making it known to them every half hour or so that I was more than ready to take the kids off their hands. But the kids didn't want to be taken off their hands. Activities were flowing happily along from one to the next. Finally, Max put it to me bluntly.

"Why don't you just go . . . take a walk?"

I smiled. As Ellie led the parade up to the attic, where she had two big trunks of "dress-up clothes," Max remained at the kitchen table, up to his elbows in pumpkin guck. They were planning to roast the seeds, but first Max had to clean off all the slimy strings.

"A walk where? I'm too pooped," I responded.

"Then go take a nap!" he snapped.

I don't take Max's snaps personally. Snapping is what he does. He's like my dad that way.

"Sounds like you're the one who needs a nap," I shot back.

"Aw, get out of here," he said. "Stop bending my ear."

So I kissed him on the cheek, a kiss he squirmed away from, and left him alone with his pumpkins.

I was just drifting off to sleep, wrapped up in an afghan on the couch, when the phone rang.

I reached up to the table behind me, grabbed the receiver, and glanced at the number. Was it Julian?

"Hello?" I said.

"Anza?"

"Yes."

"This is Esther Winslow."

"Oh!" I struggled up to a sitting position.

"Am I catching you at a bad time?"

"No, no." It was inevitable, really—you finally get a half hour to yourself, and the minute you close your eyes, the phone rings.

"I just wanted to let you know that I talked to my sister."

"You did?"

"Yeah. She thinks she might have the book."

"Really?"

"She's got some boxes in her attic that she's going to go through. I gave her your number. I hope that's all right."

"Sure," I said. *No problem at all*, I thought. *I'd be thrilled to hear from the psycho who nearly gave me a heart attack a few days ago.*

"Did you tell her about Mr. Grady?" I went on.

"I had to," said Esther. "It wasn't a secret, was it?"

"No, no! How did she respond?"

"I don't think she believed me at first. Not until I mentioned Millie." Esther paused. "Anyway, she's going to look for the book over the weekend. She said she'd call us both tomorrow or Monday."

"All right. Great. Thanks so much."

"No problem. I'll talk to you soon. Oh, and Anza?"

"Yeah?"

"If you see Mr. Grady before we talk again, give him my love."

"I will," I said.

All hell broke loose on Saturday night. It wasn't supposed to happen that way, but it did.

At about five o'clock, I could hear through the upstairs doorway, the one that connects our third-floor hall with Ellie and Max's, that the kids were beginning to whine and bicker. It was about time, really; if not for Ellie's angelic good cheer and apparently limitless enthusiasm, it would have started to happen in mid-afternoon. In any case, it was time for me to step in and reclaim my grouchy charges.

They put up only a halfhearted fight, which told me they actually were ready to come home. I put on the DVD of *101 Dalmatians* and had them take turns in the bathtub. By seven thirty, they were clean and restored to relatively good spirits, and we were eating spaghetti and meatballs by candlelight. The candlelight was Nell's idea and might have been responsible for Henry's next brainstorm.

"Can we make a campfire?" he asked. "And toast marshmallows?"

"Where?" I said.

"In the backyard."

"No. Sorry."

"Why not?"

"Because the trees are too low out there. The branches hang way down."

"So?" he said, freshly.

"So?" I responded, freshly. Sometimes he brings out the five-year-old in me. "You want to set a tree on fire?" I doubted this was likely, given the rain we'd had in the past few days, but it was the first thought that came into my head. It should have occurred to me that a five-year-old boy would like nothing better.

"That'd be *cool!*" Henry said.

Nell giggled.

"Well it wouldn't be very cool to burn the house down," I went on. "I don't think you'd be very happy about that."

In a gesture of sisterly solidarity, Delia said quietly, "We do it at the lake . . ."

"I know, honey, but you have a place to do it there."

"No we don't," Henry argued. "We do it right on the beach."

"I know. That's what I'm saying. It's fine if you're right by the water. But you have to be careful if you're building a fire right underneath a whole bunch of trees."

"We *will* be careful. I promise! *Please?*"

"Please?" echoed Delia and Nell.

And this was when I started feeling bad, particularly with the girls pleading. Despite the fact that they'd had a perfectly wonderful day, a day 99 percent of the world's children would consider really first-rate, I suddenly felt it had not been enough. To make matter worse, Dec and Kelly *could* give them a campfire, not only at Lake Sunapee, but right in their own backyard.

"I've got an idea," I said, trying to excite them with an excess of enthusiasm. "How about we make chocolate chip cookie sundaes and you can eat them out in your fort! In the dark! With flashlights!"

"Yeah!" said Nell, who was always easy to please. Henry's initial expression suggested that he suspected they were being conned somehow, but when Nell got behind the idea, followed by Delia, he went along.

So out came the ice cream and the cookies, and the jar of fudge sauce and the bottle of cherries. I didn't have cream for whipping, but I had red sugar sprinkles left over from Christmas baking and half a package of M&Ms.

I produced a tray and three juice boxes. I turned up a couple of flashlights for them to share, of immense interest to the girls because they were the wind-up kind that don't need batteries. An hour later was when it all went south, after the sundaes had been finished and darkness had really fallen and they were still out there in the dim backyard, playing a primitive version of flashlight tag.

I had been cleaning up the kitchen and having a glass of wine, one ear attuned to their happy shrieks. The sounds had brought me back to the summer evenings of my own childhood, dusky interludes involving Jay and Joe and five or six other neighborhood kids: the Davios and the Cunninghams and Frankie Lobelli. We usually played hide-and-seek. A memory as clear as a film clip came back to me: I was crouched behind some kind of evergreen bush, bursting with excitement over the fact that no one—not even the *big* kids—could find me. I was using every fiber of self-control I possessed not to swat at a pair of humming mosquitoes that had found me behind the bush.

Suddenly, I heard a little scream and then another. Then Henry bellowed, "Mama!"

I was out the door and down the steps in a flash, but I was not fast enough.

Attracted by the kids' voices and the flashing lights, Homer had trotted over to get in on the action. Cambridge has a leash law, but we all knew and loved sloppy old Homer, who took his pick of front porches for his afternoon nap. No doubt he was trying to protect the kids when he buried his nose in a bank of hostas and began to bark with gusto. And who could blame them for crowding around, to see what the excitement was all about?

By the time they figured it out, it was too late. The skunk had been rooted out from its leafy sanctuary and had sprayed them all.

Homer took the brunt of it. As the perp toddled off, its little white toupee vanishing between the boards of the fence, the dog began to whine and threw himself down into the grass, trying to rub the oily spray off his snout and face. The spray hadn't gotten into the children's eyes, and for that I was truly relieved, but they hadn't escaped lightly. I wouldn't fully realize until I got them into the house later how bad it was, but when I did, there was absolutely no doubt—it was really, really bad.

Ellie, who had been sitting in her kitchen, phoned Homer's owners, a couple in their thirties named Susie and Bud Coughlin, and they came racing over. I was already imagining my bathtub full of tomato juice and trying to figure out how many cans I was going to have to buy to fill it up. I could ask Ellie to stay out in the yard with them while I ran to Star Market in Porter Square. Twenty large cans ought to do it, I figured, wondering briefly if V8 juice would be a better purchase, in case I miscalculated the amount I needed and had a lot left over. I like V8 juice better than tomato.

Bud and Susie knew better, thank goodness. It wasn't the first time Homer had been skunked, and apparently there was a magic formula known widely to dog owners, some combination of hydrogen peroxide, baking soda, and dishwashing soap. The mix was miraculous, Bud claimed; it completely killed the odor. Susie was falling all over herself apologizing, clearly believing that Homer was responsible for the whole mess. I didn't agree. Racing around like banshees with their flashlights, the kids easily could have scared a skunk into spraying, even without Homer's help. But I was thrilled when Susie offered to hop on her bike and make a quick run to CVS for multiple bottles of hydrogen peroxide, the ingredient we were both missing. Bud took Homer home.

Having little idea how truly foul they smelled, the kids milked the situation for every bedtime-postponing minute it was worth. Back outside, Henry was stomping around with a stick, proclaiming how he'd really like to "get" that rotten skunk, and while Nell and Delia were initially swept up in his fury and out-rage, they soon plopped down on the steps in a desolate little huddle.

Nell's lip began to quiver and she put her thumb in her mouth. "I want my mommy," she said, tears spilling over.

Delia slid over and put her arm around her little sister. "It's okay, Nelly-belle," she said. "Mommy'll be back tomorrow."

Max had appeared at their kitchen door. Wisely, he'd kept his distance during all the high drama, but now he joined the rest of us as we waited on the porch for Susie to get back.

"What's wrong with you?" he asked Nell.

Nell shook her head and refused to reply.

"We got sprayed," Delia explained.

"Yeah, no kidding," Max said.

"She wants Mommy," Delia went on. "They're in Maine."

Max nodded seriously. "She can probably smell you from up there."

Nell looked up quickly, instantly snapped out of her self-pity. When she saw Delia begin to giggle, she put on a madder-than-ever face and smacked her sister on the arm. Nell was not going to smile. She was *not*.

She flew to her feet and headed toward me.

"Eee!" I said, scooting away. "No! Get away from me!"

This brought a smile to her face, as first she, then she and Delia, then she, Delia, and Henry swarmed after me like bees to honey, determined to contaminate me with their skunky stink. I could only dart and swoop for so long before they managed to bring me down with a three-kid tackle. Oh well. At least I had on an old shirt.

"Why weren't you in bed, anyway?" Max asked.

"We wanted a campfire," Henry said. "We wanted to toast marshmallows, but Mama said no."

"How come?" asked Max.

"Because we might set the trees on fire."

Max nodded, surveying the huge, ancient silver maples at the back two corners of the yard.

He glanced over at me. His look said, *What kind of cockamamie excuse was that?*

I shrugged. Surely he wasn't too old to remember the kind of cockamamie excuses he'd come up with on the spur of the moment and fed to his own gullible children.

A few minutes later he disappeared inside, and a minute or two after that, he reappeared through the bulkhead to the basement, an entrance we never used. He was dragging a standing charcoal grill, a rusty old relic that looked as though it hadn't seen the light of day in twenty-five years.

"What in God's name are you doing?" asked Ellie.

Max climbed the porch steps, went into the kitchen, and came back out with an armful of wood. He began to pile logs into the grill.

"I'm building a campfire," he said.

Chapter Twenty

It was a relief to be back at work. This is one of the dirty little secrets of parenthood: if you have a decent job, one you basically enjoy, it's often far, far easier to be among grown-ups at your place of employment than home with an utterly dependent and mercurial little person (or in the case of this past weekend, three). Then again, you miss out on all the fun when someone snorts chocolate milk out of his nose.

The de-skunking had taken until two o'clock on Sunday morning, and when the people in front of us in church—yes, I had to get them all to Mass on Sunday—started peering around and whispering, I realized that the magic formula hadn't been quite so magical. We were all so inured to the odor that we couldn't smell it on ourselves. So, after a stop at Verna's for a consoling box of doughnuts and another at CVS for yet more bottles of hydrogen peroxide, we went at the process all over again. And that took up the rest of the day, between the baths and the hair and the clothes, bumping our plans for a trip to the Children's Museum into sometime next month.

They were all good sports. I felt bad, though, as if I had really blown my chance to repay Dec and Kelly and to give the girls a memorable weekend. No, strike that; it would definitely be remembered. But for all the wrong reasons.

"Believe me, it could just as easily have happened up at the lake," Kelly insisted. "There are skunks all over the place."

Dec just kept shaking his head. I think he found it amusing.

I had been so happy to be left alone with Henry. We got pizza about six o'clock and ate in the living room watching *Pinocchio*. I fell so soundly asleep on the couch that Henry put himself to bed. He probably intended to stay up really, really late, with no one pestering him to turn off the light, but I doubt that lasted long. When I woke up at ten fifteen, he was dead to the world.

Chandler was at a conference in Chicago for the week, so Sylvia and I were spared his glowering omnipresence. All I wanted to do was to reimmerse myself in the orderly calm of the Cicero project, and I was able to do that for most of the day. As Sylvia worked beside me on an eighteenth-century diary, I brought her up to date on Declan's progress as of Friday and shared the broader outline of my day with Julian, omitting, of course, the details of how it ended. I made no reference to the roses. As soon as I could, I brought the conversation around to the skunk episode.

The whole day felt awkward, though. The two of us had met Julian at Café Algiers with Sam, both of us single women with an interest in antique books, and Julian had called me. Twice, no less. It was Sylvia's work with Finny that had brought him into our orbit in the first place, and yet he hadn't invited her to get together. Also, I was now way more involved with the Winslow family than she was—I was working to help John Grady, I had been out to the Berkshires to Esther's house, and I was presently awaiting a call from Josie. I felt really torn. Part of me longed to make a clean breast of things, spilling all the details of my encounter with the butler's ghost and everything that had resulted from that.

But another part of me, the stronger part, it seemed, was continuing to hold back. I wasn't sure why. I hoped I'd understand it soon.

The monks paid us a visit at about three thirty. They said nothing at first, but their whole demeanor screamed, *Well?*

"I haven't heard back yet," I said.

The abbot's thoughts flew past me. It was something about an excuse and an apron.

"Pardon me?" I said.

The Irish rushed by again. This time I caught it.

Is gaire do bhean leithscéal ná a naprún.

"An excuse is nearer to a woman than her apron."

I took a deep breath as some possible retorts raced through my mind. Did they think I had nothing else to do but worry about their book? Wasn't it generally considered polite to give a person who was doing you a favor—a monsignor, no less!—a couple of days to get back to you before you started hounding him for results? Hadn't they heard a word he'd said when he scolded them about the way they were treating me? And anyway, just what century did they think this was, *the eleventh*?

It was the look on the young monk's face that made me pause, that and his helpless shrug and the wry little smile that tugged at the corners of his mouth. His thoughts reached me loudly and clearly: *You think you've got it rough? Imagine putting up with him for hundreds of years!*

"I was planning to call Monsignor Dolan," I said quietly. "I just wanted to give him the weekend."

"It's Monday," the abbot said, punctuating this pushy observation with an upward thrust of his chin.

"I'm aware of that," I answered. "Look, I'm doing my level best here. If you could just find it in your heart to drop this sexist—"

I stopped myself. I was as frustrated as they were, and worn out from the weekend, but losing my temper with these guys wasn't going to help. I took a deep breath, thinking they probably had no concept of what the word *sexist* meant, anyway.

"I'm sorry," I said. "Forgive me."

"Forgiveness may be extended on behalf of Our Heavenly Father," the abbot pontificated, "but a sin is only forgiven if the sinner is truly penitent."

"Yes," I said, struggling not to rise to the bait. "I know. I made my First Communion. And my Confirmation."

"And now?" he sneered.

"*Now,* I'm preparing my son to make *his,*" I shot back. This was stretching the truth a bit. First of all, Henry wasn't going to make his First Communion for two more years. Second, one of the great advantages of sending a kid to Catholic school was that the teachers did all the heavy lifting as regarded religious instruction. According to one of the third-grade moms, all I would have to do would be to show up at a couple of meetings and buy my child a white suit.

In any case, I thought I was practicing remarkable self-control, especially given the fact that Sylvia was no help at all. She seemed unable to make a peep.

"All right," I said calmly. "I know I'm just a regular person and I'm sure you didn't have much to do with people like me back in your monastery in Ireland. So I understand how difficult this is. But we do have one thing in common: we both care an awful lot about your book."

I couldn't tell whether this was getting through to them, because at that moment, the abbot began to pace. Since they hadn't disappeared, though, I forged right ahead.

"This woman here, you have no idea what she's been through trying to look out for your manuscript." Sylvia didn't seem to enjoy having the attention drawn to her; she shook her head anxiously and took a step back toward the wall. "It could very well have fallen into the wrong hands, and she's risked her job, if not her entire career, to protect—"

The abbot wheeled furiously around and bellowed, "*Protect?* You call that protecting?"

I glanced at Sylvia. She looked almost as pale as the two robed figures hovering opposite us.

"Leaving that glorious treasure lying right there on the shelf," the abbot went on, "to be sliced up and carted off like so many pieces of—"

A shiver ran through me. "What do you mean, *sliced up?*"

The younger monk nodded furiously, and said, "Cut out the pages with a—"

"A knife!" interrupted his superior.

"Who?" Sylvia whispered. "When?"

"And now it's gone," the abbot said slowly. "And for that, we have yourself to thank."

Sylvia shrunk before his gaze.

"Now, hold on right there!" I said, rising to Sylvia's defense. There was no point in uttering another word, though, because he faded before our eyes.

The younger monk hesitated just a moment longer. "A flint, it was," he whispered. "A flint was the instrument used."

Josie Winslow lived in Cambridge, in a carriage house tucked away behind one of the mansions on Brattle Street. Brattle is one of the prettiest streets I have ever seen, and in Cambridge, it's one of the quietest. Citing the area's architectural and historical significance—during the Revolution, George Washington made it his base of operations, after terrified Loyalists abandoned their homes—the residents have succeeded in banning commercial truck traffic from their street, thus forcing the noise and the fumes and the general inconvenience onto their less significant neighbors.

But as I walked to Josie's house in the afternoon, I noticed no shortage of large vehicles in the neighborhood. On one stretch of hill linking Huron and Brattle, construction vans lined both sides of the street, the vehicles of landscapers and contractors and masons and roofers and plasterers all apparently readying a house the size of a small hospital for human habitation. I wondered how many people were going to be moving in there. Maybe there was an Olympic-size pool in the basement.

As I turned down the lane that led to Josie's house, though, I saw none of the excess in evidence a few streets away. The modest carriage house, brick and shingle and surrounded by bushes of rosy hydrangeas, reminded me a little of Esther's place in the Berkshires. I wondered what combination of familial or marital forces had turned Tad toward the aesthetic of the single pear and Josie and Esther toward houses like those in which Goldilocks ate the bears' porridge and slept in their beds.

The Lexus SUV with the "COEXIST" bumper sticker was parked on the flagstone driveway. I paused for a moment before lifting the brass knocker, remembering with a chill the shrieking and smashing that had frozen my feet to their spots on the Winslow home's landing just over a week ago. Josie had been nice enough, if a little cool, when she phoned to let me know that she had found the book, and with it, the deed. But as I heard the sound of her footsteps approaching, I fought my urge to cut and run. She opened the door slowly.

"Anza?"

I nodded, surprised into silence by the sight of the slender, calm figure damply glowing in her exercise clothes. Could this really be the same person I'd encountered last week?

"Come in," she said.

"Thanks." I stepped inside. There was no hallway in her residence, so I found myself in an expansive room that apparently served for cooking, dining, and sitting in front of the fireplace. It felt vaguely Southwestern; I noticed Navajo blankets and smooth stones in clay bowls and the startling, bleached skulls of a couple of former desert dwellers. The place seemed peaceful and uncluttered and smelled of eucalyptus, or menthol, or one of those medicinal oils you always smell in spas. Her bedroom had to be somewhere else, probably up where they used to store hay. I'd have bet there was also a room up there devoted to yoga and meditation.

"Can I get you some tea?" she offered.

Bitter, watery tea, tea made of boiled twigs, came to mind.

"No, thank you," I said. "I just had a coffee."

She steered me over to one of the chairs by the fireplace, then fetched a book off the dining table. I thought she might hang onto it until I had answered a hundred questions or so, but she handed it right over. She seemed expectant, like a child waiting to be told a story. I glanced down at the book.

Sure enough, there was the cover that Esther had described: children playing ring-around-the-rosy and butterflies fluttering around an apple tree. The youngsters were appealingly old-fashioned, all wearing little leather shoes, the girls in smocked dresses that tied behind their waists and the boys in short pants held up by suspenders. They were all apple-cheeked and flaxen-haired, healthy, outdoorsy Anglo-Saxons working up hearty appetites in the autumn air.

"He'll be so happy," I said, opening the yellowed envelope I had found tucked inside. This explained why the deed had escaped notice for so long: folded into thirds and again in half, the envelope was smaller than a page of the book. I skimmed it quickly, resolving to read it later. Apart from the offer of tea, Josie had yet to utter a word, so I guessed she was waiting for some kind of explanation.

"I was at your house," I began. "The house on Comm. Ave., I mean."

She frowned. "Doing what?"

"I'm a bookbinder. I work with Sylvia Cremaldi. Your brother had some books he wanted appraised and he asked her to stop by. We were walking that way together."

She was nodding, so I paused.

"My sister tells me you're a psychic," she said.

"Depends how you define *psychic*."

"How do *you* define it?" she asked, sitting down on the couch and pulling her legs up under her.

I cleared my throat. "It's one of those words that means different things to different people."

"Can you read minds?"

"Live people's minds? No."

"See into the future?"

"Nope."

"Can you communicate with people in . . . the afterlife? Heaven?"

She certainly was direct. I shook my head and began my usual explanation. "You know when people have a near-death experience and afterward, they talk about seeing the white light?"

"I've seen it."

"You *have*?" I said. This might not be as hard as I thought.

"I was in a car accident when I was nineteen." Josie pulled up her tank top to reveal a long, jagged scar across her torso. "I had a Jeep convertible and I flipped it, up near Plover's Beach on the North Shore. When they got my heart started again, I didn't want to come back. Wherever I was being drawn to, it was so beautiful and peaceful."

"That's what everyone says."

"It's true. So I have a hard time imagining why anyone who felt what I felt wouldn't just give in to it. It's not that I wanted to die—I didn't! I was nineteen years old! But when it happened, I *wanted* to be released by life. I just wasn't strong enough to fight the forces pulling me back."

"Nor are they."

"The people you talk to? The ghosts?"

"Yeah. It's not always a doctor in an emergency room holding them here, though. Sometimes it's a person or a place or even an object they love too much to leave."

Josie didn't respond. She seemed to be staring at the pattern in her rug. Since I didn't really want to get into a more personal conversation, it seemed smartest to change the subject to the ghost in question.

"I don't have the whole story, but from what I understand, Mr. and Mrs. Grady—"

"John and Mairead."

"Yeah. I guess they must have saved enough money to buy a little cottage in Wales."

"Well, they didn't have many living expenses," Josie said. "They were basically part of the family, and I think my mother's parents had set something up."

"He mentioned some arrangement."

"But why Wales?" Josie asked. "I don't remember them ever going there. To tell you the truth, I don't remember them ever taking any time off. I do know they took my mother to Wales when she was little, during the war."

"Your mother and Gwennie."

"Who's Gwennie?"

I hesitated. "Uh, their little girl."

Josie shook her head. "No, they never had any children."

"I think they did."

"No, no way. I'm absolutely sure about that."

I didn't enjoy challenging Josie's knowledge of the people she'd lived with all her life, but the strangeness of the situation called for some measure of honesty.

"He told me," I said gently, "that they'd had a daughter named Gwennie. He said that she and your mother were like sisters. I don't know what happened, but I have a hunch she might have died while they were there."

Josie appeared to struggle for words. "In Wales?"

I nodded.

"But Mummy—they—never mentioned anything. A little girl? Oh, my God. How old would she have been?"

"Five, maybe six. My guess is that the house is somehow connected in his mind with his daughter, and he doesn't feel he can leave this world until—"

"Until what?"

Here, I was stumped. It's not as though he was going to be going on any vacations. What use was a house to him?

"I don't know," I answered. "I really have no idea. All I know is, this is why he's still here."

Josie stood up, walked to the fireplace, and took a smooth black stone off the mantel. As though to calm herself, she rubbed it between her palms, breathing long, deep breaths. Before she could speak again, we heard the squeal of tires as a car took a nearby corner way too fast. Whoever was driving it roared up to the house, killed the engine, and slammed the car door.

Josie walked to the window and peered out.

"Shit," she said.

I didn't have time to ask her what was wrong before the door flew open and revealed the presence of one enraged human being: Tad. Back, apparently, from London.

⸺

"What are *you* doing here?" he immediately shouted, slamming the door behind himself and glaring at me.

I glanced from Tad to Josie, but before I could speak, she stepped between us. "She's my guest, Tad. And this is my house."

"The hell it is," he said viciously. "It's not yours until it's paid for, and it won't be paid for until I release the freeze I've ordered on all your accounts."

"You can't do that!" she said.

"I can't? Watch me."

He walked over to the fridge, opened it, and pulled out a beer. He didn't offer me one. I definitely would have accepted.

"You're damn lucky I don't have you arrested for breaking and entering."

"I'd like to see you try," Josie shot back.

I had to hand it to her. The girl didn't back down.

"Would you?" Tad said. "Would you really? Better be careful what you wish for."

"Daddy's house is as much mine as it is yours," she said.

"That may be true in the long run," Tad said, "but at the moment, it's not. Right now, Esther and I are the only people authorized to have keys, as you'd be aware if you'd taken the time to read the letter I sent you!"

I glanced around, looking for a back door.

"Why should I read your ridiculous, condescending letter?" Josie sputtered. "Why should I give a shit about what you have to say?"

"Because I happen to hold the purse strings right now. So unless you've recently won the lottery or maybe started to look for a job—for the first time in a very long time—you might want to think twice about destroying valuable private property."

Tad took a long draught of beer and glanced over at me. I sensed that he was about to turn his fury in my direction, but Josie jumped back in.

"And what did you destroy, Tad? Answer me that! Did I ever express interest in a single thing of Mummy and Daddy's?"

"Besides the money," he said coolly.

"Fuck you! You knew that *The Wyndemere* was only thing I cared about having, and you didn't even have the courtesy to let me know what you were doing."

"I didn't need your permission, Jo." He paused for a moment, as though questioning the wisdom of taking things further, but he decided to go ahead.

"I did what Father asked me to do."

This startled Josie into silence. She glared at her brother for a few moments, blinking rapidly, as though someone was shining a flashlight in her eyes, then she went over and sat down in a wooden rocker. She pulled her knees up to her chest, wrapped herself into a gangly knot—a position that would be excruciating to any person who didn't do yoga—and buried her face in her knees. She got the chair rocking.

Tad got up, flipped through some mail and magazines on a table, and took off his jacket. He threw it on the couch.

Josie whispered something.

"What?" he said.

She didn't answer.

"I didn't hear what you said, Josie," he insisted.

She looked up. "He asked you to?"

Tad let out a sigh and threw a look in my direction. "This is neither the time nor the place."

Meaning, I guessed, in front of me.

"That's okay," I said, sensing my opportunity and hopping up. "I have to get going."

"No!" he said firmly. "If you wouldn't mind, I would really like an explanation."

His words were like a heavy hand on my shoulder.

"Of what?" I asked, stalling for time, sinking slowly back into my seat.

"Of why you seem to be . . . right *there*, every time I turn around!"

I glanced over at Josie, half hoping she was secretly revving up for the kind of tornado I knew she had in her, but she was in another world. I was on my own with Tad.

I took a deep breath. "You want the long version or the short?" I asked.

"Short," he said curtly.

"Okay. This may sound a little strange, but I have the ability to see ghosts. And talk to them. I always could, from the time I was a little girl. When I was at your house that day, I was able to talk to the ghost of your family's butler."

"John?" Tad asked.

"He was in the upstairs hall when I went to use the—"

The word *toity* popped into my mind. I don't know where it came from, I hadn't heard it used since my great-aunt Kathleen went to her heavenly reward, but I was able to catch myself.

"Ladies' room," I went on.

"*Right,*" he said, skepticism in his eyes.

"Okay," I responded. It was really fun to do what I was about to do. It just tickled me to be able to wipe the smirk off the face of an ignorant, obnoxious blowhard. I sallied forth.

"Esther had an imaginary playmate named Millie, and you liked to read Hardy Boys books. You used to pretend you were Frank and make one of your sisters be Joe."

At this, Josie perked up. "You did!" she said.

"You broke your ankle at sleepaway camp. They asked you what color cast you wanted, and you said red. You and Esther had chicken pox at the same time, but Josie never got them. You wanted to change your name when you were little; you asked everyone to start calling you Tom. And you loved skeleton keys. Mr. Grady gathered up a whole bunch of them and put them on a ring for you, and you took them everywhere you went."

I paused. Tad didn't speak for a moment or two. I was gratified to notice that his mouth was hanging open, and tiny beads of perspiration were appearing on his temples.

"But . . . how did you . . . ?" he eventually managed to say.

"I told you. I spent time with him." I didn't add that much of this time was spent after I had, shall we say, gained unlawful entry into his family's former home. During the hour in which Johnny and I had sifted through the last of the family's books, the ghost had kept up a running commentary filled with nuggets of family history triggered by the volumes I held in my hands.

But it was a good thing Tad was coming around. I'd all but reached the limits of what I knew about his childhood.

"Should I go on?" I asked.

"No, no," he said. "I'm not saying I believe you about Woolsie."

"Woolsie?" I asked.

"That's what we used to call him. On his days off, he always wore a sweater vest."

"And socks Maimie knit him," Josie said.

"Yes," said Tad. "But I still don't know why you're here."

So I told him about *The Butterfly's Ball* and the deed and the journey out to Esther's and her phone call to Josie.

"I remember this," he said as I handed him the book. He silently flipped through it, pausing at various pages. He pulled the deed out of its envelope, and as he read the text on the yellowed page, I was suddenly overtaken by a fear that he might just fold it up, put it in his pocket, pick up his keys, and go. *Then* what would I do?

But he didn't. He put the deed back into its envelope, tucked the envelope into the book, and handed the book to me.

"What do you plan to do with it?" he asked.

I shrugged. "Bring it over to him, I guess."

"And how were you planning to get into the house?" he asked.

I answered honestly. "I didn't have a plan."

Tad seemed to mull this over. "I can meet you there. I can let you in. But under one condition."

"What's that?"

"I want to be there when you give it to him."

"Sure," I said. "Esther asked me, too."

"Me too," said Josie. "Can I come?"

"It's your house. You can all come."

"Will I be able to see him?" Josie asked.

I shook my head. "You can talk to him, though. And I can tell you what he says."

Tad let out a long, deep breath. "This is really, really strange."

I shrugged. I was a little unnerved at how he was staring at me. Finally he spoke.

"So answer me something: what's in this for you?"

"What do you mean?"

"I mean," he said, "what do you get out of this?"

"I don't get anything."

"Oh, cut the crap," he said. "You expect me to believe that you're not working some kind of angle on this thing?"

I scrutinized his features. Finny had been right not to trust him with the manuscript. Tad was an operator, through and through.

"I'm not," I said. "I have gotten paid before, plenty of times, but I'm not getting paid for this. I'm just . . . trying to help."

The look on his face said he didn't really believe me, but he wasn't going to say any more.

I glanced at my watch. Henry would be standing on the steps of the school. The rest of the kids would be gone by now, and one of the teachers would be waiting there with him, annoyed by the fact that yet again, a preoccupied parent had lost track of the time.

"Oh my God," I said. "I really have to go."

As I gathered up my things, Tad asked, "So when are we going to do this?"

"Any time," I said.

"Don't you work?" he asked.

I felt like asking him the same question. "Yes," I said pointedly, "but I have a flexible schedule. Why don't you find out when Esther can come and then call me."

Tad fished a BlackBerry out of his coat pocket.

"Let's make a tentative plan," he said, fooling around with the device. "How about this Friday?"

"Friday night could work," I said. "I drop my son off at his dad's at suppertime."

"All right. I'll call Esther and get back to you. What's your phone number?"

I recited it for him while I pulled on my coat. Though it was clear that I needed to leave, and soon, he seemed reluctant to end our conversation.

"So he's in the house," Tad said. "Woolsie is. Right now."

"Correct."

"Where does he—"

"Hang out? He can go anywhere he wants, but I met him in the upstairs hall."

"Could he hear me if I called out to him?"

"He could."

"Can he read my mind?"

"No."

"But he could hear me," Tad said, "if I talked to him."

"He could hear you," I answered quietly, "if you talked to him."

Chapter Twenty-One

Declan called at about ten. I knew it was Dec because no one else ever calls me at that hour. I also know that some people get anxious with late-night phone calls, assuming the caller will have terrible news, but neither Dad nor Nona believes in delivering bad tidings at night. The phone ringing at seven in the morning is what gets *my* heart thumping.

"You still up?" he asked.

"Barely," I answered. I'd been flipping TV channels, but nothing had drawn me in. I'd been trying to decide between making cinnamon toast, conducting a thorough search for my favorite silver earring, which was lost, but was definitely in the house someplace, or getting all the recycling and trash outside so I wouldn't have to deal with it in the morning.

"How are you?" I asked.

"How are *you*?" he said. "Helluva weekend, huh?"

"Yeah. I felt bad for the kids."

"Oh, they loved the drama. Nell couldn't stop talking about Max and the campfire and the pumpkins and all the play clothes up in the attic."

"Really?"

"Really."

"Well, I'm glad. I know they were disappointed about the Children's Museum."

"It's not going anywhere," Dec said. "So listen, we've got something unfolding here."

"What?" I sat up.

"Might turn out to be good luck for us after all that Scully was sprung. He can do more for us on the street than he could from a cell."

"Yeah, if he still feels like cooperating," I said.

"Oh, he's on the case, you bet your life he is. Before he left, I put the fear of God into him—I'd dug up some old parole violations and spoken to a guy up in Hamilton, a retired cop in his seventies who just can't seem to leave a couple of old cases behind. And a new one, come to that."

"What kind of cases?"

"What kind do you think?"

"Paintings?"

"You got it. Guy's name's Mullen, and he hasn't a doubt in the world that Scully had a hand in a theft from the Biggs Gallery, up there at Danforth Academy."

"When was this?"

"Six or eight months ago. They've shut the place down for a big renovation, moved a lot of stuff into storage, and somehow, during the move, one of the crates went missing."

I wasn't really following. "How does that help us?"

"Well, Scully may be a luckless bastard, but he's no fool—he knows he's got some things coming at him, down the pike. Especially if Mullen ties him to this Andover heist; with everything else Scully's already on the hook for, poor sod'll be collecting Social

Security by the time he gets out. So he went to work for us over the weekend."

"You're kidding."

"Nope. He called half a dozen people from here down to Florida, people he knew had dealings with Van Vleck. Sure enough, Van Vleck's on his way to Nantucket."

"Does he have the book?"

"He does."

"Oh my God! Why's he going to Nantucket?"

"To meet whoever commissioned the theft. They've got the use of somebody's vacation house for the weekend."

"You're kidding!"

"Serious as hell, darlin'."

"So how do we find him?"

"We?"

"You, me—I don't know! I'd like to help."

Dec laughed. "I don't know what I'm doing yet."

"Well, when you do know. Please?"

"We'll see."

"*Dec!*"

"We'll see! These guys play for keeps, sweetheart. I'm not putting you or anyone else in harm's way."

I loved it when he said things like that.

"Isn't there anything I can do?" I pleaded.

"Yeah. Convince Sylvia to file a report. It's a hell of a lot easier when you don't have to be sneaking around. Remind me again why this all has to be so hush-hush?"

"I told you."

"Tell me again."

"There are lots of reasons." I paused. I had been coming to my own theory, though, and it had nothing to do with Tad or the

Athenaeum or Sylvia's being afraid of getting fired or drummed out of the profession for questionable conduct.

"Because I'm not really buying it," Dec went on. "All that clatter about art history and the barbarian son."

This is why Dec is a great detective. I had to smile.

"So any time you want to let me in on the real story . . . ," he said.

"I think—she thinks—that *is* the real story," I said.

"And you've got a brain in your head," Dec said. "What do you think?"

"It's just a theory," I answered.

"That's where it starts."

"It's not even a theory. It's barely a hunch." I paused.

There was silence on the other end.

"I'm all ears," he finally said.

I took a deep breath. "Okay." I felt kind of disloyal to Sylvia, but Dec was really out on a limb here. And after all, he was the father of my son.

"I think she couldn't bear to part with it. She couldn't let anyone have it, not Tad and not the museum, because it was something she and Finny had shared, something beautiful and meaningful that belonged to just the two of them."

Declan didn't comment. He was still listening.

"And?" he finally said.

"And," I said, "I think she was in love with him. And he wasn't in love with her. He probably didn't even know how she felt."

"What makes you say that?"

"Because if he had been—in love with her, I mean—he might have left her the book. He would have trusted her to pass it on if the time came."

"Bingo," replied Dec.

Father Fran came through on Tuesday. Not only did he come through, he came through big: with an auxiliary bishop. The Boston area is big enough, and Catholic enough, that the cardinal can't do everything the top man of the Church is expected to do, so there are five bishops appointed to help him out, one for each of the regions into which the Archdiocese of Boston is divided.

The one who had agreed to come and help us, who was assigned to the area northeast of Boston, was named Bishop Soares. I am not a good enough Catholic to have heard of him—I don't read the Catholic paper or keep up on church events—but Father Fran assured me that he knew Soares pretty well; they'd served together on something called the "Migrants and Refugees Subcommittee."

"How'd you convince him to help us?"

"It didn't take much. He's had a couple of encounters himself."

"With ghosts?"

"Not exactly," Father Fran said. "But he leads meditation retreats and pilgrimages to Laus and Avila, so he's no stranger to the mystical experience. I had a hunch he might be open to this, and he was."

"Gosh, thanks so much," I said.

"Anytime."

"Should I call him?"

"He's coming into town on Wednesday."

"Wednesday, as in tomorrow Wednesday?"

"He'll be in meetings at the Chancery all day, but he said he could stop by to see you before he heads back up to Gloucester."

"That'd be fantastic," I said. "Should I call his office?"

"I'll put you on hold and have Rosemary pick up. She'll give you the number."

"All right. Great. Oh, and one more thing."

"Shoot."

"What's the protocol? For when he comes?"

"Don't worry about it," said Father Fran.

The stress was taking a toll on Sylvia. I doubted she'd ever been hale and hearty, but the circles were darkening under her eyes and her collarbones, and the bones in her face appeared sharp and angular. She was starting to look like someone who lived on Cream of Wheat.

"I can't sleep," she confessed. "I keep thinking of . . . that *person* being in my bedroom. And that incredible manuscript being God knows where."

"Is there someone you could talk to?"

"Who?" Sylvia demanded. "There's a therapist I used to go to, but I haven't seen her in a couple of years. It would take me forever just to *explain* everything. Besides, you think she's going to believe that I've been hobnobbing with ghosts?"

She had a point. In the psychiatric manual on which psychologists relied, "seeing ghosts" could get you diagnosed as anywhere on the spectrum between delusional and psychotic.

"What about Sam?" I asked. "At least he knows about the book."

"Maybe," she said, in a tone that made me doubt she was going to call him.

Thinking of Sam made me remember Julian and the roses. I hadn't called him yet to thank him. Nor had I figured out what to say.

"If it would make you feel better to tell Sam the whole story, I could go with you." I paused. "At least then you'd have someone you could talk to."

She shrugged.

"Or ask him to come by," I urged her. "Nobody's here but us. You know how he loves to come visit."

"Maybe," she said, looking slightly more hopeful. Involving me would take the pressure off her; she wouldn't be the one claiming the ability to speak with ghosts. I would.

"Call him," I said. "I really think you should."

"Maybe," she said again.

The wedding of *Q* and *U*, I learned that evening, was happening next week.

"Next *week!*" I said. Had that invitation come? Had I missed it? I didn't think so.

"Yeah," Henry replied. "Wednesday. I signed you up for cupcakes."

"Oh. Okay. How many?"

"Lots!"

"Lots like—what? A dozen?"

"How many is that?" he asked.

"Twelve."

He shook his head. "More."

"Two dozen? Twenty-four?"

"*Way* more. It's in the *cafeteria*, Mama."

As Henry used the back of his spoon to create a volcano top in his mountain of mashed potatoes, I tried to figure out what relevance this fact had to the number of cupcakes I was now expected to bake. He reached for the gravy and poured it into the crevice, continuing to pour until the lava had swamped Pompeii.

"That's enough," I said, a little too sharply. I took the pitcher out of his hand.

He glanced up quickly. Even I was surprised at how harsh

my tone had been. I wasn't really angry about the gravy. I knew he loved gravy. I was feeling just a little annoyed that he hadn't checked with me before he volunteered me for "lots" of cupcakes.

Of course I could always buy them. But that would be cheating.

"Are other people bringing food?" I asked.

"Yup." He began to stir the gravy into his potatoes.

"And there's a cake, right?"

"I *told* you." He maneuvered a massive pile of brown mush toward his mouth. I helped myself to a slice of meat loaf and attempted to spoon some carrots onto his plate.

"No!" he shouted, pulling his plate away. Because his mouth was full of gravy and mashed potato, the sound came out like "Moo!"

"Five bites. You know that's the rule."

He shoved his bread plate my way, and I realized he had no objection to carrots. He objected to carrots mixed in with the mush.

"I'm sure there'll be plenty of desserts," I said. Judging from the cookies and doughnuts brought in to celebrate every conceivable occasion, and lots of nonoccasions, I could already envision the buckets of Dunkin' Donuts Munchkins and plastic trays of muffins and scones.

"We have to have enough," he finally managed to say.

"For everybody? Not everyone's going to eat a cupcake, honey."

"But what if they want one and they're all gone?"

"Then they can have a piece of cake."

"No! We need to have enough!"

"And how many people are you expecting at this shindig?"

"It's not a shindig," he said, looking hurt. "It's a wedding!"

"This wedding," I conceded.

"Maybe like a hundred. Or two hundred."

"Two *hundred*?"

"Miss O. said we could invite anybody we wanted."

"Well yeah, but how many people did you invite? Just one—me."

"No. I invited Daddy and Nat."

"You did? When?"

"When they were here. They said they would come. And Kelly and Nell and Delia, too, cause Dee-Dee's starting kindergarten and Nell might come to pre-K. And Ellie. And Max."

"You asked all those people?" I said. "And they all said yes?"

He nodded and speared a carrot. "I want to in—"

"Don't talk with your mouth full."

He finished the carrot. "Can we call Pop?" he asked. "I want Pop to come."

My irritation about the cupcakes had turned to amusement, and I found myself feeling surprisingly touched. He was doing all right, Henry was. He knew I would have said yes to the cupcakes, to as many cupcakes as he needed me to provide. He didn't have to check with me, any more than he needed my permission to try to round up all the other people whose love he took for granted.

"We can call Pop," I said.

I watched Henry finish the rest of his potatoes and start in on the carrots and meat loaf.

"And I'll talk to Miss O.," I promised him. "I'll make sure we have enough."

He smiled, sat back, wiped his mouth, and let out a long, contented sigh.

"Thanks, Mama," he said.

We called my father at about eight thirty and were off the phone within minutes. He doesn't like to talk on the phone. He's never really shaken a lesson he must have learned very early in life, at a time when long-distance calls were wildly expensive and reserved for the brisk communication of important facts. Dad likes to get right to the point, take care of whatever needs taking care of, and get off.

"*Who's* getting married?" he asked, after Henry had handed me the phone.

"It's not a real wedding," I said. "It's a party at his school. But he's excited about it."

"Okay," my father said.

"Okay what?"

"Okay, I'll come."

"But it's next Wednesday, Dad."

"What of it? I haven't got anything better to do. I'll take the train."

"Wow! Well, great! That's fantastic."

My father had only been to Boston once, just after I gave birth to Henry. The trip had been hard for him, every part of it— meeting Declan, seeing me all blotchy and teary, accepting the fact that his only daughter was going to be raising a child on her own, hundreds of miles away from any help he and Nona might have been able to give me. He never came back. Then again, I never asked him. Maybe all I had to do was ask.

"I'll call you when I know the schedule," he said.

"We'll come pick you up. You can stay here."

Eavesdropping, Henry shouted, "For as long as he wants." And then, because I didn't cut my dad off to deliver Henry's message immediately, Henry grabbed the phone right out of my hand.

"For as long as you want, Pop," he said. "You can sleep in my bed."

He paused as my father said something I couldn't hear.

"I don't think so," Henry said earnestly.

I had been about to scold him for snatching the phone so rudely, but as I listened to him talk, and watched the smile that was spreading across his face, I bit my tongue.

"I don't think I do," he said seriously. He turned to me. "Mama, do I have stinky feet?"

"He's teasing you, honey."

Henry smiled and nodded.

"Okay," he said quietly. "Okay. Okay, Pop. I love you."

And then, abruptly, he hung up.

"I knew he'd come," Henry said.

Next, we called Nona, but as we waited for her to pick up, I wished I had thought about this a little more before dialing her number. Things could get complicated. While it would be great to have her here for a visit sometime, this was not the time. This was the time for Henry and Dad to connect.

Fortunately, voice mail picked up. For a moment, though, I wasn't sure it was hers. She used to rely on the impersonal, prerecorded message from the phone company, but now her greeting was warm and friendly and was prefaced by a snippet of . . . *waltz* music?

"Hi, Nona," I said. "It's me—and Henry. Just calling to say hi. Hope all's well. Maybe you're out."

"Tell her!" Henry demanded.

I ignored him. "Everything's fine here," I went on.

"Tell her!" he shouted. "Ask her!"

I shot him a stern glance and finished leaving the message. "We'll try you again tomorrow. Lots of love. Okay, bye."

I hung up.

"You didn't ask her!" he shouted, all revved up with urgent excitement. "Call her back!"

"Now wait just a minute, mister!" I said. "You don't grab the phone out of a person's hands and you don't scream at somebody when they're leaving a message!"

"You didn't tell her!" he said angrily.

I took a deep breath and delivered my threat coolly.

"Do not talk back to me, or I'm going to call Pop back, right this minute, and tell him not to come."

"No!" Henry shouted. "You can't!"

"I can, too, Mr. Smart Mouth, and I will, unless you sit right down and listen to me."

He turned away, stubborn. "You're mean," he said.

I let it go.

"Look," I said. "I know you're excited about this, but I'm not sure we're going to invite Nona."

"Why not?" he said, pouting.

"Because I want it to be special. For Pop. And you. Okay? Kind of like boys' time."

He turned around and looked at me.

"If Nona's here, I'm not saying it won't be really nice, but it'll be—different. I think Pop would have more fun with just you and you'd have more fun with just Pop."

"But she might be sad," Henry said.

Suddenly, I knew where all of this was coming from. Late in the summer, Henry had found out that a birthday party had taken place for one of his friends from nursery school and he hadn't been invited. Though it hadn't been a *real* party—it was a low-key trip to the aquarium for a total of four kids, including the birthday boy's younger sister—Henry had been crushed.

I had alternately wanted to murder both the parents and the boy and to cheer for the levelheaded grown-ups, who had opted not to engage a circus troupe or rent the use of a hotel pool for a five-year-old's birthday party. But Henry felt only one emotion: despair.

"We'll pick another time for Nona to come," I said.

He slumped onto the couch. This was complicated business. He'd no sooner learned how to put himself in the place of a person who was being left out than a new and more intricate set of social considerations was presenting itself to be learned.

"Maybe my birthday," he said.

Chapter Twenty-Two

Our first order of business was to make sure that no one surprised us in the bindery while Bishop Soares was meeting with the monks. I had spoken with the bishop's assistant, Father Quinn, during their lunch break at the chancery. He and the bishop would be arriving at the Athenaeum at about five fifteen. While most of the library's employees would be heading home by then, and few had reason to come down to the bindery anyway, I thought we should play it safe. I suggested that Father Quinn park in the garage beneath the Boston Common and told him I would come and escort him and the bishop to the library. I planned to bring them in through the back entrance.

"Let's put a sign on the bindery door," I said to Sylvia.

"Saying what?" Sylvia asked. "Nobody ever comes down here." Then a rueful smile appeared on her face. Someone certainly had come down here. According to the monks, someone had been using a "flint"—whatever the heck that was—to destroy the book we thought no one even knew about.

"Warning!" I dictated, as Sylvia grabbed a pen and paper. "The bindery of the Boston Athenaeum will be off-limits to all staff members today between the hours of five and . . . seven?"

"Let's say eight," Sylvia said. "In case they're late."

They had better not be, I thought. I had arranged for Henry to go home from after-school with his friend Calvin, and to have supper at Calvin's house, but I had to pick him up by eight o'clock.

I proceeded to dictate the rest of the notice. I gravely exaggerated the risks associated with inhaling the fumes of hot paraffin wax, *significant* amounts of which, I said, were going to be in use in the bindery between five and eight.

While it's true that inhaling these fumes is a little like breathing in diesel exhaust, and that daily, prolonged exposure can wreak havoc on the respiratory system of people with asthma and allergies, the amount of wax that's actually used in bookbinding is small. Anyway, we weren't using it.

We sent out the e-mail notice, then put a huge, scary sign on the door. Then, when five o'clock approached, we'd lock the door from the inside. For good measure, we might even find a can of the smelliest substance on the premises and leave it just inside the door. With the top off.

The only thing we hadn't anticipated was a surprise visit from Sam, who arrived unannounced at five minutes of five. I glanced over at Sylvia, who shrugged helplessly. I could hardly blame her. I was the one who had urged her to call him. She obviously had. And here he was, happy as a clam to have been invited to drop by for a visit. The timing could not have been worse, but what could we do?

"Come in," Sylvia said, as I hurried to close the door behind him.

"What are you doing with paraffin?" he asked.

The look I shot her said, *Be my guest.*

The look she shot back said, *No. You!*

I let out a sigh.

He glanced back and forth between Sylvia and me. I must have looked as hangdog as she did, because after a minute, Sam said, "Would someone please tell me what's going on?"

I took a deep breath. "Sam, can I ask you something?" I rolled a chair toward him.

"Yeeessss . . ."

"Do you believe in ghosts?"

"No," he said confidently. "Definitely not."

I glanced at the clock. Four fifty-eight. There were several ways to do this, but given the fact that I had to leave in a couple of minutes to meet Father Quinn and Bishop Soares, I opted to be direct.

"Well, then, you might find the next hour a little . . . unsettling. Because in about fifteen minutes, I'm going to be back here with two, plus a bishop and a priest, and—"

I looked over at Sylvia. She was nodding.

"And the four of us—or five, if you stay—are going to have a . . . a visit."

Sam smiled, glancing from me to Sylvia and back.

"Aw, go on," he said.

I nodded. "I don't have time to explain now. I'll be happy to later, but you have to decide pretty soon if you want to stay or not."

"You're pulling my leg," Sam said.

"No, she isn't," Sylvia countered.

Sam's smile began to fade. "Is it like an . . . exorcism?"

Given my mention of a priest and a bishop, I supposed his question made a certain amount of sense. I shook my head.

"A séance?"

"Nope, just a regular old conversation."

"Between whom?" He gave me a tilted, suspicious look.

"Between . . . well, actually, it's between the bishop and the monks, but since the bishop won't be able to see them, I don't *think*, I'll speak for the monks. He's coming because they don't trust me."

"Who? The ghosts or the monks?" He shook his head and said, "I can't believe I'm asking that question."

"The ghosts *are* the monks," I said, pulling on my coat. "Or rather, the ghosts *were* monks."

"They're the monks who created the manuscript," Sylvia volunteered. "They've stayed with it through all these centuries. They know some things they'll only tell a bishop."

I could see Sam trying to add two and two, and continuing to come up with three. "But . . . the manuscript's not here," he said slowly. "Is it?"

Sylvia shook her head. "We hope they know something that might help us find it."

"Uh-huh," Sam said.

I glanced at the clock. Five after five. I had to leave. Now.

"So you're welcome to stay," I said, "if you want. But if you're not up for it, you can walk out with me."

Sam turned to Sylvia. "Are *you* staying?" he asked.

She nodded. "I can explain a little more while she's gone."

"Okay," Sam said, "I guess I'm in." And then he added, "Wow!"

<hr />

Father Quinn and Bishop Soares were standing beside a dusty green Subaru Legacy. I don't know what model of car I expected, but I certainly expected it to be black. Priests always drove black cars. A bishop's car, by rights, ought to have been really, really black.

I felt an unwelcome breeze of doubt blow into the underground garage. I knew that bishops who had been ordained as Jesuits sometimes continued to wear the robe of their order even after they were promoted, but the cleric who stood before me looked like the monk stirring the oversized vat on the label of Trappist jams. Could he really be a bishop? He seemed awfully . . . regular, an average man in his sixties with thinning gray hair. I wondered if maybe it was like returning as an adult to a room that loomed large in childhood, only to discover that everything about and within it seemed shrunken. I hoped he had some really convincing props in that bag he was carrying, in case the monks demanded proof of his ecclesiastical stature.

Father Quinn locked the car, but not before the ghost of a wan young woman had drifted out of the backseat. She looked sixteen or seventeen. Her long, curly hair hung in two thick braids, and she wore a flowered blouse with a little round collar and a jumper made of corduroy. The outfit appeared home-sewn. I didn't make eye contact with her, though. I already had enough on my plate.

"Thank you so much for coming," I said.

"Monsignor Dolan is a good man," said Bishop Soares. "When he asks me to go somewhere, I go." He spoke with a slight accent; he might have been Brazilian or Portuguese.

"It's a very valuable book," I said, "the book that's been stolen. We think it might be the Book of Kildare."

The bishop nodded slowly. Father Quinn didn't look too thrilled to be here; the mention of the manuscript barely seemed to register. "His Excellency has had a very long day," Father Quinn said, relieving the bishop of the satchel in his hand. "So if you'd be so kind as to lead the way."

In other words, Cut the chitchat, sister, and let's get this show on the road.

"It's only a couple of blocks," I said as we emerged from underground into the fading daylight.

Bishop Soares looked around, a smile spreading over his face as he took in the skateboarders and three-card monte hustlers and the rushing commuters envisioning the moment when they would be home, opening their doors to a wife, or a boyfriend, or a child, or a drink, or a long, lonely night in front of a glowing blue screen.

"Fall," Bishop Soares said, pausing on the edge of the common and drawing in a slow, deep breath. I paused, too, and the breath I drew was cold and edged with the wood smoke of the season's first fireplace fires, and there was the scent of coffee, good coffee, from No. 9 Park, and the odors of urine and fallen apples and pine mulch banked under the nearby bushes.

"It's beautiful," I said. He had quietly led me to a moment I would have missed, a moment in which I had stood absolutely still amid the beauty and bustle of the city in early evening and realized that I was alive, here, on earth, right this minute, as one season, in one of the finite number of years of my life, gave way to the next.

I no longer doubted that he was a bishop.

———— ⊷⊶ ————

I had to go looking for the monks. You would have thought, given that they had been waiting for nearly nine hundred years to have a conversation with a live cleric, that they would have been all over the afternoon's activities in the bindery. But no, they were nowhere to be seen. I found them in the first-floor reading room, hovering beside John Singer Sargent's portrait of Annie Adams Fields.

The young monk saw me first. "Herself is here, Father," I heard him whisper.

The abbot turned around. Fortunately, given the hour, there was no one in the room to observe me talking to the air.

"They're waiting for you," I said, trying to keep a exultant tone from creeping into my voice. "And they haven't got all day."

"Who?" snapped the abbot.

"His Excellency Bishop Esteban A. Soares, of the Diocese of Boston," I informed him coolly. "And a senior member of his staff."

"Where?" the abbot demanded.

"They're down in the bindery," I said.

As I probably could have predicted, the abbot was impatient and rude. Did he thank me for delivering what he had requested, or rather, *demanded*? Not a chance. Wasting not a fraction of a millisecond, he disappeared. The younger monk, on the other hand, gave me encouraging proof that some mothers, even those in twelfth-century Ireland, manage to impart impeccable manners to their sons. He floated across the room, then silently kept pace beside me as I made my way down the hall and then down the stairs. I had no doubt in my mind that if he could have, he would have held open the doors.

It had been lucky, after all, that Sam had shown up, because when we entered the bindery, he was entertaining our guests with a charming history of the Athenaeum, describing the eccentrics and artists and visionaries and kooks who had all played their parts in its history. I would have loved nothing better than to have sat down and listened, but Father Quinn greeted my arrival with a curt little nod and a glance at his watch. It would have been so much fun to watch him fly out of his chair, if he could have seen the abbot pacing furiously behind him. On a couple of occasions, the older monk had reminded me of Rumpelstiltskin, but today he made me think, with a giggle I could barely repress, of Yosemite Sam.

"Maybe we should start with a prayer," I suggested.

The bishop nodded. "Let us pray."

The two monks fell to their knees, fairly quivering with anticipation.

"May Almighty God have mercy on us," intoned Bishop Soares, "and guide our hearts and hands to the accomplishment of good, the appreciation of the day, and the adoration of God, our eternal Father in heaven. In the name of the Father, and of the Son, and of the Holy Spirit, amen."

"Amen," we all said, the Catholics among us also making the sign of the cross. The monks returned to a standing position, and everyone turned their attention to me.

I addressed the bishop and the priest. "Uh, I don't know how much Monsignor Dolan told you about . . . how he and I met."

"He told me enough," said the bishop.

"So there's nothing you'd like me to explain, before we start?" I asked.

"Ready to go," said the bishop.

Father Quinn couldn't resist a grumpy interjection. "You know, of course, the Church's official position on ghosts."

"I do. But once you've had an experience with an earthbound spirit—" I shrugged. "It's the Church's doctrine versus what you've seen with your own eyes."

I could tell he didn't like my answer. I wouldn't normally do what I was about to do, but we really didn't need ants at the picnic. I had to pick up Henry by eight.

I focused my attention on the spirit who had floated out of the car in the underground garage, and who had remained near Father Quinn ever since.

"Who are you?" I asked her.

"His sister," she answered.

"What's going on?" asked Father Quinn.

"What's your name?" I asked her.

"Kathryn Quinn," answered the ghost. "But everyone called me Kat."

I looked Father Quinn in the eye. "You had a sister named Kathryn. But she went by Kat."

The expression drained from his face. He glanced around nervously. "What are you . . . ?"

"Why are you here?" I asked her.

"Because he blames himself for the accident. We were hiking in New Hampshire, seven of us. We took some chances. But it wasn't his fault, what happened. If it was anyone's fault, it was mine."

It was kind of intense just to lay this on the poor fellow, here in public with everyone around, but I couldn't have him mucking up the works.

"She says it wasn't your fault, the hiking accident. She says that if it was anyone's fault, it was hers."

"Kat!" he cried, spinning around. "Kat? Are you here?"

"She's here," I said quietly. "If you like, we can have a conversation with her later, in private."

Instead of what I'd expected, a meek admission that there was something to my claim of being able to speak with spirits, the priest turned on me. "This is a trick," he said. "A cruel trick. I don't know where you dug up this—"

I glanced at the spirit of Kat. She understood that I needed help.

"Tell him that . . . say, 'Tickles toppled the tower!'" she said, smiling at the memory of what had to be a private joke.

I didn't have a clue as to what these words meant, but I did as she said.

Before our eyes, Father Quinn seemed to crumple into a much smaller and older version of himself. He closed his eyes and nodded.

I glanced around. The bishop wore a compassionate look of concern, and Sam looked panicky. Sylvia slid her chair over beside his and took his hand.

I sighed and glanced at Bishop Soares. "Should I go on?"

"Please," he said.

I took a deep breath. "We're in the presence of two monks. We think they died in Ireland in the twelfth century. We're pretty sure they created the book that was stolen, and we think that book was the Book of Kildare."

"You think," said Bishop Soares. "If you're able to speak to them, why don't you know for sure?"

"Because," I answered, "earthbound spirits are kind of stuck in the period of time in which they lived. And died. The monks are uncomfortable revealing information to me. They wanted to speak with a person from the Church."

"All right. So, here I am. Speak, dear friends!" Bishop Soares glanced around the room, but of course he couldn't see them. "Where are they?" he asked me.

"Over by that table," I said, indicating a table by the far wall.

Bishop Soares stood up and crossed the room. He held out his hands. "Speak, brothers," he said. The younger monk made a gesture of yielding to his superior; the abbot would speak for both of them.

I could tell that the old ghost hated to rely on me, being compelled to pause every sentence or two while I related his story to the people in the room, but we soon fell into a rhythm. Here is the story he told, just as he told it.

"Saint Brigid was my patroness; the monastery at the Church of the Oak—Cill-Dara—was our home. Welcomed the traveler did we, with 'a clean house, a big fire, and a couch without sorrow.'

Lived we by the words of our grace before meals, to us come down through the ages from our saint of saints:

> *A great lake of finest ale should we like*
> *For the King of Kings.*
> *A table of the choicest food should we like*
> *For the family of heaven.*
> *Of the fruits of faith shall the ale be made,*
> *Of love shall be made the food.*
>
> *Welcome the poor to our feast should we,*
> *For the children of God are they.*
> *Welcome the sick to our feast should we,*
> *For the joy of God are they.*
> *With Jesus at the highest place should the poor be seated*
> *And with the angels should dance the sick.*
>
> *The poor God bless.*
> *The sick God bless.*
> *And so our human race.*
> *Our food God bless,*
> *Our drink God bless,*
> *All homes, O God, embrace.*

"Simple was our daily life, and clear were our tasks. From the hands of our brothers in God came parchment, from the breeding of the beasts with the lightest of fur, and the lightest of skins, beasts delivered, shorn of these skins, back to God their Creator in the month of the Feast of the Harvest, Lunasa. For one Bible, needed we the skins of hundreds of beasts: into His Kingdom may God welcome them, and so my brothers for the cleaning and the stretching of the skins.

"Ogham was our alphabet, but soon learned we the Latin and the Greek. A spell for the eye weaved we, letters of magic to sanctify the page as the flower sanctifies the meadow and the song of the bird the air.

"Nightly came the angel to my cell. In sleep, opened he my eye to the vision of the beauty of the Kingdom of God. By day held he my pen, flowing the lines of my ink, pressed by my brothers from the lees of the wine, and the rind of the pomegranate. With my pen wove this angel his spell from the tombs of Valley of the Boyne, the spell for the eye of no circle, but a spiral, of no line as is the line between the sky and land, but alone as the curve where wave meets sand.

"Then, by night, come the Vikings and with sword and fire consume our earthly shells. Fly our souls inland with the horse and, on his back, the devil, our ransacked book in his cape rudely wrapped. To this place, tonight, come we, shades of our earthly forms, as in the song of the psalmist, through a thousand years, which is as yesterday when it is past.

"For the fields of heaven long we. For the table of Saint Brigid long we. For the embrace of our Lord God long we. Yet stay we in the shadows of this earthly world until the will of Our Lord be done: to the abbey of Cill-Dara is returned its jewel."

This was easier said than done. First of all, the abbey didn't exist anymore. Bishop Soares stepped in at this point, assuring the ghosts that he would *personally* safeguard the manuscript's journey, right into the hands of Pope Benedict XVI, if need be. This was all very well and good, an earnest promise if there ever was one, and one that visibly delighted the monks, but the fact remained that we didn't actually have a book for the bishop to safeguard.

Then came the second worst news we'd had in the past ten

days: someone—a woman, we eventually figured out—had lately been coming into the bindery in the middle of the night and using a "flint" to remove individual pages from the book. By a process that resembled a game of charades, we managed to ascertain that a flint was the twelfth-century equivalent of a razor blade.

"Oh my God," said Sam.

"What?" I asked.

"Oh no, nothing," he said. "I'm just . . . taken aback that someone would . . . to a priceless manuscript like that." He shook his head in dismay.

The bishop was due at an important dinner in less than an hour, so we thanked him profusely for coming, accepted a round of blessings, and made arrangements to keep in touch. As he reached for his coat and gathered his belongings, I pulled Father Quinn aside.

"I'm really sorry I sprung that on you."

He nodded and shrugged.

"If you like, I could meet with you some day, alone. You could talk to her; I could help you."

"I'm confused," he said. "I never knew . . ."

"How could you? But she hasn't crossed over for a reason, the reason being that she's not at peace. I'm sure you want that for her."

"It *was* my fault," he said. "All these years, I—"

"When would you like me to come?" I asked.

And so it was agreed. He would call me in a couple of days and we would figure out a time and a place. In the meantime, I told him, he should speak to her.

"She can hear every word," I said.

"You're absolutely sure she's there?" he whispered.

"I'm sure," I said.

It was Amanda, Sam informed us. She was the one who was cutting up the book. There wasn't a shred of doubt in his mind.

"What?" said Sylvia. *"Amanda?"*

A wave of anger swept through me as I remembered that day in the bindery, how she had been checking me out over her precious little glasses. Wearing four-inch heels.

Sylvia turned to me. "Then why aren't the ghosts hounding her?"

"Maybe they are, or trying to, at least," I said. "Not everyone feels their presence. Besides, the manuscript's been here in the bindery, with you, and before that, with Finny and you. You're the person associated with the book."

Sam looked on gravely. I glanced at the clock. It was seven twenty-two, and I really should have been on my way, in case there were delays on the T, but I sat tight. This was a story I had to hear.

"It's not the first time," he said, pacing sadly. Sylvia and I exchanged shocked glances as we waited for him to continue. He didn't speak for a long time. Finally he stopped and looked up. With a tone of steely resolve in his voice, he said, "But it's going to be the last."

"Sam!" Sylvia said. "What do you know? Tell us!"

Sam took a deep breath, then sighed. He came back over and sat down.

"Two years ago," he began, "I was at an antiquarian's conference in Seattle. There are often two parts to these things, a symposium where people present papers and give talks, and a market, where dealers offer prints and books and such for sale. Anyway, I had some time on my hands, and I stopped by the booth of a well-known dealer, an English fellow who's been in business for decades. On the walls of his booth, obviously the showpieces of his current collection, were some stunning prints, gorgeously matted and framed."

"For sale?" I asked.

Sam nodded, took a breath, and continued. "I recognized them! I was sure I had seen them before. There were eight in all. Four were maps, eighteenth-century maps of Japan and Indochina, and four were copper plates. A plate of the whole Celestial Planisphere, and one each of the constellations of April, May, and June.

"Now, this dealer's not a fly-by-night guy. He's been in business for . . . oh, probably forty years. He had to have a provenance on the prints, or he couldn't have been asking the prices he was asking—people aren't going to plunk down thousands, or in a couple of cases *tens* of thousands, of dollars if there's a chance the prints are just reproductions and not first editions.

"Anyway, I chalked it up to my having spent too many years staring at books of prints, all the ones I worked on and too many others. But I couldn't let it go. Where in the *world* had I seen them?

"One morning, a few weeks later, I woke up and I knew. It was like my brain had been searching my memory, day after day, and had suddenly come up with the answers. We *owned* the books that the prints were in! They were the property of the Athenaeum!

"I couldn't wait to get to work. I came right in, didn't have breakfast, didn't even have coffee—just hopped on the T and got here as fast as I could. I knew exactly where the books were. And when I opened them, sure enough, the pages were gone. Removed with a razor blade."

Sam broke off briefly, then repeated a version of his last sentence, to make sure we understood its importance. "The prints I'd seen framed on the walls of Cecil Kennedy's booth had been removed with a razor blade from valuable first editions owned by the Athenaeum."

He broke off for a minute, shaking his head.

"I didn't tell anyone. I closed the books and put them back on the shelves, went about my business as though nothing at all had happened. But I started doing a little detective work. I went to London and paid a visit to Kennedy. I knew he'd been taken in by somebody, and somebody very, very savvy. He's a top guy; he's got no interest in selling stolen goods. It'd be the end of his reputation if word got out, if not the end of his business. He immediately took the prints off the market and agreed to help me trace them."

"And the trail led back to Amanda," I guessed.

Sam nodded. "I should have gone right to the police. Right then and there. But I didn't. It was the biggest mistake I ever made. I went to see her first. I wanted to give her a chance to explain. To tell you the truth, I couldn't really believe she was involved in this. I just couldn't get my head around that fact."

Sam went over to the watercooler and poured himself a glass of water. He had a long sip.

"She didn't even try to deny it. It was as though she always expected to be caught. Oh, she made all the excuses: she was deeply in debt, she'd made bad investments, her divorce had ruined her. To tell you the truth, I always thought there was something a little *off* about her: she was two years here, two years there, never staying in a job for very long. There was an incident at the Tate that I got wind of. All very hush-hush, but I know they let her go, under a cloud."

"So why didn't you bust her?" I burst out.

"I couldn't," he said.

"Why not?" asked Sylvia, glancing at me.

"Because she had a secret weapon. Something she could use

against me." Sam paused for a moment and then went on. "I rebound those books. Most people on staff didn't know they existed, and even if they did, they wouldn't have been able to tell when pages were missing. I was the only one who'd really worked with the books—handled them, taken them apart and put them back together."

"But what could she have on you?" Sylvia asked. "You're one of the nicest and most honest—"

Sam held up his hand, closing his eyes and shaking his head. "You know. Ben," he said quietly.

"Of course."

"My son," Sam continued, looking now at me, "has a drug problem. He's been clean now for over a year, but it was tough sledding for a very long time. Two years ago, he was in rehab at a program in Connecticut, and he was doing really well. He made it through the whole twelve weeks, which was a first, and when he got out, he came to live with me. His mother and I are divorced."

I knew all this, of course. Sylvia had told me the story. But I acted as though I hadn't heard it before.

"I got him a job here," Sam continued. "Nothing too difficult, just a pleasant, easy job to give a little structure to his life. He was doing really well, but then, around the holidays, this girl he'd been seeing broke up with him and he . . . slipped. He started using again. To finance his habit, he stole—and fenced—a couple of small items from the library."

"Books?" I asked.

Sam shook his head. "A Greek bronze, a bust of a young boy. Ironically, it could have been Ben at the age of four or five—looked just like him. He also took some letters and sketches. And small amounts of money from some staff members' purses.

"Amanda suspected Ben and confronted him. He admitted it and offered to try to help get the objects back. Out of respect for me, Amanda said, and all the years I'd worked here, they wouldn't go to the police. She'd handle it internally. In the end, they were able to retrieve the bust, the sketches, and one of the letters. I paid back the money, and that seemed to be the end of it.

"At the time I was enormously grateful. Little did I know that it was all part of her plan, in case I ever discovered what she was doing."

"She blackmailed you," I said.

Sam nodded. "When I confronted her about the plates in Cecil's collection, she claimed to know about more things Ben had stolen—claimed she had absolute proof of his having gotten away with stealing an antique coin collection, book of Audubon engravings, and a folio of architectural drawings by Alexander Parris."

"Which *she* stole," I suggested, catching on.

"That'd be my guess," answered Sam.

He slumped down into a chair.

"So let me get this straight," I said. "You confronted her about the prints—the maps and the constellations." Then I lost the thin thread I was following.

"And she said that if I went to the police, she'd reveal what *she* knew about Ben. Not only about the bronze and the letters and the sketches, but a slew of other thefts only she knew about."

"But she was lying!" Sylvia said.

"I know," Sam said sadly. "But who knows what 'evidence' she had cooked up? Ben could have gone to jail. He could have served time! He couldn't have taken it, not just then. We would have lost him once and for all. Besides, I needed my pension. I needed my health insurance. I was sixty-six years old. She gave me a choice: keep quiet, take an immediate, voluntary retirement, or—"

"Or *what*?" I asked, feeling my fury gathering into an impotent storm.

"Or she'd go public with everything. She had files, she claimed. She had friends. If I wanted to end a long and honorable career with my reputation and my retirement package intact, I had only one option—announce my decision to step aside. If I refused, she'd bring down the whole house of cards."

"That bitch!" I said. "Pardon my French."

"No, no," Sam said. "It took two of us to dance that dance. If it had only involved me, I think I would have taken her on. It just about killed me to see her getting away with this."

"But there was Ben," Sylvia whispered.

"There was Ben," echoed Sam.

We sat in silence for several moments.

"How could I not have noticed?" Sylvia finally said.

"Oh, come on," I answered. "You can't blame yourself for this."

"But I do."

"What was the book, four hundred pages?" I glanced at Sam, whose expression was sympathetic.

"Three eighty-six," Sylvia said sadly.

"And how thick was the vellum?" I asked.

She shrugged. "Some pages were like leather, others were as thin as tissue paper."

"Right. And it probably wasn't the leather pages she cut out. So unless you were going through the manuscript regularly, page by page, there'd have been no way of noticing."

"I tried to handle it as little as possible."

"Of course you did!" said Sam. "As you should have done!"

Sylvia nodded but seemed unconvinced.

"What I don't get," I said, "was how she knew where it was—how she actually found it."

"Well," Sylvia said, "she had that phone call from New York, probably from Paola Moretti. She told me about that when she called me into her office that day. And we know she ran into Wescott at that Harvard symposium and he apparently mentioned *something* about a manuscript."

"But he didn't believe us," Sylvia said. "He didn't believe there *was* such a thing as a Book of Kildare."

"No," I said, "but it was still a valuable manuscript, Kildare or not. It was still a book that the Athenaeum had been lucky to get, assuming it had actually come with the collection."

"There was nothing in the database, though," Sylvia said, "because she told me she tried to look it up."

"I'll tell you just exactly what she did," Sam said firmly. "She came down one night when no one was here and just started snooping around. Believe me, I've seen it all before. If she took the book, someone would have noticed, so she couldn't do that. So instead, she took plates and left the book."

Chapter Twenty-Three

Hᴇɴʀʏ ᴡᴀs ɢᴏɪɴɢ to be a hammer.

How he and Ellie had arrived at this decision, I had no idea. By the time I got to see the kitchen/costume shop in full steam, Max had been promoted to chief construction officer, having made a series of ill-advised cracks criticizing Ellie's efforts with plywood strips, a stapler, and chicken wire.

The idea had been to create a tube that would enclose Henry up to his head. The tube would then be covered with brown fabric, and the fabric painted to mimic wood grain. The head of the hammer would be a separate piece and would sit on Henry's shoulders. Ellie was a whiz with a glue gun. She was confident that she could fashion a wire frame out of old coat hangers, which she could then upholster with hot adhesive and gray felt.

I immediately saw some problems.

First of all, Henry would roast inside a hammerhead of felt.

Second, he would not be able to sit down, or even visit the boys' room, if need be.

Third, his arms would be pinned to his sides, which would be particularly tricky because he would not be able to see, given that he would never, ever agree to cut eyeholes in the hammerhead. This would immediately give it away as a kid's costume and not a *real* hammerhead.

If there was one thing that drove my son crazy on occasions that called for costumes, it was anything that compromised the illusion he hoped to create. He wouldn't wear a jacket over his Halloween costume when he was three, because bees didn't wear jackets, nor when he was four, because Batman needed only his cape. Efforts to reason with him failed. The cape was for flying, I insisted, to no avail. Nor would he wear a sweater *under* his costume, because that would make him feel—if not look—like a baby, and not the grown-up four-year-old trick-or-treater he was.

He wouldn't troll for candy in rain boots. He wouldn't be caught dead with an umbrella. Nor would he carry a flashlight or let me walk beside him with *my* flashlight. I had to stay way behind, preferably out of sight, because to have your mother hovering around when you are trying to pass for a bee or Batman, well, that gave everything away.

What *I* had given away, though, in enlisting Ellie's help with the costume, was the right to butt in every two seconds with my opinions about armholes and eyeholes and provisions for the needs of Mother Nature. After all, Ellie and Max had managed to raise two kids of their own. They'd work it out with him. And if not, well, how long could the wedding of *Q* and *U* actually last? He'd definitely take the hammerhead off for cupcakes.

Sam was a man on a mission. Within twenty-four hours, he'd made contact with nearly two dozen colleagues on both sides of the Atlantic, enlisting their help in canvassing their region's dealers in rare prints and books. The purloined plates had yet to surface. But thanks to the dragnet that Sam had laid with his colleagues, they wouldn't go on sale in London, Paris, Amster-dam, Tokyo, Dubai, Düsseldorf, Berlin, Zurich, or New York with-out raising huge red flags. Contacting the Art Loss Register, a massive online database, and the Art Crime Team of the FBI were the steps Sam had wanted to take next, but we'd convinced him of the ongoing need for discretion.

Eighteen hours later, we had our first concrete lead. Sam had been waiting for Sylvia when she got to work on Thursday, and an hour later, when I arrived, they sat me down and Sam repeated his story to me.

He had a friend who worked at The Cloisters, a guy named Florio Something. Florio had been in touch with a rare books dealer in Manhattan, a man called Bruno Dollfus. Dollfus had apprenticed with his uncle Hans in Vienna before opening his own business in New York in the eighties.

In 2006, he had been the curator of "Royal Devotions," an ex-hibition of forty-five illuminated manuscripts that had been on display for a month at the Waldorf-Astoria. Having trained at the elbow of his famous and reclusive uncle, one of the world's premier dealers in illuminated manuscripts, Dollfus had radar he never doubted. And his radar had recently been triggered.

According to Florio, Dollfus had received a call within the past week or ten days from a man looking to sell him some medieval plates. After a lengthy conversation, some snooping around on the Internet, and a day or two spent poring over his reference collec-tion, Dollfus had walked away from the deal. Either the plates were forgeries, he'd concluded, or the seller was reaching out from the darkest, dimmest corners of the black market. In neither case did Dollfus want anything to do with him.

"Does he have a name?" I asked Sam. "Did Dollfus keep the guy's number?"

"We're trying to find out. I have a call in to Florio right now."

"What if he does?" Sylvia asked. "What'll we do then?"

"I'll ask Declan," I said, as my mind raced forward through the possibilities. In the best case, we'd be able to track down the man with the plates. If the wary Viennese book dealer was willing to help, it would make things even easier.

But there was only one person who would be able to verify that the plates in question were the plates cut out of our book: Sylvia. Maybe she could pose as the book dealer's colleague. How would the seller know?

"If you had to pick up tomorrow and go to New York," I said to Sylvia, "could you go?"

"For what?" she asked suspiciously.

"To verify the authenticity of the plates. They might not be the ones from our book."

"What? Meet some thug in an alley? No way!"

"No, no," I assured her. "It wouldn't work like that."

"I'd go with you," said Sam. "There's nothing I'd like better than to—" He broke off with a little growl.

"Let's hear that again, Sam," I said.

Sam smiled as he growled again. Then again, more loudly. Then with the addition of a couple of punching motions. "Pow!" Sam added.

"Right in the kisser," I said.

"You got that right, baby," said Sam. And for the first time in almost two weeks, Sylvia laughed.

There were two messages on my machine when I checked it after dinner. Henry was in his room, working on his homework, copying the numbers zero through nine, ten times each. The numbers were printed on the left side of the worksheet. Henry's task was to keep his pencil from going outside the lines on the page.

The first message was from Julian, whom I kept forgetting to call, and the second was from Declan. I decided to call Julian first. I could call Declan's cell phone any time; apparently he was working until midnight.

I picked up the phone and dialed the number I had copied down. Just as I thought the call was going to his machine, he answered.

"Julian? It's Anza."

"Anza!" he said. "Nice to hear your voice."

"The flowers are gorgeous. Thank you so much."

"Oh, good."

"Some of them haven't even opened yet. They get prettier every day."

"I'm glad," he said. "I'm so glad." There was an awkward pause, which, as usual, I jumped in to fill.

"You really didn't have to. Honestly, there—"

"Oh, no. I did. I absolutely did. I'm so sorry. I didn't handle that well at all."

"Don't worry about it," I said.

"Well, it's just that it really caught me off guard."

"I know. I shouldn't have said anything. I mean, you were the one who planned the whole trip out there, and here I am, in the middle of the day—"

"No, no," he said. "It was fine, really."

There was another awkward lull. I suppose he was waiting for a cue from me; would I suggest that we get together again? Would I pretend that what had happened was like someone's spilling a glass of wine on me, a clumsy, accidental lapse that had nothing to do with who he really was?

I felt tongue-tied. He was trying, he really was. But I felt confused. He was nice, and thoughtful, and funny, but he had also been condescending and rude. I knew I could prove to him that ghosts really did exist, that was the easiest thing in the world to do, but why would I? To prove I was right? I didn't care about being right. I cared about being myself. It was as though I had told him I was a Catholic, or a Jew, or a Republican, or a Democrat, and he had said, *Oh! In that case, never mind.*

"You know," he began. "I really would like to know more."

Now I was the one who was caught off guard.

"More about what?" I asked.

"About you. About your...your...what it is you... experience."

"But I thought you didn't . . ." Now I was *really* confused.

"I was startled, I'll admit. It's just that I've never seen a ghost myself and I've never known anyone who did."

"Or who admitted it."

"Yeah, maybe."

I let out a sigh. He'd apologized. He'd sent flowers, for which I, rudely, had not even called to thank him. Maybe, just maybe, I should give it one more try.

"Look," I said, "the next few days are kind of crazy. But maybe we can we have a drink sometime—soon."

"I'd really like that," said Julian.

Chapter Twenty-Four

"It's on," Declan said. "The meeting. The handoff on Nantucket."

I let out a little shriek, and he said, "Okay, okay, hold your horses there, girl."

"Tell me! Tell me!" A moment ago, I'd been sitting in my living room pondering the truly boring question of whether I should have a touch of brandy before bed or a cup of chamomile tea. And now, suddenly, excitement!

"Scully got confirmation a couple of hours ago."

"Do you have an address?"

"Working on it."

"And a time?"

"That, too."

"Can I come?" I pleaded. "I *really* want to come."

Ignoring me, he said, "We got damn lucky in one respect."

"What's that?" I asked.

"Interpol had Van Vleck in its sights. They think he's been trafficking in what they call 'cultural property'—statues stolen from a museum in Kabul."

"Looted?"

"Exactly."

"So why is that lucky for us?"

"Well, they want him, and we found him. Two lads are on a plane right now, guys who work out of Europol, in The Hague. They have all the paperwork they need."

Maybe I should have had the brandy. My synapses weren't firing.

"I'm not following," I said.

"They can enter the premises legally, Anza," Dec went on. "They can arrest him. We couldn't do either one, since your girl-friend there wouldn't agree to sign a friggin' piece of paper."

"Oh my God! Dec! That's fantastic!"

Amazing. So it would probably happen this weekend. So I could go! Henry would be with Dec and Kelly—no, wait. Dec would be . . . on Nantucket.

With me!

No, I told myself sternly, most definitely *not* with me! I couldn't let myself go down that road again.

But an *island*.

I had to stop this *right now*.

"But we will get the book back, right?" I asked. After all, that was the whole point—to carry out Finny's wishes and send the miserable ghosts on their way. I was all for rounding up interna-tional art thieves, but not if it meant that our precious manu-script had to disappear down the black hole of an evidence locker in The Hague.

"You should, if all goes well. Interpol's only interested in the Afghani statuary, and in apprehending Van Vleck. After they make the arrest, I'll simply relieve the unlucky bastard of our book. He'll hardly be in a position to protest."

"And what about the person he's meeting—the person he stole it for? Can you arrest him? Or her?"

"Nope."

"You're kidding."

"You can't have it both ways, darlin'. No official report, no arrest."

He paused and then, probably anticipating what I was going to come back to next, said, "You really don't want be getting involved in this, love."

"But I do! You have to let me, Dec! Come on! If I hadn't come to you with this, you never would have leaned on Scully, and you never would have learned about Van Vleck. You're cracking a case for Interpol! Think of it!"

"We haven't cracked anything yet, Sherlock! There's every chance in the world he'll get wind of this somehow and slip right though our sweaty little hands."

I hadn't thought of that.

"Let's talk tomorrow morning," Dec said. "I'll have more info."

"When's the meeting supposed to happen?"

"Saturday night. We think."

"I'm coming, Dec."

"We'll talk about it tomorrow."

"We can talk about it tomorrow, but I'm coming."

He laughed.

He said, "I ought to have my head examined." What he didn't say was no.

———⟡———

I was fixing scrambled eggs for Henry when the phone rang. I glanced at the clock as my heart began to thump. It was 7:05. It had to be Dad or Nona. I took a deep breath and reached for the receiver.

"Anza!" said Sylvia. "You won't believe it!"

I sighed with relief. "Won't believe what?"

"You know that guy Dollfus?"

"The art dealer? The one from Vienna?"

"He's flying up on the shuttle."

"What?"

"I know!"

I dropped a pat of butter into the pan and watched it sizzle across the hot surface. I picked up the pan and swirled it around, but before the surface was evenly coated, the butter had disappeared. "What's going on?" I asked.

"Sam heard back from his friend at The Cloisters," Sylvia explained. "That Florio person. Florio went to see Dollfus last night. They know each other from working on that exhibit. Dollfus wasn't anxious to get involved in this, *until*—"

Sylvia hung on that word. I had a hunch where this was going. I poured the eggs into the pan, and as they sizzled and popped, I said, "*Until*—let me guess: he found out that we thought we had the Book of Kildare."

"Right," answered Sylvia. "See? That's what I was saying about the art world: everybody wants to be the one to break a story. It can make your career, to turn up a painting or a drawing that no one knew existed or that was somehow *lost*."

"At this point," I responded, "the only thing that matters is getting the book back. Who cares who gets the credit?"

"I know I don't," she said.

"So what happened?" I put some bread in the toaster as Henry padded over to his place at the table. Balancing the phone on my shoulder, I poured him a glass of juice and set it down.

"Dollfus agreed to call the guy back," Sylvia explained. "The seller had given his name as Windsor Atlas."

"*Windsor Atlas*? Give me a break. That can't be real."

"Real or not, that's what he called himself. Dollfus told him that he'd given it some more thought and decided that he'd like to see the plates after all. Atlas offered to bring them right down to New York, but Dollfus told him he that he wasn't going to *be* in New York until the end of next week. He said he had to come up to Boston for some meetings. He didn't, really, but they took a chance, figuring that if Amanda was involved, then maybe—"

"Don't tell me: the guy lives here."

"Chestnut Hill," Sylvia replied.

Chestnut Hill was a bucolic and exclusive section of Brookline. In the eighteenth and nineteenth centuries, wealthy Bostonians had built their summer homes in its green, rolling pastures. Nowadays, these homes belonged to players for the Celtics and the Red Sox, and CEOs and hedge-fund managers who summered somewhere else.

My heart beat rapidly as I buttered Henry's toast, spooned the scrambled eggs on top, and cut everything into strips and squares, the way Dad had always done. I set the plate down as Sylvia continued.

"The meeting's on for six o'clock tonight."

"Where?"

"The Charles Hotel. Can you call Declan?"

"He's probably not up yet," I said. "He worked until midnight. Anyway, what's Declan going to do?"

"I don't know, arrest them?"

Acting on the information Declan had given me last night, I said, "He can't arrest anybody. No one's reported a theft. No one's pressed charges."

I had a sip of my coffee and watched Henry play with his toast and eggs. He wasn't a big breakfast eater, but then again, neither was I. While I would urge him on at lunch and dinner, I wasn't about to hector him first thing in the morning. I considered my responsibility fulfilled when I put something vaguely healthy down in front of him.

"Look," I finally said. "The point is to recover the plates, right? So we can put them back in the book."

"Right. But Sam would like to put Amanda out of business."

"That's fine. I'll call Declan and see if he or one of the guys can meet you at the hotel."

"Me? What about you?"

I hesitated. She wasn't going to like this, but there was nothing I could do.

"I can't come," I informed her.

"Why not?" There was a petulant tone in her voice. I felt like saying, *Excuse me, but I do have a life!* I decided to let it go.

"I . . . I've got something I can't . . . get out of." Once again, I debated bringing her in on the truth: tonight was the night I was meeting Tad and his sisters. Tad had confirmed earlier in the week that Esther was coming in from the Berkshires. After I dropped Henry off with Kelly, I was driving into Boston. At seven thirty, we were all coming together at the house on Commonwealth Avenue.

Once again, I decided not to tell Sylvia.

Fortunately, I had even bigger news with which to change the subject.

"Declan thinks he's found the book!" I announced abruptly. "He called me late last night."

"Oh, my God!"

"I don't have any details," I lied, "but if all goes well, he thinks we'll get it back over the weekend."

"That's so fantastic! Oh my God! I can't believe it. That's so great."

"As for the plates," I said, "there's really no point in my being there. You're the only one who can identify them."

"But what'll I do?"

"I don't know. Maybe . . . pretend to be Dollfus's partner. Do a really close inspection."

"And then what?"

"Well, confront 'Windsor Atlas'!"

"Me? I'm not going to confront him! What if he has a gun?"

"He won't have a gun. Look, let me get Henry to school and I'll meet you at the bindery. We can call Dec together and figure this out."

There was silence on the other end. Then Sylvia said meekly, "I don't know about this."

"I'll see you soon," I said.

⸻

By three o'clock, it was all arranged. Declan was working until midnight, so he couldn't freelance at the Charles, but he put in a call to a cop friend in Cambridge, a detective named Karl Bryson. To Sylvia's relief, Bryson took it from there. Dollfus was instructed to reserve a suite at the Charles, one with two bedrooms and a living room.

When 'Atlas' arrived at the hotel suite, Bryson would be waiting in one of the bedrooms. When Dollfus answered the door, he'd introduce Sylvia as his colleague and business partner, and after some book chitchat, and maybe a drink, they'd turn their attention to the plates. Once Sylvia was satisfied that the plates were from our book, she would begin to cough and excuse herself to go into the bedroom—for a cough drop or a glass of water. Once she was safely inside the bedroom, Bryson would step out into the living room and Sylvia would lock herself in. Dollfus would duck into the second bedroom and lock himself in.

Bryson would then show his badge, identify himself as a Cambridge detective, threaten the seller with immediate arrest, and take possession of the stolen plates.

"What if he won't turn them over?" Sylvia had asked.

Declan had laughed. Bryson was big, Declan said. Actually, what he said was, "Bastard's built like a brick shithouse." And besides, if there was any trouble, well, Bryson would be carrying.

"But I thought you couldn't arrest somebody if there wasn't a report," Sylvia said.

"Who told you that?" asked Dec.

"Me," I admitted. It was more like a guilty little peep.

"Brilliant," he muttered.

"Is this legal?" Sylvia asked.

There was a slight pause before Dec responded.

"Legal enough," he said.

Chapter Twenty-Five

"He's already here," I said quietly.

They couldn't see him, of course. We were sitting in the living room of Finny's house: Tad, Esther, Josie, and I. The space felt forlorn—dismantled and strangely hollow—but in a gesture I would never have predicted, Tad had proposed that we light a fire in the fireplace. As Esther and I had assembled chairs, and Josie had made a good faith, though futile, effort to reassemble parts of the boat model she had smashed in her fury, Tad had gone down to the basement and returned with an armful of wood.

All this time, Johnny was right there with us, his expression eager yet somehow subdued. It was not until the fire was crackling merrily and we had each settled into a chair that the nervous chatter gradually subsided.

"So," Tad finally said. "How do we do this?"

I turned to Johnny. "Why don't you sit down?" I suggested, motioning to the chair nearest the fire, which we had placed there for him.

"Woolsie!" said Esther, spinning around, trying to glimpse the shadow she would never be able to see. "Woolsie? Where are you?"

That's when I said, "He's already here. He's sitting right there in that chair."

"We miss you!" Josie cried, glancing in the direction of the chair. "You and Maimie! We all miss you so much! You were like . . . it was never the same after you . . ." She was already crying. Her words were coming out in little hiccups. She couldn't bring herself to utter the word *died.*

Tad had grown very pale.

"Tell her it's all right," Johnny said. "Tell her I miss them, too."

I relayed his message and Josie dissolved into little sobs.

"Josie," Tad said. "Get ahold of yourself." Esther stood up and went over to her sister. She sat on the arm of Josie's armchair, but the fragile antique couldn't bear her weight. It pulled right away from the body of the chair and Esther barely saved herself from landing on her somewhat ample bottom.

Johnny made a wry crack and I relayed it:

"You always *were* after more pudding. See where it got you?"

"I was not!" said Esther, stifling a grin as she inspected the damage to the chair. "Tell him it was only the butterscotch I loved! And only if Maimie had cream!"

The ghost of the butler was smiling now, and he seemed like a much younger man—or rather, the ghost of a much younger man. I had a sudden vision of what this house must have been like when the wallpaper was fresh and the draperies were bright and sturdy, when the adults now sitting before the fire were half their present size and were sliding down banisters, dressing up the dog, and begging for seconds of Maimie's desserts.

Half an hour passed easily as first Esther, then Josie, then Tad slipped into the triangular rhythms of our conversation: they gradually began to address "Woolsie" directly, then he would respond and I would repeat his words to them. They seemed, this evening, like different people. Tad was shy and reserved, Esther dealt with her feelings by making a lot of jokes, which were usually pretty lame, and Josie—well, Josie was basically an emotional mess, though tonight she wasn't smashing boat models or picture glass. She just cried a lot.

I noticed as we chatted that they related to Johnny as polite children do to adults. There seemed to be a line they wouldn't cross, confining their questions and reminiscences to episodes remembered from their own childhoods: the time Esther and Josie decided to paint the fourth-floor bathroom purple; the time Tad cut the hair off Josie's Chatty Cathy doll. It happens this way sometimes. If a person was a child when the earthbound spirit left their lives, they feel like a child when he or she returns. They can't or don't want to make the adjustment for the years that have passed, and I can understand why. I think I would feel the same way if I ever met the ghost of my mother. I would long to be her child again, though I am myself now a mother and her equal in age.

"We found the deed," I finally said, hoping to move the evening forward. "And you were right, it *was* in the book."

Tad got up, crossed the room, and reached into a leather bag he had laid on a table. He retrieved the book, brought it over to us, and handed it to me expectantly.

I removed the deed from the book and held it up.

"Here it is," I said. "Safe and sound."

I would have handed it to Johnny, but he wouldn't have been able to hold it. Instead, I pressed the folds of the paper open and laid it on the arm of his chair.

He was overcome with emotion as he gazed at the paper, so overcome that he didn't say anything. One by one, the siblings turned to me, with questions in their eyes—What was he doing? What was going on? Wasn't he happy?

"He's overjoyed," I said, and Johnny nodded.

"Why Wales?" Esther asked him. "There has to be a reason."

"There is," he said.

"You told some of it to me," I said to Johnny. "But would you like to tell them?"

He nodded and began.

"Your mother, God rest her soul, was born in 1937. Maimie and I, we had a little girl. Born just two months before your mum."

"Woolsie!" Esther cried. "You never told us."

He shook his head. "We couldn't . . . speak of her."

"Can you tell us now?" Josie asked gently.

The ghost nodded. "Her name was Gwennie. Gwendolyn Winifred Grady—Winifred after Maimie's aunt Una."

"Una," said Tad. "I've heard of her. Wasn't she a cook for Mummy's family?"

"She was," answered the butler. "It was Una who brought Maimie to work for your mother's parents. I'd been working in the house for almost a year. That's how we met. A year later, we were married.

"Anyway, you've heard me tell about the war—how your grandparents had Maimie and me take your mother to Brighton, during the evacuation."

"And then to South Wales," Tad continued.

"Right. See, we had a cottage on the water. A right little snug of a place. Four rooms—kitchen, sitting room, and two bedrooms. We were there for three years."

"Three years?" said Esther. "I had no idea it was that long. I thought it was like . . . a month or two."

"No. We stayed until just before the blitz on the Swansea Docks. Your grandfather, of course, was involved in the war effort and couldn't leave London, but he arranged for our return. I suppose he could do things other people couldn't, having the grand position and all. But only three of us came home."

"What happened?" Josie finally asked.

"Gwennie . . . she was swept away by a wave. The girls were playing on the shore. It was a Sunday in June and Maimie had packed us a picnic. If you could call it that; there wasn't much to be had in those days but what you could grow yourself. That day, I remember, we had brown bread and boiled potatoes and some jot—bacon bits and onion with scraps of wild rabbit.

"The sky was clouding over, but we didn't give it a thought. It all happened so fast. Next minute we heard a bit of a rumble and the wind was getting cold, so we were packing up to head home. We think Gwennie had her eye on a bird. There was a flock of little grebes, young ones, all fluffed out on the water, and one of them flapped up and took flight. Gwennie ran right into the water, took a spill, and was pulled down and out by an undertow. Maimie started screaming and we both ran into the water. Neither of us was much of a swimmer, but we went right in after our baby. Thing was, we couldn't see where she was—she was underwater. It held her there, the undertow did. Maimie ran back to care for your mum while I kept diving under the water, trying to see where Gwennie was. Other people came in, too, five or six men, I recall, and it was one of those men that finally found her. Not twenty-five feet from where I was. But it was—"

Johnny broke off.

"Too late," said Josie sadly.

The ghost nodded. He paused to collect himself and then went on.

"We had to leave her there," he said softly.

"Gwennie's buried in Wales," Tad said softly.

"She is."

"And that's why you bought a place there?" asked Esther.

The ghost nodded. "Right near the one your grandfather rented for us. We planned to settle there, Mairead and I, after you kids was up and out."

"But she got cancer," Josie said kindly. "And then you did."

"I never could give up the smokes," he answered. "Nerves, I s'pose. But I had to find that deed. That place is our only connection to Gwennie. It's near the churchyard where we laid her."

"And you own it?" I asked. "The house? Free and clear?"

"We do. We put everything we had into that place."

"What would you like us to do with it?" I asked.

You would have thought, given all the years he spent trying to bring about this very moment, that he would have had a plan. But he didn't.

"Well, I don't rightly know," he said.

Tad stood up. "Woolsie," he said, "you will never know what you and Maimie meant to me and my sisters." Astonishingly, he then had to stop talking. His voice was cracking.

"That's right!" said Esther.

"It is," cried Josie.

"Even more than my mother and father," Tad continued, "you made this place a home. You taught us to count. Maimie made our birthday cakes. You fixed our bikes. Maimie knitted us sweaters. You didn't tell my father when you caught me smoking—"

"And you didn't tell Mummy," Josie interrupted, "when you caught me climbing up the fire escape at two in the morning."

Hmmmm, I thought. *You're braver than I am.*

Johnny smiled. "You were good kids, all of you," he said. "You were like Maimie's and my own."

"If you leave it in our hands," Tad said, "we'll figure out what to do with the place. We'll think of something good and we'll do it. Do you trust us?"

"Sure I do," said the old ghost.

"Who's been paying the taxes?" Tad asked.

"Oh, I paid them right on time, every year," answered the ghost.

Tad glanced awkwardly at me.

"So they haven't been paid—recently," I suggested.

"No," admitted Johnny sadly. "Oh, dear God, you don't suppose . . ."

"Don't you worry about it," Tad said firmly. "If taxes have to be paid, we'll pay them. Whatever it takes, we'll work it out. I promise you."

I don't know exactly when my opinion of Tad had begun to change, but I was beginning to feel sure pretty sure I'd misjudged him. After all, it was Sylvia who had set me up to dislike him so much, and she certainly didn't know him very well. Maybe she had convinced herself that she was closer to Finny than he was to his own children. Maybe she needed to feel at the center of Finny's life, and saw his kids as a complication. Maybe she simply wasn't a good judge of character and disliked anyone who overwhelmed her. In any case, I found myself warming to Tad.

"I give you my word," Tad said to the ghost.

"Me too," cried Josie.

"And me," said Esther. "We all promise!"

"I'm not sure how we'll do it," Tad said. "The deed's in your name and you're . . . gone. I'll have to talk to someone who knows about Welsh property law."

"I'm sure you'll figure it out," said Johnny. "You've got a good head on your shoulders."

"I'll try," Tad said. "I'll do everything I can."

"God bless you, lad," said Johnny. "God bless you all."

Tad let out a sigh and looked at me. Gradually, so did Josie and Esther.

"Johnny," I finally said. "Are you ready now to leave?"

"I am," he said.

"Is there anything else you want to say?"

"Tell them we loved them all to pieces. Tell them not to work so hard and not to fight with each other and to remember me and Maimie and make us proud: to be good people and kind people and do a good turn when they get the chance."

They all dissolved when I repeated his words. I'd be doing them all a favor to get this over with as soon as possible.

"Anything else you want to say?" I asked. "He's going to leave now, so it's your last chance."

"I love you!" shouted Josie, tears spilling down her cheeks.

"I love both of you!" said Esther. "Tell Maimie I love her!"

Tad alone could utter not a word. He kissed his hand and held it over his heart.

"All right, Johnny," I said, "here we go. Look over at that wall. In a minute, you'll see a white light and a doorway."

I closed my eyes and envisioned the light and the opening.

"I see it!" I heard him cry.

"Walk toward it," I said. "And when you're ready, walk through it."

I held the image firmly in my mind as I opened my eyes. Johnny was floating toward the light.

"Maimie!" I heard him cry. "Gwennie! Oh, my darling baby girl! I'm coming! Daddy's coming!"

He approached the glowing door, walked through it, and was gone.

The fire flared up with a burst of snaps and crackles. The ghost's departure had disturbed the energy in the room. Esther was now the one crying, and Josie crossed the room to hug her sister. Tad sunk down into a chair.

"That was the most amazing thing I have ever seen," he said. "I just don't know what to say."

"You don't have to say anything," I responded.

Tad stood up, walked over to where Johnny had been sitting, and fetched the deed from the arm of the chair. He shook his head as his eyes scanned the faded lettering. Finally he looked up.

"What'll we do with this?" he asked. "What would be the right thing? The thing he'd want us to do."

"I have an idea," I said.

"Let's talk about it," he answered, smiling.

I nodded. "Okay. There's something else I want to discuss with you, too."

I'd seen a whole different side of Tad in the past few hours, and I no longer believed that he was just a crass and thuggish opportunist. Esther embarrassed him by telling me, as we sat there watching the embers die down, that since Monday, when Tad learned through me that Johnny was still in the house, Tad had basically been living here, talking to the spirit he couldn't even see, just keeping the old ghost company though his last days and nights on earth.

Her brother had also set in motion a plan to try to get the boat back, Esther later confided. He hadn't really known how much the boat had meant to Josie. He'd also been doing what their father had instructed. Finny had been worried about Josie's safety. She'd had her psychiatric ups and downs, and her father had been deathly afraid that she would take the boat out by herself one day, while in the throes of one of her manic swings. He'd been terrified that she would drown.

Anyway, sitting in the quiet living room as the fire burned down, I knew that I could trust them. So I told them everything. The whole story. How their father had left the manuscript in Sylvia's possession. How she had promised him that she'd keep trying to trace its history and assemble proof of its provenance, and how she'd hid it in a false cover when the books were unexpectedly donated to the Athenaeum. How she'd ultimately tried to safeguard it by taking it home, and how it had been stolen. I told them about the monks, and about Dec, and about what was going to happen this weekend on Nantucket.

I only avoided one part of the tale, the part that might really hurt them.

Your father didn't trust you, was what I kept to myself. I wasn't even sure, anymore, if this was true. Here, too, Sylvia might have put her own spin on things.

They were silent for a very long time. It was a lot to absorb, this huge long saga; it would have been a lot to absorb even if we hadn't already passed an emotional few hours. But if not for the intimacy of these past few hours, we would never have been able to speak heart to heart.

Tears came to my eyes when Tad finally spoke.

"How can I help?" he asked softly.

That was how we found ourselves heading down to Police Headquarters on Berkeley Street, where Tad filed a report on the stolen object and gave Dec the signature he so urgently needed. And Tad's good deeds didn't end there.

Bruno Dollfus looked nothing like I'd expected. I'd been prepared for a giant moose of a guy—distracted, ill-shaven, thoughts fixated on another century; in other words, an outsized version of Sam. But the man who answered my knock on the door of a room at the Charles Hotel was a trim, compact athlete in a gold silk tie and a navy silk suit. Judging by his appearance, I doubted there had been any need for the protection offered by Karl Bryson. I imagined Dollfus whipping off his tailored jacket, crouching with concentration, raising his hands like lethal paddles, and decking the hapless Atlas with a couple of well-placed kicks.

Sam and Sylvia sat side by side on a sofa upholstered in cranberry brocade. They were beaming. One champagne bottle sat upside down in an ice bucket, and Sam grabbed a second from another silver canister as he flew to his feet. He reached for a champagne flute on the coffee table.

"Anza!" he cried. "We've had an extraordinary evening."

That makes four of us, I thought.

My gaze was drawn to the table off to our left, which someone had covered with a cloth of chocolate-colored velvet. There they were, on the table, eight or ten loose manuscript pages.

I glanced at Sylvia as Dollfus's cell phone began to chirp. My heart was racing; I could almost feel the adrenaline coursing through me.

"Are they . . . ?" I asked.

She nodded. Then smiled.

"Good Lord!" I said.

I walked over to the table and caught my breath at the beauty of the pages spread out across it. On the fragile yellow sheaves of parchment were intricate golden letters, green within their borders, and tiny, crosshatched chains that seemed to form the marrow of an oft-repeated paisley pattern. The hand lettering of the text remained crisp and dark. It had survived the centuries well. I felt dazed at the actuality and nearness of these priceless pages, at the warmth and brightness of the room, and at the scent of aftershave in the air, Bruno's no doubt, something sylvan and astringent, like bark and lemon. I glanced over at Sylvia. Her cheeks were flushed and she looked childlike, sitting beside Sam on the couch with her knees pulled together and her toes turned in.

Bruno stepped into the adjoining room to have his phone

conversation and handed me a glass of champagne. I had a sip. It was icy, and it sent a worrying jolt of pain up one of my back teeth. I sat down in one of the armchairs.

"It went just the way we hoped," Sam said.

"Only better!" Sylvia added.

"Really? Well, tell me!"

"You tell her, Sam," Sylvia said.

Sam needed little urging. He cleared his throat and leaned forward.

"I was down in the lobby," Sam said. "Bryson had me wait down there while he came up here for the meeting. So there I am, sitting in the corner, reading a magazine and minding my own business, when who should come prancing across the room?!"

Sam was grinning.

"Who?" I asked.

"Guess!" he said.

"I don't know."

"Amanda! She walks right into the Noir."

"What's the Noir?" I asked.

"It's a bar off the lobby," answered Sylvia.

"No!" I said. "So what did you do?"

"Pulled my chair back into the shadows so she wouldn't see me, but I could still see her. She sat right down at the bar and ordered a drink. Didn't move for an hour, hour and a half. Probably had three or four drinks. She kept checking her cell phone over and over.

"Finally, the elevator doors open and Bryson steps out. He's got a guy with him, big fat fellow in a navy blue blazer. There's no love lost between the two of them, you can see that right away. Bryson's got him by the arm and the cop's looking around the lobby for me. But I don't *want* him to see me! I want to keep my eye on Amanda. Bryson marches the guy out, and I see he's got him in handcuffs. But Amanda doesn't see any of this. She's just sitting there, working on her drink.

"I race outside, and Bryson's just putting the guy in the car. I tell him Amanda's inside, so he comes back into the hotel with me, hauling the guy in the handcuffs.

"We walk right into the Noir. We walk right up to her. She whips around. She doesn't seem to get it. She's looking from me to Bryson, to her pal there, and he's speechless, he's just shaking his head, afraid to say anything. So I say, 'Amanda, this is Detective Karl Bryson. He works for the Cambridge Police Department.'

" 'Detective?' she says, acting all sweet and innocent. But she knows.

"I look her straight in the eye and I say, 'It's over.'

" 'Madam,' says Bryson, 'I'm afraid you'll have to come with us.' "

Chapter Twenty-Six

WE CROSSED NANTUCKET Sound on the high-speed ferry. I couldn't help wondering, as the boat headed out of the harbor toward open sea, past the small cluster of neat and modest cottages referred to grandly as the "Kennedy Compound," what the old whaling captains would have thought of our zippy little Mustang of a boat. I prefer the slow ferry, the one that makes the trip in a couple of hours. I like standing on the upper deck, watching the coastline of Massachusetts get smaller and smaller as the wake churned up by the boat's groaning progress foams and swirls, fanning out behind the ferry in a mesmerizing flow.

Today, though, we had opted for speed: one hour, dock to dock. We were set to meet up with the folks from Interpol, who had taken a room at the Jared Coffin House, an old inn right on the main square in Nantucket proper. Since Interpol didn't have jurisdiction over the island, they'd had to coordinate their efforts with both the Massachusetts State Police and an art theft task force of the FBI. Based on information Declan had obtained from Scully, the State Police, working with officers on the Nantucket force, believed they had pinpointed the house in which the meeting was set to take place: an *Architectural Digest*–type home built in the past few years in a secluded area of Madaket, on the western side of the island.

Dec had refused to let Sylvia come. It was bad enough, he'd insisted, his being responsible for the presence of one "civilian" (me); there was no way in the world that he would consent to Sylvia's tagging along. For that matter, he hadn't wanted me to come, either, but I had leverage, and I'd begged. Mercilessly.

"Who'll identify the book?" I had asked.

"You."

"But I've never seen it. What if it's the wrong one?"

"The wrong twelfth-century illuminated manuscript?" He gave me a wry look.

"Yeah."

"I guess we'll just have to take our chances," he'd said.

The location was on our side, he explained as we nursed burned coffee and split a bag of chips in the ferry snack bar. I wouldn't have minded having a beer—being on the boat made me feel almost as though I was heading off on a vacation—but as it was, I had barely talked Declan into letting me come. I had to be on my best behavior. He wouldn't have looked kindly on my nursing a brew at eleven o'clock in the morning.

"First off," he said, "it's kind of a hilly, duney part of the island. At least that's the word I got. And there's a lot of private security in that area. Guys patrolling the dune roads in cars pretty much nonstop."

"How come?" I took a sip. God, how could this coffee be so bad?

"They're all high rollers out there, in that area. New money. Big money. They want their privacy, and they spare no expense building the dream house on a big plot of land. But they're vulnerable, too, being way out there in the dunes. Off-season, the houses are sitting ducks."

"What does this have to do with us?" I asked.

Dec finished his coffee, stood up, and tossed his Styrofoam cup into the trash. He sat back down. "People are used to seeing guys on the local force, and guys from the private security companies, crawling around the dunes in their cars. Nobody'll give a second thought to a couple of black Crown Royals."

I nodded, gazing easily at the familiar features of the man sitting opposite me. That was the moment when I realized that I was not going to go out with Julian again, not even for a drink. Sure, there had been a buzz between us, and that had felt really, really nice. I wasn't angry about what happened, not anymore, and certainly not after the roses. But when you've been lucky enough in your life to have had the real thing, you know it when you feel it again. And if you don't, and you're pretty sure you never will, what, really, is the point of a drink?

I was trying to act blasé, but I was anything but. The Interpol agents had booked several private rooms at the historic inn, which wasn't the sort of place built for business travelers needing to rent impersonal spaces for semiprivate work meetings.

Nope, I was in a bedroom. A frilly, overheated bedroom, with fancy French wallpaper and Mary Cassatt reproductions on the walls and a massive mahogany four-poster bed taking up most of the space in the room. The bed looked so inviting, with its stiff, white sheets and down comforter and what looked to be a whole range of pillows, all the way from fluffy to firm. I wanted nothing more than to lie down and close my eyes for just a few minutes. But I wasn't alone. There in the room with me were two burly State Police Officers. You know the kind—huge, intimidating, all decked out in their jodhpurs and black leather motorcycle boots.

They weren't especially . . . chatty. At least not with me, whom I gathered they had been assigned, at least unofficially, to babysit. They had set up shop on the far side of the room, commandeering a delicate ladies' writing desk. They looked like figures in a Norman Rockwell illustration, or in a children's picture book: two grizzly bears having a tea party.

That left me the wing chair by the window overlooking the street, so I sat down and tried to pay attention. To what, though, I wasn't sure. I had no idea what was going on. Busy and serious-looking men, and a couple of women, could be heard chatting on phones and with one another in the room beside ours and the one beyond that. Cell phones were ringing and walkie-talkies were crackling, but I could rarely make out more than "Copy that."

Dec poked his head in once or twice, winked at me without smiling, and left. Gradually, as the hours wore on, I found it harder and harder to fight the soporific hum of all those quiet conversations from which I was excluded, and the heat we had tried to turn down, and the lingering effects of all the champagne I had drunk with Sam and Sylvia and the restless night that had followed, as I tossed and turned, worrying that I would oversleep and Dec would leave without me. I lay my head back against the wing of the chair and decided to close my eyes for just a couple of minutes.

"Anza," I heard a man say.

My eyes flew open and I sat up. It was dark out. Where was I?

"Time to head out," the officer said.

"Oh! Sorry. I—"

I stood up so abruptly that I almost lost my balance. I was still half asleep. The state police guys were standing by the door, and I had that sick, disoriented feeling you sometimes have when you've fallen dead asleep during the day, and when you wake up, it's dark.

One of the cops flipped the switch that killed the bedside lights; the other was jangling his keys, watching with not a hint of amusement as I fumbled around in a daze, trying to locate all my things.

Damn! How long had I been asleep? Where was Dec? I was furious at myself for having drifted off and furious at Dec for having let me! How could he have left me in the mortifying position of being conked out in a chair while I was supposed to be helping? He and the Staties had probably had a good laugh about that, shaking their heads at the useless wannabe, fast asleep in the chair. I hoped to God that my mouth hadn't been hanging open and that I hadn't been snoring.

"Where are we going?" I asked, stumbling down the hall behind them. Everyone else seemed to have left.

"Madaket, ma'am," came the reply.

Two hours later, I couldn't have been more awake. For one thing, I was deathly cold. I was sitting in the backseat of the cruiser, which was tucked just out of sight in one of the Madaket dunes. I had all I could do to keep my teeth from chattering, but there was no way I was going to ask them to turn on the heat, not after they probably spent the afternoon making jokes about Sleeping Beauty in the chair. I'd die of frostbite before I'd request any special treatment.

I could see the house a little way off. It was a beautiful, modern place with decks all around and big glass windows overlooking what the cops said was Capaum Pond. There were a couple of cars parked outside the house—one that looked like a nondescript sedan and another that had to be a sporty Mercedes or some kind of Jaguar. I had gathered from hearing the police chat that there were three other unmarked cars in our immediate vicinity and two more cruisers back on Madaket Road. I didn't know exactly what we were waiting for, but I wasn't about to ask.

Suddenly, I saw three black cars with their headlights off crawling slowly toward the house. My heart began to beat wildly, and I found myself praying that Declan was not in one of them. He always downplays the risks of being a cop, but there in the darkness, I had a terrifying feel for the danger and uncertainty that are part of his job. I bit my lip and leaned forward, squinting to see as much as I could. The cars pulled to a quiet stop and twelve or fourteen people piled out. They didn't close the car doors. They quietly approached the house on foot and seemed to fan out around it, maybe blocking the other exits.

The moon had not yet risen, so I couldn't see very much. Occasionally, there would be the flash of a reflective vest. I heard a dog begin to bark. That was all.

"What's happening?" I whispered.

"They're going in," the policeman whispered back.

Then there were shouts of "FBI! Police! Open up!" There was a lot of commotion outside, and the cops turned on the engine and flicked on their lights. We heard shouts, and people yelling, and the splintering of the front door as the agents gained entry. Thank God we heard no shots. But suddenly, I glimpsed a shadowy figure on one of the second-floor decks.

"Look!" I said. "There's someone up there. Look!"

In a flash, not waiting to see if any other officers or agents had caught sight of the fugitive, the cops were out of the car. They pulled their guns and shouted for the man to stop, but he didn't. He dropped down awkwardly from the deck and stumbled off in the darkness toward the edge of the pond. I caught a flash of silver hair.

The officers took off after him. I could see him struggling to get away, but his progress was hobbled by deep sand and grass.

They all disappeared over a dune. I wanted to get out of the car, but I was afraid; both that something might happen to me and that I would do something to piss off Declan, when I'd promised to stay out of the way.

I wasn't in suspense for long, though; in less than a minute, my buddies reappeared, half-dragging the man, who was handcuffed and held firmly by the arms, up over the ledge and toward the house. He was tall and slim and appeared vaguely familiar to me. But that was crazy. No, it had to be a movie star I was thinking of, someone like Richard Gere.

I watched them all climb the steps and disappear inside. Then I sat there alone, shivering, for what felt like half an hour. Finally, Declan appeared on the porch, hopped down the steps, and headed toward my car.

"All clear there, love," he said, opening my door. "You can come in."

I got out slowly and threw my arms around him.

"Are you all right?" I asked.

"Course I am," he said, shaking his head as though I was silly to have worried. All of a sudden, I wanted to cry. I paused and took a breath, and forced back the tears that were gathering in the corners of my eyes. Seeing this, Dec put his arm around me and gave me a squeeze.

Inside, he steered me right down the hall toward the back of the house. Cops and agents wearing FBI jackets were talking on phones and taking notes, drifting around the house and checking out the art and the furnishings.

And there, suddenly, was the manuscript, right on the dining room table. I felt a wave of faintness, but I took a deep breath and crossed the room.

The book was larger than I had expected—maybe a foot by fourteen or fifteen inches. I didn't want to touch it. I gazed in awe at the dazzling variety of shapes and colors that had been squeezed into the four rectangular panels of the cover.

I looked up at Declan.

"That's your book, then?" he asked.

"Could be," I said, smiling. "Looks about right."

Declan grinned. "All right. Let's get out of here. Leave the boys to their work."

"Can we take it with us?"

"No."

"Can I just peek in?" I asked. I was suddenly dying to see what was going on in the front room, and more important, who it was that my officer pals had tackled in the dunes outside.

Declan nodded curtly. The gesture said, *Make it quick.*

I crossed the hall and walked toward the room with all the noise and activity. A man I took to be Van Vleck was sitting there, dressed in a caramel-colored sports jacket and tight beige jeans. He looked oddly disengaged from the swirl of activity around him, as though he had imagined this scene many times before and was now rewatching a dull and familiar film.

With all the bustle and noise, it took a minute for me to locate the other man the officers had arrested. I almost did a double take as my brain struggled to make sense of an image that didn't seem right. It couldn't be . . . wait a minute . . . no, this was wrong . . . it was a mistake. I recognized the person in the chair, and he couldn't possibly be involved in this! He was respected all over the world! He was important! But he was handcuffed and sitting in the chair in the corner, surrounded by men and women in FBI vests.

It took several moments for me to believe that I really could trust my eyes.

It was Jim Wescott.

We learned the story in bits and pieces. We didn't know everything for close to a year, when a long article on the tawdry little scandal in the art world appeared in the *New York Times Magazine*.

Amanda was serving time by then, at a regional women's correctional facility in Chicopee. She'd made a deal with federal authorities: in exchange for helping them to recover all the plates she had stolen and sold in the course of her career, she received a reduced sentence: three to five years, with the possibility of parole for good behavior.

It made a certain amount of sense, once a couple of important facts came to light.

From the time that James Wescott received Finny and Sylvia's letter, he had set his sights on acquiring the Book of Kildare for the British Library. From the details in their description, from his knowledge of comparably dated manuscripts, and from extensive research he had swiftly undertaken in European archives and scholarly journals, Wescott had arrived at a firm conviction that the manuscript in Finny and Sylvia's possession was, indeed, the inspired treasure of the Irish scriptorium.

He wanted it. He was consumed with frustration that such a valuable and important work of art should be in the hands of a rich American dabbler. Where it belonged, he believed, was with him, in England, at the British Library. Trinity College had the Book of Kells, and come hell or high water, he decided, *he*, Jim Wescott, was going to get the Book of Kildare into the British Library. He was coming up on retirement. The Harrison Collection had slipped right through his fingers, and the Henry Moore pieces and the Banville papers. The "discovery" of this precious lost volume and its acquisition for the British Library would get his train back on the tracks.

First, he composed a dismissive letter, designed to convince Finny and Sylvia that a "Book of Kildare" had never actually existed. Many scholars shared that opinion, so it wasn't too hard to add two more naysayers to his chorus: Julian Rowan and Susan McCasson. Wescott hoped that Finny would decide, in his disappointment, simply to sell the manuscript at auction. Wescott could then snap it up for the British Library, legitimately and easily, with honest cash changing hands.

That didn't work, because Finny passed away. Informed by Tad that the collection had been donated to the Athenaeum, Wescott went next to Amanda. It was Wescott's inquiry that tipped Amanda off to the possibility of a valuable, not-yet-catalogued manuscript on the Athenaeum's shelves. She went searching through the bindery when no one was there. She couldn't actually take the book, of course—Sylvia would have been certain to notice—but she could take pieces from it when no one was watching. No one, it turned out, but the ghosts.

Informed by Amanda that there was no book matching his description in the Athenaeum's collection, Wescott began to wonder if Finny had willed it, or given it as a gift before his death, to Sylvia. She had signed her full name to that initial letter, so it wasn't that hard to find out where she lived. She was listed in the Boston phone book, with her street address. One had only to scan the eight names on the polished brass mailboxes in the foyer of her building to know precisely where she resided.

Wescott's attendance at the Harvard symposium was a cover; that was why he had stayed in Cambridge for only a day before heading up to "Vermont" to see the foliage. He had never gone to Vermont. He had come to stay in a house in Madaket, owned by a contact of the man he had enlisted to help him, the infamous Jannus Van Vleck.

There was a third player in the game, a man named Sanford Suffield. Born in New York, he was the son of a British teacher and a modestly successful merchant in the garment trade—his father manufactured overcoats for the armed services. Suffield, bright and keenly ambitious, had risen quickly through the ranks of his father's company and become enormously wealthy through partnerships with Chinese and Hong Kong–based clothing manufacturers. He had also fallen in love with and eventually married a British magazine writer. They'd decided to live in London.

Suffield struggled to adapt to his new surroundings; he took to dressing in custom-made suits and bought a country place in Scotland. Branching out from the garment business, he began to make a name for himself locally by buying buildings in fashionable areas of London, and eventually, a few restaurants. He bought horses. He invited his wife's colleagues for weekends in the country and he and Sophie began to pop up in the "Party Scene" pages of *Tatler*.

What Suffield couldn't manage to engineer, though, was full inclusion of a social sort. He could own every restaurant in London, he finally realized, and lots of posh apartment buildings, and he would still be seen as a rich American throwing around his money. Socially, his nose might forever be pressed to the glass.

Wescott was acquainted with Suffield and, of course, understood all this. He invited Suffield to dinner and broached the prospect of a unique and, just for the moment, clandestine collaboration. Would Suffield consider providing the capital to "acquire" a priceless, long-lost manuscript, the ownership of which was presently "in flux"? Wescott described his research and whetted Suffield's desire to help make "art-world headlines." If all went as planned, Wescott promised, he, *Sanford Suffield*, would receive much of the credit for one of the most important gifts the British Library had ever received, a priceless treasure long believed to be lost.

It would change everything for him in London, Wescott whispered. To put it bluntly, Suffield would soon find himself being invited to a whole different class of party.

After a day or two of thought, Suffield got back to Wescott. He'd be more than happy to finance the venture, he said. He'd like nothing better than to present a substantial gift to the national library of his adopted home.

Wescott took it from there.

Suffield's case is still making its way through the British courts. His defense maintains that he was deliberately defrauded. As for Wescott, his quest ended in professional disgrace and prison. Van Vleck's serving eight to ten in MCI–Concord.

Chapter Twenty-Seven

THE WEDDING OF *Q* and *U* went off without a hitch, not counting the fact that I'd run out of confectionary sugar at two a.m. and had to dash out to Store 24. All in all, I baked six dozen cupcakes, finally hitting the hay at close to three thirty. But the look on Henry's face that morning made it all worthwhile.

"Mama!" he said, running his sleepy gaze over platter after platter of cupcakes, all lined up on the counter. "When did you make these?"

"After you went to sleep." I said.

"They look great! Can I have one?"

"Sure," I said.

The cafeteria was already bustling when we got there. I glanced around a little nervously for Kelly and Dec, but they weren't there yet. This was the only part of the morning I was dreading. I hoped that having so many people in our little group would normalize what was bound to be a kind of weird meeting between Declan and Dad, who had arrived by train on Monday night. I knew they'd shake hands and pretend to be glad to see each other and slip right into small talk about the Red Sox and the Reds, but I still wasn't looking forward to the moment.

Miss O. presided with her usual aplomb as children trooped in with their parents and loved ones. Most of the kids were already in costume—Minnie Mouse, a butterfly, Superman. I had not been allowed to see Henry's finished costume; he'd wanted it to be a surprise. I glanced around to see if my nemesis, the pristine Julia Swensen, was in attendance. Sure enough, there she was in the back, wearing a killer pair of brown suede pumps and tapping away on her BlackBerry.

Henry, who was coming with Ellie and Max—my backseat having been full of cupcakes—arrived not a moment too soon. Dad and Dec had greeted each other heartily, spoken for all of ninety seconds, and were now seated as far away from each other as possible, on the two opposite ends of the row of folding chairs we had reserved for the Henry contingent. Nat didn't show. I should have called her to remind her; Henry had probably left out a crucial detail or two, like the date, time, or location of the great event. Ellie slid in beside me just as a trumpet processional began to blare out of a set of speakers.

And in came the costumed letters, two by two: an Apple, with the aforementioned Butterfly; a Crayon, barely able to walk, beside a very short child doing the Queen Elizabeth wave, all decked out in what looked like a very expensive Dog costume. There was a fairy . . . no, an elf! With a fireman. And a little girl wearing a box decorated with wrapping paper; her head was sticking out of the top and in her hair was a large red bow. I guess she was a Gift.

And there was Henry. A huge grin spread over my face. I glanced at Dad, who didn't seem to know what to make of all this.

"There's Henry!" I said.

"Where?" he asked.

I pointed to the hammer and Dad laughed out loud. I reached over and took Ellie by the hand. She was beaming. She had done a fabulous job. The handle of the hammer looked loose and pliable, and the fabric resembled wood grain. And in the silver cloth-covered hammerhead were . . . eyeholes!

The hammer strutted proudly to the end of our aisle. Completely ignoring the rest of us, he leaned right over Declan and Nell and yelled, "Hi, Pop!"

My father waved and pointed to the front of the room. "Pay attention!" he said.

The letters made their way to preassigned seats. Then they turned, stood, and sang a song about spelling, to the accompaniment—and I am not kidding—of a Broadway-style sound track blaring out of the speakers. This was wild! It was a musical revue! There were songs, and skits, and finally a strange and oddly sweet little wedding ceremony in which the queen promised never to leave the side of her umbrella, who wore an honest-to-goodness umbrella top affixed to a hat. Then they all stood and sang a little love song to spelling and reading, screeching with enthusiasm as they slipped and slid toward a fevered crescendo.

I didn't know whether to laugh or cry.

As for the cupcakes, Henry was right. We ran out.

Dad stayed with Henry while I drove into town. I would normally have taken the T, but I just couldn't imagine riding the Red Line with the Book of Kildare in my backpack. It scared me to death even to have it in my possession, but given our plans, this was unavoidable. Tad was given temporary custody of the book last night, after the police had photographed it. Tonight, after we let the monks have one last look, Sylvia was going to go right to work, creating calfskin folders to protect the detached plates. The manuscript could fall apart if we tried to disassemble it in order to reinsert the severed pages. It was just too old and fragile and we didn't dare take the chance.

As though they were aware of all the events that had recently transpired, the monks were waiting for us in the bindery when we switched on the light.

"We have it," I whispered. "The book." I laid my backpack on the central table and carefully removed the manuscript.

"Glory be to God!" said the abbot.

"And all the pages," Sylvia added. "We recovered everything! Every single piece."

"The blessings of God be upon you," said the young monk.

"Thank you," I said. They were both staring at the manuscript on the bindery table and tears had come to their eyes.

"I'd love to open it up for you," I said, "but we probably shouldn't touch the inside pages. The less we handle them, you know . . ." I glanced at Sylvia and shrugged. She appeared pained.

"Of course, of course!" said the abbot.

Sylvia let out a sigh, then opened one of the drawers in a nearby filing cabinet and pulled out a pair of white cotton gloves. She slipped them on. I immediately understood where she was going with this and quickly came to my senses. Forget the rules we had both learned at North Bennet Street. These poor, devoted ghosts deserved a long last look at the object they so cherished. Why, they clearly loved this manuscript as much as many of the ghosts I've worked with had loved their husbands and wives and children! I wouldn't have denied any of those earthbound spirits the chance for one last experience with who or what had kept them tethered to this world. The monks deserved no less. I was a little ashamed of myself for not having realized this. I was glad that Sylvia had stepped in.

For nearly half an hour, as she quietly flipped the pages, they whispered to each other and laughed at shared memories of the other monks who had worked on the book: Brother Alphonse, with his secret recipe for black encaustic gaul; Brother Marcus, who raised the geese prized for the sturdiness of their quills, attributing his success to his habit of serenading the geese nightly with a one-monk concert of lute music. When we came to the end of the book, Sylvia went to her briefcase and pulled out the individual plates. She laid them, too, out on the table.

"That woman had fine taste," the abbot said. "These were among the very best."

I stepped up to the table. The golds and greens and reds were unaccountably vivid, given the centuries that had passed since the monks' pens and brushes had made contact with the parchment. I suddenly had an urge to ask them about the production of their inks and their methods for curing vellum and their preferences in the matter of pens—quills or iron nibs? But that wasn't fair. This was not about me, this moment in time, it was about them. The abbot waited patiently while the young monk perused the last of the plates. When the young ghost was finished, he stepped back and looked to the abbot.

There was silence in the room for several moments. I hadn't really liked the old coot, but I suddenly felt sad. Looking at the younger monk, I felt tears pricking my eyes. He was Henry. He was a boy, really, no older than eighteen or nineteen. He had probably entered the monastery when he was twelve or thirteen, an age Henry would be reaching in the blink of an eye.

It all went so fast; too fast! In no time at all, my son would be the age at which the young monk had died, and I would be forty, then fifty, the age I ascribed to the abbot. Death could cut either one of us down at any moment, slowly or quickly, and even if we both lived to a ripe old age, our years together on this planet were numbered. As were mine with Dad, and with Nona—even fewer in her case. I might be separated from a loved one tomorrow, or in a year, or in ten years. At some point, I would be separated from them all.

The tunnel of light would exist for me, too, one day, and for everyone I cherished in this life. While I didn't fear death, as many people did, I prayed to God that when my time came, the white light would lead me to the people I loved and lead the people who loved me, to me.

I let out a sigh and addressed the monks. "Are you ready to cross over now? I can help you, if you are."

"We've been ready, my dear, for a long, long time," said the abbot. "But before we leave, let me thank you with one last blessing."

"All right," I said. "I could use a blessing."

"Not as much as most," said the abbot, and for the very first time, there was a twinkle in his eye.

He closed his eyes and began to intone the words I passed on to Sylvia:

> *Deep peace of the running waves to you.*
> *Deep peace of the flowing air to you.*
> *Deep peace of the smiling stars to you.*
> *Deep peace of the quiet earth to you.*
> *Deep peace of the watching shepherds to you.*
> *Deep peace of the Son of Peace to you.*

"Thank you," I said, and then I closed my eyes and brought up an image of the white light. I kept my eyes closed as I asked them, "Can you see it? Can you see that door right there on the wall, the door with the light all around it, and the really bright light shining through it?"

"Yes!" cried the younger monk. "I see it! I do!"

"Glory be to God!" whispered the abbot.

"Walk through it," I said. "Walk right up to it and into the light."

The younger monk went first. He seemed apprehensive, so the abbot put his arm on the spirit's shoulder and walked him up to the light. The monk drew in a breath, then sighed rhapsodically at sights he alone could see, deep, deep within the light. The abbot followed, turning to face me before disappearing forever. He raised his right hand to bless me with the sign of the cross.

As the tears ran down my cheeks, my thoughts flew from Henry to Dad to Nona, to my mother, smiling through the years in that sepia photograph, smiling with Dad on the beach.

I crossed myself. The abbot nodded, smiled, and stepped into the light.

It would be nearly as hard, I suspected, for Sylvia to let go of the manuscript as it had been for the monks. It was the symbol of her connection with Finny.

I would have offered to stay with her while she put together the calfskin binders, but I really had to get back: Dad and Henry were waiting at home.

"Want me to call Sam?" I offered. "He'd probably be glad to come in."

She shook her head. "No, thanks. I'll be fine."

I doubted she would be fine. She'd probably cry her way right through the job, but at least she had something concrete to work on. Maybe, as she sewed and glued her way through the creation of the individual binders, a job that would easily take her nine or ten hours, she would be able to come to terms with some of her feelings.

I'd once heard it said that accident victims who receive modest injuries, like broken bones and lacerations, sometimes recovered more completely from the effects of their experiences than other trauma victims, whose wounds are purely emotional. As witnesses to their own physical healing, people perceive themselves—*them*, not just their broken arms and legs—to be moving toward health and wholeness.

Maybe the creation of the binders would foster in Sylvia a sense of completion and closure, slowly allowing her to come to terms with the end of a precious chapter in her life.

I hoped so.

Chapter Twenty-Eight

Dad and I flew on Aer Lingus to Shannon.

I'd tried really hard to convince Sylvia to accompany me, but she was positively phobic about flying. I suggested Valium. I suggested alcohol. I suggested she take one of those courses at the airport, where they try to get you over your fears. But she was adamant. She was not stepping foot on a plane. When I told this to Tad, who had already purchased the tickets, he said I could take anyone I wanted. The person I wanted was Dad.

My father was excited, if slightly suspicious—a free trip to Ireland? What was the catch? Would we have to listen to pitches for time-shares? Were we guinea pigs of some sort, being hood-winked with free airline tickets and hotel rooms? What were they going to ask us to do?

"Nothing," I said. "Or rather, nothing you won't love."

He loved every minute of it, and so did I: the first-class flight, the hired car meeting us at the airport and taking us right to a beautiful B and B on Galway Bay. What he loved most of all, though, was the trip to Kylemore Abbey, up in Connemara, not far from where he was born.

The Benedictine nuns of Kylemore Abbey had for years run one of Ireland's loveliest private boarding schools for girls. The number of boarders has been dwindling in recent years, though, as have vocations to the monastic sisterhood, and the Benedictines had recently announced the regrettable decision to close the school. The board of directors of the order, deeply in need of money with which to care for the elderly members of their community, had been approached by an English real estate developer. The castle of the abbey and its historic gardens had caught his eye. He wanted to turn the place into a four-star conference center and hotel.

That was when Tad stepped in, not only donating the Book of Kildare to the impoverished sisters, but making a sizeable commitment to establish at the abbey a study center dedicated to the preservation of monastic manuscripts.

There would be more of these manuscripts coming, he wrote in the letter, which Dad and I delivered to the ecstatic old nuns. At this very moment, Tad was in the midst of a search for a full-time director.

The Kildare monastery no longer existed, Tad had explained to me. These gestures were as close as he could come to giving the book back to people from whom it was stolen, which he really believed his father would have wanted. But that wasn't enough, Tad had explained. The sisters would only have to sell the manuscript in order to save the abbey and to support the ill and elderly of their order. If he was really going to help—and, I privately suspected, prove somehow to the watchful spirit of his father that he was generous and altruistic and worthy of being trusted—Tad would have to do more. More was what he intended to do.

Dad stayed in Connemara while I flew Ryanair to Swansea, in Wales. I'd learned of Children's Center, a shoestring operation in the toughest part of town, serving children in foster care, babies of the drug addicted, and quite a few orphans. I take the credit for this bit of Internet research, but Tad made the phone call. Could Children's Center make use of a seaside cottage?

The first time he phoned the director, she hung up on him. She was sure that someone was playing a sick trick. No, Tad insisted when he called back, it wasn't a trick. The offer was genuine. If Children's Center would like to have what Tad believed to be a cozy little cottage within sight of the water—for picnics, for a camp, for whatever they wanted to use it for—the place was theirs. He would have all the paperwork verified and get the deed into their hands within the month.

The director broke down on the phone, he said. And Tad broke down telling me.

I called the director of Children's Center from a pay phone on the outskirts of town. No, I insisted, there was no need to organize a dinner or a ceremony or anything formal or official. I'd drop off the deed and be on my way. It was, I was sure, what Johnny and Maimie would have done.

Before leaving town, I did one more thing I knew they would have done. I stopped by a rundown florist shop near the train station and purchased the prettiest assortment of flowers I could assemble. I took a walk through the village, found the quiet little churchyard within sight of the water, and laid the flowers on Gwennie's grave.

***

Back in Galway the following morning, I was sitting over an Irish breakfast with my father, trying not to gag as he tucked into a couple of thick slices of black pudding, sausage made of cow's or pig's blood, cooked with fillers until it congeals. It's black as midnight, and in my opinion, just as scary.

"How can you *eat* that, Daddy?" I squealed.

He shook his head. His mouth was full. He swallowed, had a sip of tea, and said, "You don't know what you're missing."

"Oh, I know," I said. "I know exactly what I'm missing."

He smiled, cleared his throat, and pushed his chair back from the table.

"I've been thinking of staying a while, Suzy-Q," he said, startling me with a nickname I hadn't heard in years.

"What? Staying here?"

He nodded. "Just for a . . . visit. Maybe a couple of weeks."

"Well, sure."

"It's good to be home," he said. "I didn't know how I'd feel, but honest to God, it's great. I could stay with the boys for a bit."

"The boys" were his two brothers, Martin and Joe. They were both married and in their sixties.

"I'm sure we can change your ticket," I said. "We can call the airline as soon as we're done."

I sighed and reached for his hand. My father looked happy. This was a good idea; it had been years since he'd spent any amount of time with his brothers and cousins. Maybe, just maybe, there would be a girl he used to know way back when.

"You'd be welcome to stay yourself," he said, though I'm sure he realized it was out of the question.

I smiled at him and shook my head.

I had someone to get home to.

ACKNOWLEDGMENTS

The amazing love I get from my husband, Ted, and our daughters, Amber and Tara, makes my work so enjoyable. I cannot thank them enough.

To Jennifer Gates, my literary agent with Zachary Schuster Harmsworth, for your great book sense and friendship, and to Lane Zachary for all of your support. I am so grateful to both of you for introducing me to Maureen Foley—how ingenious of you to know we could work together so well.

To Maureen Foley, you have a wonderful gift for bringing life to everything that you put on paper, and your work ethics are to be envied. Thanks to your husband, Rob, and your children for sharing your time and talent with me.

To Three Rivers Press and our current editor, Heather Proulx, and our original editor, Carrie Thornton, for making us feel so welcome and believing in this project.

To Scott Schwimer, my Los Angeles entertainment attorney. You always keep me on the right path (which is not an easy task). Thank you for doing it with such love and humor.

Thanks to relatives for the support and encouragement: son-in-law Stephen Hastings, Mary Lou Drsek, Matthew and Diana Weber, John and Betty Ann Hanzl, Robert and Sherry Slepecky, Kristen, Joette, Brenda, Angela, and Nick.

To friends Charity Ingraham, George and Dottie Janes, Elizabeth Joy, Gary and Grace Jansen, Richard and Mary Kruzel, Christine Kurfis, Dr. Issam and Kathy Nemeh, Kevin and

Eleanor McLaughlin, Kati Russell, Dr. Mark and Cindy Schick-endantz, Larry and Phillis Townes, Helena Ward, and all the nuns at Incarnate Word, especially Sister Monica.

A huge thank-you to Gina Kruzel and Wendy Lister for helping out with my ghost clearings, allowing me to have time for writing.

To every earthbound spirit I have ever met: thank you for sharing your unique stories. Most of all thanks to God for all of His blessings and the gifts that He has given me.

—MAW

I wish to express my deep gratitude to Lane Zachary, Mary Ann Winkowski, and Jennifer Gates. Warmest thanks are due to Carrie Thornton, Heather Proulx, Cindy Berman, Laura Duffy, Jo Anne Metsch, Sibylle Kazeroid, and all the talented artists and wordsmiths at Three Rivers Press.

For professional guidance and cheerleading, I am grateful to Ken Weinrib and Gary Ungar. For their gifts of friendship, I thank Sarah Baker, Alec Baldwin, Vicky Bennet, Tim and Sara Cabot, Terry and Catherine Doyle, Seamus Egan, Tim Grafft and David Hacin, Sandy Jaffe and Jay Blitzman, Gillian McManus, Jeff Perrotti, Avery Rimer, Larry Reynolds, Jamey Rosenfield and Debi Zilberman, Billy Smith, Eve Stern, Victoria and Nicolas Thierry, and Michael Williams and David Collins. To Anna Bensted and Lino Pertile, I offer thanks both for their friendship and for the use of the Eliot House Library at Harvard University.

I am blessed beyond words to go through life with my sister and brother, Peg Pitzer and Tom Foley, and all the wonderful members of their families: Fred, Nancy, Sarah, Kevin, Jill, Adam, Owen, and Max. I honor with infinite appreciation our much-missed parents, Charles and Mary Foley.

I thank, above all, my dearest children, Charlie and Grace Laubacher, whose wit, good cheer, and enthusiasm for life bring joy to mine, and my beloved husband, Rob Laubacher, with whom I feel extraordinarily blessed to share this journey.

—MF

ABOUT THE AUTHORS

© Louis McClung / Lassos Photography

MARY ANN WINKOWSKI is the author of *When Ghosts Speak*. She is a paranormal investigator who has collaborated closely with several federal agencies and is the high-profile consultant for the CBS series *The Ghost Whisperer*. Visit her online at www.maryannwinkowski.com.

© Gabriel Amadeus Cooney

MAUREEN FOLEY is the acclaimed writer, producer, and director of the films *American Wake* and the award-winning *Home Before Dark*. Visit her online at www.hazelwoodfilms.com.